To
Bice and James

THE BAT
THAT FLITS

NORMAN COLLINS

BLOOMSBURY READER

LONDON · NEW DELHI · NEW YORK · SYDNEY

This electronic edition published in 2012 by Bloomsbury Reader

Bloomsbury Reader is a division of Bloomsbury Publishing Plc,

50 Bedford Square, London WC1B 3DP

ISBN: 978 1 4482 0117 4
eISBN: 978 1 4482 0249 2

Visit www.bloomsburyreader.com to find out more about our authors and their books
You will find extracts, author interviews, author events and you can sign up for
newsletters to be the first to hear about our latest releases and special offers
Printed and bound by CPI Group (UK) Ltd, Croydon, CR0 4YY

NOTE

There is no Government Station for Anti-Bacteriological Warfare at Bodmin. And there are no real-life counterparts of any of the characters—English, German or American; male or female; Protestant or Catholic; Communist, Labour, Liberal or Conservative. The only person, therefore, who could have any possible excuse for kicking up a bit of trouble for alleged defamation of character is the author—but that is a risk that is inevitable with all tales told in the first-person-singular.

The Bat that flits at close of Eve
Has left the Brain that won't Believe.

WILLIAM BLAKE

Contents

Chapter I

1

To get to the house you go straight up over the moor. And, if you like moors, you could probably search the entire northern temperate zone without finding a better one. There are several families of buzzards; one or two quite interesting moths; a sub-species of mosquito as fierce and almost as large as flying Alsatians; and a half-excavated Early British settlement, complete with the gate-stone still in situ, which is not bad considering that the whole thing is a collector's piece left over from a previous civilisation. Add to that some beautiful sunsets by Turner out of Technicolor, a china-clay pyramid or two, various wandering posses of suspicious and distinctly inedible-looking sheep, and the list of rural charms is just about complete.

It was the elderly, moustached barmaid at the Tremant Arms who said that the moor is at its absolute best in springtime. I wasn't in a good position to judge. When I got to Bodmin the whole of the West Country winter stood in between me and the spring, and I had already decided that I was allergic to moors at any season.

But perhaps I wasn't in the right mood for enthusiasm of any

1

kind. Bodmin is two hundred and fifty-six miles from London, and I had been on the go ever since eight-thirty that morning. The dew had still been on the pavements when I had paid off my landlady in Maida Vale and placed myself, body, digestion and soul into the care of British Railways.

As it happened, body and digestion were all right. The food was a bit better than I had expected—grape-fruit, a piece of perfectly recognisable fish, a reasonably ripe Camembert—and a steward who did not seem actually to dislike serving it. It was the soul that was starved, not the body.

And that was entirely my fault. At Paddington, I had bought two American thrillers, *Picture Post* and a copy of *Lilliput*. I usually start with the pictures first, and I had opened *Lilliput* while the train was still drawing out of the platform. Eve Unashamed was the title to one of the illustrations, as though Unashamed were the young lady's family surname, and she reminded me vaguely of someone I'd known up at Cambridge. I began to wonder what had become of her. And that started me off. From then on as far as Exeter I thought about the past. I went over the whole thirty-five years three months of it.

For a start, I am an only child. I have wondered at times if perhaps that has had something to do with it—no proper community spirit fostered in the nursery, and that sort of thing. At my prep, school I was about averagely average. At Harrow, which nearly broke my father in sending me there because clergymen even then couldn't afford that kind of nostalgic luxury any longer, I was a bit more promising. Then came Trinity, where I foxed them all by getting a very middling sort of Second when everybody had predicted something pretty brilliant in the way of a First. And after that I joined the Research side of World Drug Proprietaries Inc.

I had left home by then and moved into digs. Remarkably uncomfortable ones, too. They were in Bloomsbury on the Gray's Inn Road side. The smell of boiled cabbage fairly knocked you back as you came in through the front door, and you had to sit on the flannel in the bath-tub to avoid being shredded by the chipped enamel.

The War interrupted most people's lives. But not mine. I remained with that bath all through. My work was in Gower Street—on tropical diseases. And I never got nearer to the tropics than occasional visits to the hotter dance halls in the Tottenham Court Road, in company with miscellaneous probationer nurses from University College Hospital. When the War finally packed up I went back to World Drug Proprietaries Inc. at my old salary of six-fifty. And then came the row—the big one—over scientific integrity versus the Publicity Director. We parted company, World Drug Proprietaries and I, with three months' salary in lieu of notice and an air of mutual relief that was like a reprieve from the Home Secretary. And now there was this Government job at Bodmin.

That's really all about me, except that the full name is James Wendell (after my mother) Hudson, and that I have a scar right down one side of the face from a motor accident when my brakes failed on me.

As I went over this piece of natural history, I felt that sitting there in the train I could have dictated a whole manual, complete with glossary and testimonials, on How to Side-Step Success and Antagonise People. The rest of the reading matter that I had with me was just no good at all. I found I had already seen *Picture Post*; and the two American thrillers were probably written for the English market in some back bed-sitter in Bournemouth or

Cheltenham. They were full of cops slugging dames and private investigation agents making love to nymphomaniac oil-heiresses; and by the time the train had reached Oke-hampton I'd had enough of all of them.

There was nothing for it, therefore, but to get my bag down off the rack and start in on some of my homework. It was quite an interesting little volume that I had with me, published by the Foreign Languages Publishing House in Moscow. The title was *Materials on the Trial of Former Serviceman of the Japanese Army Charged with Manufacturing and Employing Bacteriological Weapons*. That's my line, you see, bacteriological warfare. And the Government Station at Bodmin was where most of the advanced work was going on.

I had just got really interested in a bit about plague-infested fleas being dropped in fragmentation bombs on Russian prisoners tied to stakes driven into the ground, when I heard an ex-G.W.R. stationmaster calling out "Bodmin." That shook me.

Fleas and all, I nearly got carried on to Truro.

2

It was as I was getting into the hire-car after my drink that I realised how far Bodmin really is from the centre of things. The car was like something in a Transport exhibition, and the interior was full of blinds and tassels and tortoise-shell handles. There was even a bottle of smelling salts close alongside a cut-glass vase full of artificial flowers. By the time we'd done a hundred yards, I felt like some faded Bodmin beauty having a last bash at the altar before the deep Cornish night finally closed down on her.

I hadn't bothered to ask how far it was. It was consoling enough to find that anybody except the War House and the Min. of S. had ever heard of it. I had been quite prepared to discover that the whole thing was simply a typing error somewhere in Whitehall. All the same, I was relieved when the car finally lurched to a standstill. And the fact that we had really got there was announced by the appearance of a perfectly convincing-looking commission-aire in a blue uniform and a regulation peaked cap. It was like meeting a traffic-cop in the Sahara.

Because it was our first meeting everything was a bit on the formal side. And this was silly. The commissionaire certainly knew who I was because he said that he had been expecting me. And I might have been presumed to know, too, because I had got there. But he evidently wanted to be quite sure. There was apparently some sort of white Pass, marked "SECRET: VALID FOR ONE VISIT ONLY" that I dimly remembered when he began talking about it. I must have put it into my other suit. And that meant that it was somewhere underneath about half a hundredweight of miscellaneous junk in my suit-case. So, finally, I had to show him the letter of appointment that I still had with me in my pocket. The letter seemed to satisfy him, however. I think that it must have been the first real letter that he had ever been allowed to hold. He even tried to read it right through, including all the bits about salary and compulsory pension fund deductions, before I took it away from him again.

Then with a lot of snorting and clankings, the double gates of Penmawr were swung open and the wedding-hearse from Bodmin passed victoriously through. I learnt later that there were about half a dozen other ways of getting into the grounds without enduring all that chain and padlock business. We had hikers in the paratyphoid block once, and they came straight in past the stables.

I don't think that I can have made a particularly good impression when I got to the house. The letter had told me to ask straight away for the Director, Dr. Clewes. And when I was shown into what seemed to be the drawing-room I found that Mrs. Clewes had been waiting tea for me. They had hung on, it seemed, until nearly half-past five and had then eaten a lot of leathery toast washed down by some pretty lukewarm tea. They offered to make a fresh pot specially for me. But there was too much of the no-trouble-at-all-it-won't-take-a-minute sort of talk about it, and I said no thank you. But it was evidently a point to note: the ideal new research assistant does not hang about waiting for the pubs to open if his Director's wife is expecting him.

Mrs. Clewes did not seem a bad sort, however. A bit faded and with the air of having expected better things of life—it's funny how the wives of most scientists are like that—she had a nervous trick of using her handkerchief every other moment as though she had just been crying. But, at any rate, she was better than the other sort, the witty, Gorgon kind: Cambridge in my time had been full of them.

And the Old Man himself was all right. He was elderly and rather short-sighted, with eyebrows that were several sizes too big for his face. It occurred to me then that if they were thinned out and cut back a bit he'd be able to wear his glasses better. And later on when I saw him, all tangled and hairy, trying to look down a microscope I knew that those eyebrows were by way of being a national liability. He was like a prawn trying to do microscopy.

There was one other person there, a young woman. I took a good look at her, and then shied away. That was because I had met her sort before. She was the dark, sleazy-haired, demure

6

type; the kind that look as though they have just drowned the baby, but would rather not talk about it please. She might even have been quite good looking if she had allowed anybody to see her eyes. As it was, she sat there exactly where she knew that the lamp-light would fall on her hair, and kept her lashes drawn like Venetian blinds.

It was a rather difficult party. For a start, I was two whiskies up on all of them and, in any case, half cold tea probably counts a minus. Then I had rehearsed my own part just a shade too strenuously. I was determined to show myself as someone who was alert, intelligent, well informed. And, in the result, I talked too much. I remember that I put the Director right on social credit, war in Asia, the tsetse fly, the Georgian Group and the Marx brothers. The tsetse fly and the Marx brothers were the only two on which I was really sure of my facts, and on the Marx brothers I was more than knowledgeable: I was brilliant. There was a long pause when I had finished. The Herr Direktor's wife promised that she would make a point of listening next time they were on, and could I remember which wave-length please. We left it at that.

Then the Director got up and began shepherding me into the hall.

"Perhaps after dinner you wouldn't mind coming across to my office," he said. "Just to attend to the security side. We've had to tighten things up a bit lately."

The Director sounded quite apologetic as he said it. But perhaps that was only to avoid frightening the demure one. She was sitting there, still and statuesque, like an oiled Siamese. It was cream rather than security that seemed to be in her line.

I wasn't surprised, however. There had been another atom scientist arrested only yesterday. The papers had been full of it.

Not that the publicity means anything. The Government rather encourages all this A-talk. It's harmless, and it keeps people's minds off other things that aren't so pleasant.

Bug-warfare, for instance.

3

The bedroom that had been allotted to me was in the annexe. And instinct told me that at some point in history all the others must have moved up one in an effort to get out of it. There were even signs of hasty flight in the scratches on the paint-work. The room was small, only about eight by twelve. There was a passable divan-bed, and the electric light over it was almost in the right place. Up against the opposite wall was one of those fancy bachelor-girl type wardrobes with shelves and drawers down one side, and just enough space on the other for the heavy stuff like the three-piece and the tea-gown.

The little wardrobette was pink—easily my unfavourite colour—and the wicker armchair had been bought to match it. It was a fiendish instrument that chair. If you took a hot bath and then sat down in a leisurely sort of fashion in your nothings, you got up looking like an early Christian martyr who had gone out the grid-iron way. Apart from the torture-stool, there was nothing else except the wash-basin. This was very narrow in order to conserve as much as possible of the twelve by eight, and correspondingly deep so that it was like paddling in a goldfish tank every time you went down to capture the soap.

Just to see what sort of a night I was likely to have I went over to the bed and turned down the cover. As I did so, something on the pillow caught my eye. It was a scrap of paper, with some typing on it. That struck me as odd. A pillow is such a highly personal kind of place for leaving anything. You'd have to have a simply frightful crush on the games mistress before you'd even think of using it. But the situation wasn't half so odd as the note itself. This was typed in heavy black capitals.

And what it said was: "DON'T INTERFERE. EVERYTH-ING IS UNDER CONTROL."

Chapter II

The extreme punctuality with which the thick Brown Windsor was served up at dinner-time promised some rather pretty efficiency on the catering side, and we all got down to the dutiful lap-lap-lap straight away. Unfortunately, the cooking wasn't up to the time-keeping. The results that came through that hatch would have led to a rebellion in any works canteen.

I wondered why the others all seemed so cheerful in the face of the obvious rebuff of the food. And I found out later that there was a club bar—entrance fee five shillings, annual subscription half a crown, and both paid on the nail in my case—where they had all begun to unfocus a bit before coming in.

I wasn't saying very much. But I was observing hard. I still wanted to find out who had left that note for me. And I was trying hard to take in the whole lot of them, getting my social bearings, as it were. For a start, there was the inevitable refugee scientist, little Dr. Mann with his thick pebble spectacles. He sat himself next to me and tried to be pleasant. It was a rather irritating kind of pleasantness, however; the sort of pleasantness that a cat exhibits when it spends too long rubbing itself against your trouser-legs. I agreed politely that plees it was foggy again outside, no? And then a moment later I found myself agreeing equally politely that plees it was a long way from London, no? But after that the conversation lapsed. I wasn't sorry. They're all the same, those German Ph.D.s, a sort of laboratory version of the Volkswagen. Their chief failing is that they're as industrious as indoctrinated beavers. If let, they will go on for ever taking readings and temperatures, and drawing graphs and keeping card-indexes, when an ordinary English fox terrier could tell them that it is the wrong tree altogether that they have been barking up.

The only other squeak that I had out of Dr. Mann was when the waitress, a massive village maiden as swarthy as her remote Phœnician ancestors, dropped one of the domestic-grade-porcelain-finish-export-rejects on to the stone floor. There was a loud crash, and our refuge friend gave a jump that jarred the whole table. That's another thing about refugee scientists: nerves are an occupational disease with most of them. Even in 1952 there are still plenty of sleepless nights in places like Cambridge and Princeton all because of Hitler.

We were nine all told at that table, and it's easiest to follow the company clockwise. Next to Dr. Mann was Kimbell. He was a rather dreary Manchester product, with a lot of uncombed black hair like wire-wool and an almost imbecilely intense expression. At this moment, he looked as though he were trying to mesmerise his fish pie. Kimbell was the chess player of the camp, I discovered. He was always going away by himself into the corner with little pieces of paper about white to play and do something clearly impossible in three. His chief joy was chess by correspondence—I think that the rough and tumble of an actual encounter across the board was a bit too much for him. His nails were bitten abnormally short even for a research-worker, and seen from any angle, he looked about twice as foreign as Dr. Mann.

Next to Kimbell was a thin, yellow-faced youth who might have been a choir-boy who had been letting himself go after Lent. He looked as though he needed a whole string of early nights and no singing practice to put him right again, and I saw that when he raised a spoonful of food to his lips his hand always trembled. Swanton was what the lad was called. And, after Dr. Mann, it was Swanton who was the first to remember his manners and make me one of the family circle by talking to me.

"Excuse me," he said in his rather sweet treble, "but you're not a policeman by any chance, are you?"

I shook my head.

"Not any longer," I said, dropping my voice almost to a whisper so that he had to lean right across the table to hear what I was saying. "It was something to do with the Commissioner's daughter. It never got into the papers."

I don't think that my reply altogether satisfied him. But at least he changed the subject.

"Been in this racket long?" he asked.

"Only since I was unfrocked," I answered, still in the same half-whisper.

Everything was about all square from there onwards. He hadn't discovered anything about me. But I had picked up quite a lot about him. I had learnt for a start that he was interested both in me and in policemen. He could have been the one who had typed the note. But after another look at him I decided against it. He didn't look strong enough to type.

I couldn't see Swanton's neighbour very well because he sat upright on his chair and didn't sprawl about like the rest of us. Rogers, or something of the sort, the name seemed to be—the introductions had all been made in a quick mumble, English-fashion—and he was older and decidedly more formal than the rest of us. Rather like a respectable colonel already within arm's reach of his bowler. I found out later that he was a considerably stepped-up lab. boy. He knew his stuff all right. But he had never taken his degree, and he was very sensitive about it. In consequence, he went about with a distinct air of strain as though he were travelling on the railway without a ticket.

At the head of the table—I gathered that there was no particular seniority involved, and I came to occupy the place myself sometimes—was a plump, pink, baldish young man with very small teeth and protruding eyes, who looked rather like a baby trying to get windies up. Smith was the best that he had been able to manage by way of a surname, and he was putting in some pretty serious eating, fairly wolfing down the fish pie as though it were strawberries and cream. He was just back from the other side where he had been delivering some lectures. The real purpose of his visit, so far as I could gather from what he was saying, had been to show the North American barbarians what two millennia of European breeding can eventually do for the human race.

On his left was one of the barbarians themselves. Ulysses Z. Mellon the name was. He was tall, dark, aquiline, and with hair *en brosse* like a doorstep shoe-cleaner. If he hadn't been in the research line he looked as though he would probably have been in films. His clothes gave the impression of having just come back from the valet, and there was that indefinable air of distinction that advertisements for aftershave lotions are always trying so hard to isolate.

Alongside young Mellon sat Bansted, also a clearly recognisable research type. He was a statistician who rather fancied himself as an administrator. He wore a toothbrush moustache and a little dolly-size bow-tie, and looked every bit as much a dare-devil as a provincial bank manager. He was really just a steady, reliable calculating machine that might have been turned out by Remington. But according to gossip he had a heart somewhere, and it was already broken. He had expected to be made the Big No. 1 White Chief of the Bodmin Station, and he was a disappointed man. Rifle shooting was his only hobby. And I gathered that once a year he showed up and did some rather spectacular work at Bisley.

Last of all there was the lady of the party, Dr. Hilda Sargent. She wasn't a regular diner-in, it seemed, and lived somewhere out at St. Clynt's at the Vicarage. But to-night she had stayed on at the Institute to finish off something. She was a tall girl with red-gold hair and a good profile, and I was glad that she had stayed. By the end of dinner I had already outlined about half a dozen different ways of reforming my whole moral character so as to be able to climb up on to the red-gold girl's plane of things. The only trouble was that it looked as though it might be a bit lonely up there.

Because so far she didn't appear to have noticed me.

As soon as dinner was over I went back up to my room. It was quieter than most places for thinking in, and I wanted to sit back and go over my fellow diners one by one. But by then I had something else to think about. My advance luggage had arrived, and somebody had been through it before me. Everything was more or less as I had left it, and so far as I could see there was nothing missing. But it had definitely been tampered with. The toothpaste that I had shoved in on top of the shirts just before banging the lid shut was now where it should have been inside the little sponge-bag.

That was queer attention number two. On the whole, life in the Bodmin Institute promised to be livelier than I had anticipated. I'd certainly never had anyone who cared so much about me before.

Either that, or I'd been mistaken for somebody else.

Chapter III

1

Iwoke next day with my mind fresh and unclouded. Somebody who didn't know anything about it once said that a clear conscience is nature's quickest route to a good night's rest. That may have been true in the Middle Ages. Since then, Science has found a quicker one. It's called dormital, and I had taken half a grain before turning in.

But there was one person who was up before me. I saw him, a walking advertisement for tweeds, go striding across the lawn while I was shaving. He looked like a spaniel after its monthly condition powder.

And it wasn't all dormital with me either. This morning I had a special reason for waking up so promptly. I wanted to get on with things. The first thing that I wanted to do was to track down the typewriter on which the "don't interfere" note had been hammered out. "Find the machine on which the message was typed, and you will have found the typist who typed the message," I kept telling myself, thereby making a howler in elementary logic which would have sent the late Dr. Bradley reeling.

All the same, admitting that the major premise was false, my deductive method from there on was pretty clear. I argued it out nursery fashion. "Where there is a Director, there is bound to be a Director's secretary," I reasoned. "And where there is a Director's secretary, there is bound to be a typewriter." It seemed simpler to start that way than to begin searching round for midget portables concealed under loose floor-boards.

What's more, I hit the bull's-eye first time. The room marked "Office Private" had someone already seated at the typewriter when I came in. She was a thin-lipped, frowning sort of woman rather like a disgruntled cloak-room attendant. The only thing she had was a typewriter.

Because it was our first meeting, I used my special voice, the plummy slightly husky one.

"Good morning," I said. "I'm afraid you don't know me. I'm the new man, Hudson, and you now have the advantage of me."

I was smiling at her by now; smiling really hard.

"Morning."

The smile that bounced back was all teeth and nothing else, so I decided to cut things short.

"I just dropped in to hand over my ration book," I explained.

The teeth were covered up again by now, and only a pair of very tight-looking lips remained.

"Housekeeper second door along," the reply came back by return. "She'll attend to you."

I had got as far as the door by now, and the Director's secretary was bashing out her stuff again as though she were riveting. Then I stopped.

"Oh, there is just one other little thing," I said.

"Yes?"

"I wonder if I might use your typewriter just for a minute?" I asked. "For an envelope, you know. It's my handwriting. You've no idea the trouble it gives to postmen."

"What address?"

As she was speaking, the secretary had jerked her own top-and-two-carbons out of the Underwood, and slotted an Institute envelope into its place. It was pretty deft, that operation. And I remembered reading somewhere that all acquired skill is an attempt to compensate for natural deficiencies.

The only trouble was that I could not think of any address.

"The Commissioner of Police, New Scotland Yard, Whitehall, S.W.I," I told her at last. "And mark it 'Urgent and Personal,' please," I added. "You see it's about my wireless licence. Entirely slipped my memory. I so rarely listen these days."

I don't believe that she even heard that last bit. But I had all I wanted. And, as soon as I got outside, I compared the typing on the envelope with the words on the little slip of paper. The letters were identical. There was the same half-blind "e" and the same guttered "m." That hadn't got me very much further, however. It only showed that someone else had been using the machine. The resident Gorgonette in the private office wasn't the kind who would ever send anyone an anonymous letter.

If she had ever received one herself, I knew that the poor thing would have been filed away under "A" before it could properly have unfolded itself.

2

That little Cornish hell, our common room, promised to be the best place for continuing my researches. People give themselves away more when they are relaxing.

And I wasn't sorry that I had something definite with which to occupy my mind. The first sight that met me when I went inside

18

the common room was a pile of geographical magazines going back practically to Marco Polo—I found out afterwards that someone had carelessly failed to renew the subscription, and they stopped, too, around Drake and Frobisher. Apart from the magazines, there was a ping-pong table with some highly professional-looking, rubber-covered bats lying there all ready; a wireless, with last week's *Radio Times* lying on top of it; and a writing-table with several sheets of notepaper and no envelopes. As a studio-set for a documentary dealing with the leisure problem of the middle classes it was practically perfect.

The chairs, too, were of the type that is specially designed for common rooms. You don't see them anywhere else, and there is probably a factory somewhere with a gang of imported fakirs making them. They are all the same, these chairs; smallish with a removable spring cushion, and a back that can be adjusted to three positions. There is the upright or impossible; the middle, or merely uncomfortable; and the practically flat out, or unconscious. I set mine at uncomfortable and sat down.

The others had all come in by now. And as soon as the Phoenician flute girl had put down the coffee things with a crash that made poor Dr. Mann wonder whether the attack was coming from the east or the west, we all settled down to peaceful hive-activity.

The buzzing that night was mostly about A-bombs. Smith was saying that the New Yorkers were in a state of complete panic, and that if a fire-cracker went off in a New York subway the blast would be felt as far away as the White House. I've forgotten exactly how he put it, but I know that it was very clever.

I was only half listening, because the other half of me was watching young Mellon's face while our friend was doing his counter-Pilgrim stuff. But Mellon had evidently encountered quite a few Dr. Smiths on this side. He was only half listening. Bent forward in his chair, he was trying to listen to the wireless as well. It was a B.B.C. variety programme that was on, and there was an expression of awed and reverent incredulity on his face. Perhaps I was wrong in thinking that the films were his alternative employment. It could have been the Diplomatic Service.

Then Kimbell made a typical Manchester contribution by saying that panic was characteristic of all unheterogeneous peoples, and promptly went back to a scrap of paper on which he had just written B—K Kt 3, or some such piece of purely inspirational gibberish.

This was Dr. Mann's big moment. He was apparently aching to add his crumb of mid-European confusion. According to him the Americans were suffering from an outsize in guilt complexes for having used the A-bomb at all.

"Plees, you cannot understand how the mind works or you would never say such foolish things," he went on, going very white round the gills while he was speaking. "In every Western religion murder and suicide are both wrong, no? Hiroshima was not only *mass* murder"—here his stuffy little voice rose to a bleat as he uttered the word "mass"—"it was also an intense expression of the American people's own death wish." He paused as much for breath as any other reason, and then shaking his peculiar pear-shaped head as he reflected on the lost opportunity: "It would have been better if the Hiroshima bomber had crashed and everyone in it had been drowned."

Just as he finished, there was a slight creak on the other side of me and our resident calculator and memory-man came into play. It was evident that his reaction time was a bit slow this evening. Perhaps he needed a new dry cell or something.

20

"There was an outbreak of panic in New York in 1938," he said slowly, "when the Columbia System broadcast Orson Welles's version of *The War of the Worlds*. People really thought that the Martians had come. The trouble started in the Negro and Italian quarters."

That was the end of the message so far as Bansted was concerned. The wheels just stopped turning as suddenly as they had started. But Kimbell was quick to snatch at the point.

"It would do," he said approvingly. "No shared mass-unconscious."

This immediately brought a deprecatory snort from Rogers. It was the sort of snort that was intended to indicate that no matter how popular the mass-unconscious might become in the future, Rogers himself was determined to keep right out of it.

"And no education," he said firmly. "An educated mass would have recognised one of H. G. Wells's most popular books immediately."

Being self-educated himself, Rogers was always very enthusiastic about education. But he seemed to have a confused idea at the back of his mind that it was H. G. Wells who had invented it. It may have had something to do with the fact that Rogers had once met H. G. at a P.E.N. Club reception. I didn't hold this against him, but what used to irritate me about Rogers was that he would go around quoting *The Outline of History* quite seriously as if it were a reference work.

Then the choir-boy, Swanton, spoke up. He was back on the original topic.

"Well, anyway," he said, speaking in a slow rather singsong sort of drawl as though half asleep, "it won't help the Americans any having been the first to use the bomb. That was just what Russia needed. It provided her with a free field test under ideal conditions, and also demonstrated to the rest of Asia what Christian civilisation is like when put to the supreme test."

It was at this point that young Mellon said quietly that his folks were Methodists both sides of the family, and that some Middle West Methodists had written to the President in precisely the same terms. But that did not please Swanton at all. He evidently did not like being in agreement with Methodists anywhere.

So, just to show that I was still there, I decided to butt in. I suggested—I can't remember exactly how I put it—that the A-bomb was grotesquely overrated as a weapon of warfare simply because of all the mess that had to be cleared up afterwards. And I went on to say that any intelligent generalissimo would rather occupy a perfectly intact London, with all the inhabitants either dead or dying, than have to go over the rubble with a Geiger counter to find out whether there ever had been any Houses of Parliament or whether that was just another propaganda story.

It was rather a lucky note to strike, and it acted as a Class I social catalyst. Everyone was perfectly ready to agree that the nuclear physicists were a lot of publicity-hogging queens, and that the bacteriologists were the salt of the earth.

We went on, I remember, to say that bacteriologists should be treated at least as well as Russia treats her pet novelists—free motor cars, diplomatic wives, country hideouts and all the rest of it. And in that happy mood of mutual adulation, we broke off and played some rather self-consciously energetic ping-pong in which I was no good, and fat little Dr. Mann walked all over the lean American.

All things considered, the common room had turned out pretty much as I had expected. At least I was getting to know my play-mates. Dr. Mann was a humanitarian who was in favour of bomber crashes for the general good of the race. Smith had been born about two or three Georges too late. Swanton had not seemed too downcast by the prospect of a false move on the part of Christian civilisation. And the rest might just as well have gone for a nice walk on the moors while the others were talking. Fairly average, I would have said for common-room gossip anywhere on the research side of things. And nothing firm for me to go on so far. Merely hunches.

Then, as I was getting into bed, I came on something a bit more definite. It was another of those little typewritten messages, neatly deposited in the middle of the pillow. There was the same shining emphatic blackness about the type, only this time the wording was rather more exact. "COMPARING TYPEWRITERS ISN'T GOING TO HELP YOU ANY," it ran. "I KNOW ABOUT YOU EVEN IF YOU DON'T KNOW ME."

I stood looking at it for some time. It was the last sentence I didn't like. Because there was always the possibility that it might have been true. And after all, we can't, every single one of us, be pure lily-white right through.

Chapter IV

1

By next morning something seemed to be stirring. We heard at breakfast that the Old Man had called a special meeting for nine-thirty. And I learnt from Swanton that when that happened it usually meant that some senior Civil Servant had been having a nasty attack of panic up at the Whitehall end.

Anyhow, I felt strong enough to face it. And, outside a gipsy orchestra, you couldn't have seen a finer body of men than the research staff of the Bodmin Institute as we all filed into the Director's room. There was perhaps just a suggestion of the hair-dresser's assistant about some of us because we were all wearing our white overalls. And when the demure one came in and joined us she looked like something that had drifted over from the embalming counter.

There was one man whom I hadn't met before. And it turned out to be the early riser. Michael Gillett his name was, and he sat himself down beside the demure one as to the manner born. He had a good clean profile, sharply cut without being too pointed. I found out afterwards that he was a ski-er. When he wasn't working at the bench he spent all his time in Switzerland. I don't wonder. That profile was just made for a ski-cap.

On the whole, I was rather pleased to see him there because he came as England's answer to the American. So long as we could produce sufficient Michael Gilletts I didn't grudge them their aristocratic film diplomats like Ulysses Z. Mellon. The only thing that I wondered was how long a man with Gillett's profile intended to remain on research work. I formed the distinct impression, possibly wrongly, that if the right opportunity came along he would be perfectly ready to switch over to the sales side and embrace Big Business with one feverish ecstatic hug.

Then the Old Man came in and we all folded our hands in our laps. The Old Man himself wasn't by any means too bad. Largely, I suspect, because I was a new boy, he began by reminding everyone that we were an *anti*-bacteriological institute and not one of the real joy-through-glanders kind; and when he had got to the end of that bit, Dr. Mann looked as though he could have kissed him.

Even so the nature of the work was naturally pretty much the same either way. It went something like this. Some ingenious fellow in a research institute in Prague or Warsaw or Tashkent would discover, or think that he had discovered, a new means of disseminating *B. typhosus* or *B. pestis*. And some equally ingenious fellow in our M.I would get on to it. Then, after a certain amount of preliminary sifting, mostly by people who didn't know an autoclave from a Buchner's tube, the papers would be sent down to Bodmin. After that, we would go into recess for a month or so, and finally we would report back either "Could be," or "Bodmin say Tashkent all screwy-screwy." If it was "Could be" all the dope would then be passed over to the fumigation squad—the Anti-Bacteriological Device Unit was the official title—who kept their D.D.T. and Flit sprays somewhere up in a sister institute near Worcester. And if it was "screwy-screwy" we would just begin again on something else.

By now the Old Man had reached the bit we had all been waiting for. And here he did allow himself one of the routine numbers out of the effects book. Or perhaps he was just being careful. Taking out his key-ring, he selected the Chubb and went across to the safe in the corner. Then he went through the usual business of opening up the Chinese envelopes with the separate tags, TOP PRIORITY, SECRET, ONLY TO BE OPENED BY . . . attached to each one of them. He was painfully slow about it, and his eyebrows seemed to be getting in the way more than usual. But he got down at last to the typewritten part, and began to read. Then we had our surprise. Because it was our old friend, *B. anthracis*, that it turned out to be. And that, let me tell you, came as a bit of an anticlimax. Because we had all been expecting a virus—probably one of the unfilterable ones—and *B. anthracis* is not much above first-year standard.

All the same, the M.I. report said that They, the Other Chaps, had worked out a new air-delivery scheme for *B. anthracis*, which was apparently giving a lot of pleasure at the far end; and that meant that we would have to look into it.

What was more interesting from our point of view, however, was the fact that the report went on to say that the same mysterious, everlasting They had got several stages ahead of us in the preparation of the L-substance that is used in all laboratories for putting up the birth-rate in the germ kingdom. And that really did make us prick our ears up.

I suppose that everyone knows something of the speed with which bacilli multiply. From baby to grandfather within the hour is how the more popular text-books describe the process.

And that begins to mean something when you start off with several million babies in the first crèche. Because their children are having children while the old folks, the founder members of the colony, the original Pilgrim Fathers, are still lusty with the powers of increase themselves.

So if there was anything in the new L-substance—or, rather M-substance as it was referred to, just to remind us that They were supposed to be one jump ahead—there would be immediate high jinks up at the Worcester depot. Instead of sitting round doing nothing as we always pictured them, they would have to begin stockpiling penicillin and Chloromycetin and all the rest of it. Also, before they were through, somebody would probably have to go round all the seaside resorts buying up the donkeys because the best anti-anthrax serum, Sclavo's serum, is obtained from immunised mokes. . . .

The Old Man was putting the things back into their various envelopes when he paused.

"We are rather short-handed to get everything done in the time," he said speaking almost apologetically as though we were all down there simply for the week-end, and were suddenly being asked to peel the potatoes or do the washing up. "We'll have to drop everything else, but that can't be helped. And"—here there was that same apologetic note again—"no visitors until we're through, please." He paused. "In fact, I've asked for all passes to be cancelled," he added. "The department attaches the greatest possible importance to this particular piece of research and is sending an additional security man down here while we're working on it."

I was sitting next to Dr. Mann while the Director was speaking. And, when he came to the word "Security," I saw the little

German's clasped hands suddenly tighten as if he were trying to crush something together inside them. Then with a sigh, the sort of sound that a tired child makes just when it is falling off to sleep, he relaxed again.

This rather annoyed me. Because the very last thing I wanted was to begin getting interested in Dr. Mann.

2

Personally, I am allergic to all security regulations. They bring out the absolute worst in me. One of the reasons I chose Bodmin was because I wanted to be away from people. But the moment I heard that visitors' passes were cancelled, I was wondering how I could get Cousin Chloe and Aunt Hetty over for the week-end simply to show them round the works.

We all said as much over morning coffee afterwards. And Swanton even went a bit further. His was a bad case of allergy, and he talked a lot about secret police, microphones hidden behind pictures of the Coronation, and letters being read by ultra-violet light behind the counter in the little local post office.

"If we had any real guts, which we haven't," he went on, "we'd go along to the Old Man now and say that if They"—it was a different They this time, but apparently every bit as sinister—"send someone down here to spy on us, we quit."

"I don't see why. It seems a perfectly natural precaution to me." It was the great Dr. Smith, our ambassador at large, who was speaking. "If there are people here," he went on, "who can't see the significance of what they are doing, they ought to be moved on before they constitute a public danger."

This was Kimbell's opening. He had a natural habit of hanging round the outsides of conversations like a hyena, and then suddenly bolting in as soon as the blood was flowing.

"Also sprach Zarathustra," he remarked. "If you want a tame Dick on the premises you are welcome. You may be one yourself, for that matter." He paused and negligently flicked his cigarette ash half into his own coffee and half into mine. Then, like a modern Madame Récamier finding someone in her salon who had been left too long out of the conversation, he pointed his grubby, nicotine-stained forefinger at me, and said: "Or Hudson could be the new security officer. It would be rather nice timing, and calculated to allay suspicion."

That seemed fair enough to me, so I decided to buy it.

"As the old Persian proverb says," I replied, making it up hard as I went along: "'Beware the shepherd who first points out the thief.'" And for good measure I added: "Up in Uzbechistan where my people come from we say the same thing only differently: 'The unfaithful wife is she who praises chastity the loudest.' The phrasing is slightly different, but the meaning is clearly very much the same."

It was while Kimbell was working that one out that I got up. As a matter of fact, I was rather busy. So I simply edged Kimbell's match-box gently into the centre of a pool of milk that the Phoenician had spilt on the table top, and left them to it.

I had a feeling that the red-gold girl was deliberately keeping out of the conversation. If so, that was another distinct alpha in her favour.

Chapter V

1

During the next week there was enough overtime done inside the Bodmin Institute to bleach the hair of any good Trade Union secretary. We started early, and we left off when our eyes got too gummy to look through a mike. Just that. I even forgot about my mystery notes.

In a sense, it made it much easier that it was anthrax we were working on. He is a great favourite among beginners, is *B. anthracis*, because he is hardier and stands up to rough treatment better than most of his kind. And that is really the crux of the matter in bacteriological warfare—not which germs our human brother, the enemy, can deliver without catching something nasty himself, but the condition of the poor little germs by the time they have been let loose. It is the extremes of temperature that are the trouble. Because when germs get their feet cold they don't necessarily die, but they aren't up to any very serious work next morning—they have become attenuated, as we call it; and overheat them, and they've had it.

Anyhow, *B. anthracis* has always shown itself more willing than most. It belongs to the spore group which, being

30

translated, means every-germ-its-own-air-raid-shelter. For when this particular bacillus finds life a bit inhospitable, it gathers its own protoplasm together in a little ball—*B. anthracis* is a big sturdy fellow about seven thousandths of a millimetre long—and proceeds to put on armour for the winter. The only thing that *B. anthracis* does like is a breath or two of fresh air. And even then it can get along with the window shut—which is what is meant when the bacteriologist calls him a facultative anaerobe.

But even with all the help that *B. anthracis* could give us, we weren't making very much progress. Because it was round about this time that little things began to go wrong.

There is no lab. on earth where a clamp doesn't come off some time or other, or a piece of tubing break at one of the S-bends. But we had more than that to contend with. First, the thermostat on the main incubator packed up twice in a week. Then the cotton-wool that should have come straight out of the steriliser for stoppering the Pasteur pipettes was found to be supporting as many foreign strains as a camp of displaced persons. And finally the centrifuge went funny on us. That was too much, and the feeling gradually developed that it was more than the law of averages that we were fighting. It was Bodmin United versus the Gremlins by now.

I take it that everyone knows what a centrifuge is. But for the very young I will just rough in the outline. It is really no more than a wheel with little slots inside, into which test tubes can be fitted. You fix the test tube in place, press the button, and the wheel spins away at anything up to 5,000 r.p.m. Then while you are finishing a cigarette or putting in a 'phone call, the centrifuge has done your straining for you and the solids in the test tube solution have been slung right down to the bottom. It is our schooldays' friend centrifugal force that has done it, the same old faithful that tips you over into the far ditch if you try taking a corner a bit too fast.

Now 5,000 is quite a lot of revolutions. And, like juggling, it is all a matter of balance. A centrifuge is built to something a bit better than cart-wheel standards. It is real precision engineering, in fact. And before sticking in a test tube on one side and so upsetting the bearings you always weigh up a dummy and mount it opposite. There's nothing to it really, and accidents to centrifuges are in the low order of things that have built up the big fortunes in insurance. That was what made the behaviour of the Bodmin centrifuge so distinctly rummy.

It was on Monday that one of ours started to go wrong. The first tube disintegrated at somewhere round the 3,000 mark. And when the casing had been cleaned up and enough glass powder to make even a Borgia feel squeamish had been washed down the sink, the same thing happened again. And again.

It was after the third disruption that Gillett came over. In happier circumstances and without his qualifications he would have made the ideal works manager. He had a way of standing, with his shoulders very square and his hands in the pockets of his jacket, that would have given just the right note of confidence in any workshop bay. His profile, too, was at its absolute best when the forehead wore a slight frown. And there was a kind of Troop Leader efficiency about him that made the rest of us all look like very junior Wolf Cubs. While we were still saying, "My, my," Gillett was getting down to work inside the case.

"It's no good going on fooling with the damned thing," he said bitterly when he stepped back. "The Old Man will have to 'phone up the M. of S. for a new centrifuge. We can't do a bloody thing with this one."

As he said it, he slammed the tin lid back into position with the kind of noise that an angry cook makes when the soup has boiled over.

"It's the sheer waste of time that gets me," he said angrily. "It's like trying to do serious work on a desert island."

But by then the idea had begun to get around that people in general, and possibly one person in particular at our end, weren't very anxious to see us getting on any faster.

2

I'm often surprised by how much I notice about other people, and then find that I have missed something that a woman would have spotted immediately.

For example, I knew that on top of everything else that was going on, Kimbell had just started another correspondence game with someone living in Vienna and after a sleepless night of agony and indecision had just made his second move.

I knew that Rogers was having trouble with his teeth and in consequence could hardly wait for Mondays, the fish-pie day, to come round again.

As for Bansted, he was still evidently after a No. 1 job somewhere, and was hard at work pulling the wires. Twice during the past week I had seen him shut up in the telephone booth in the front hall, and the length of time that he was in there without talking suggested that he was trying to get on to something long-distance—though come to think of it, everything was long-distance from Bodmin.

Swanton, I knew too, was in the middle of some

quasi-professional dust-up connected with the Scientific Association for International Co-operation. He was one of the joint secretaries of the thing, and there was a public row going on about his opposite number. Someone had called the poor chap a fellow traveller, and Swanton was urging him to bring a libel action—though whether it was because the remark cast doubt on his hundred per cent loyalty or on his hundred per cent Communism I wasn't quite sure.

As for young Mellon, I had found that in addition to the gift of youth everlasting he possessed the secret of sex inexhaustible—which may have been what Goethe was really getting at. By now he had the resources of the whole Cornish countryside, north and south coasts alike, planned out in his mind as neatly as an ordnance survey map. Shut him up in a dark room alone and he could have filled in the iso-blondes from memory.

I had also got to know quite a lot about little Dr. Mann. He had a load on his mind, and was in the uncomfortable position of never knowing for certain that the load had not been removed rather suddenly. By this I mean that his people were living in Berlin—Russian sector. There was a mother and a grandmother and some other sort of female relative—a sister, I think. The poor fellow was always in a terrible state of nerves about them, and kept making up little parcels to help to keep them going. He sent bars of chocolate, toothpaste, even old shirts of his own that he had finished with. A parcel of miscellaneous rubbish of one kind or another went off almost every week, and about once a month he showed happy because one of them had arrived. His one hope—and it looked a forlorn one—was to get a U.S. visa somehow, and cart the whole lot off to Manhattan. He had told me so half a dozen times at least.

So I hadn't exactly been going about with my eyes shut. But

what I didn't know was that Gillett and the demure one had just got themselves engaged to each other.

Even then, there was quite a lot about Gillett's love life that I didn't know about. And I found out the other half, or rather a part of it, entirely by accident. Things had eased off a bit in the labs. And there always comes a point when about the best piece of research that anyone can undertake is to go down to the local and try to analyse the brew *du pays*.

The trouble with me was that the red-gold girl had upset my whole metabolism. I was therefore in one of those states of deferred activity, quietly sporulating in one of those unspeakable chairs in the common room. It was position number three that I had chosen, the Unconscious. And because of the draught, I had picked on the chair that was right up in the alcove, practically under the darts board.

Before I had been there for five minutes the door opened and someone else came in. That annoyed me because I didn't want to be disturbed. But a moment later I was not so sure. I was aware of some sort of high-frequency emanation that told me that the presence was a sympathetic one. And in the whole Bodmin colony that could mean only one thing. It meant that the red-gold girl was in the room with me. I was just preparing to come out of my corner all male and ruffled and tweedy when the door handle began turning again.

This time it was Gillett who came in. From where I was reclining I could just see a thin section of the doorway. And I noticed with real admiration how well Gillett was wearing his profile this evening. It was in particularly fine shape, and I think that he must have been honing or polishing it. Then the side wall of my little corner shut him off from me abruptly, and I

35

heard the red-gold girl say "Oh."

What interested me was that Gillett seemed to be expecting that kind of a reception. He used the old familiar oh-my-God-am-I-being-patient-or-am-I kind of voice that all men adopt when talking to women who don't want to be talked to. And he started in straight away.

"*Please*, don't be like that to-night," he said. "I only wanted to explain."

"There's nothing to explain. Really there isn't."

That is not an answer that I approve of. It is just *un peu trop classique*. But it has been going on for a long time, and it obviously has its points. Men who have ever lived with women for any length of time avoid giving any possibility for such a reply.

"Oh, but there is," he said, falling into the trap like any newcomer. "And you know that there is. I've been waiting for the chance to talk to you. So when I saw you come in here . . . "

This was becoming embarrassing. Even if I got up now, I'd heard too much already for either of them to be able to overlook it. There was nothing for it, therefore, but to lie doggo and pretend to be asleep.

"It's about Una," Gillett went on.

Una was the demure one. Her parents must either have had second sight when they christened her, or they had been re-reading *The Faerie Queen*.

"I don't want to hear anything about Una, thank you."

"You will when I tell you," Gillett continued, the note of patient reasonableness flaking off his voice in great chunks while he was speaking. "I tell you that she loves me. And it wouldn't have happened if I didn't love her too. I know that you think that I have just been playing with her. But it isn't true."

Gillett paused for a moment. He was no fool. He must have

36

realised that the speech was unworthy of his profile.

Anyhow, it was still the girl's scene. And she was playing it well, too. That is, if she was playing it at all.

"It doesn't matter whether I believe you," she said quietly, "and it doesn't matter whether you believe it yourself. The only thing that matters is whether Una believes it, and I hope for her sake that she doesn't."

"What do you mean by that?"

There was a slightly longer pause this time, and I could tell that Gillett was getting all ready for his second big moment, the one where he comes down l.c. with the ambers full on him. Then I heard a sound that told me that the red-gold girl was crying. That decided me.

Gillett had just got as far as: "Can't a man . . . " when my first snore interrupted him. It was a good snore, stertorous at the outset and fading away on the down stroke into a low flute-like sibilance. It was the sort of thing that has kept whole Blackpool boarding-houses awake during Wakes Week. Gillett stopped instantly. There was really no alternative. I doubt if he could have made himself heard above it. He turned on his heel—I detected the distinctive squeak of crêpe rubber on polished oilcloth—and came over to my corner.

I was ready for him. My hands were clasped in the dead crusader attitude and my lower jaw was just supported loosely by the top button of my waistcoat. There was, too, a new confidence in my snoring. Every time I gave vent to one I could feel my whole spine vibrating like a road drill.

"Who is it?"

Gillett did not reply immediately. I think that he was waiting for his lip to curl.

"I'm afraid it's not a very attractive sight," he said at last.

"It's Hudson."

But attractive or not—and there are two opinions on every-thing—I had stopped his conversation. And, as it turned out, there was no possibility of his reopening it. That snoring of mine had set up a wave pattern like the one that broke the Tacoma bridge. A moment later the chair back broke clean off at the point where the little brass hinges were screwed into it.

Chapter VI

1

When the Security Officer finally arrived from London, he did not give much trouble to anyone. And it wouldn't have been worth the while of a temporary typist to resign on his account. For a start, I think he was a bit lower in the order of things than either Swanton or Kimbell had anticipated. They had evidently been fearing some pert and awful little major, with a black brief-case and full access to all the Bodmin files, both private and professional.

What actually turned up, looking as though he had travelled steerage and the voyage had been a stiff one, was a slow sad sort of man of about sixty, with bad feet. He talked rather vaguely about a dog that he had apparently been expecting to find hanging about Bodmin station waiting for him. And he spent the greater part of his first day simply walking the outer ramparts in a sort of daze, click-clicking his teeth whenever he came up against one of the breaches that we had scooped out of the wire fencing.

It was obvious from the start that all was not well with our Security Officer. Perhaps the elevation or the subsoil did not agree with him. The first night he got himself locked out while he was making his routine inspection of premises, and he had the whole Institute roused before he had managed to get himself inside again. Then his dog, a big snarling Alsatian, with a nasty patch of what looked like mange somewhere down towards the south end, turned up at the Institute. It had been sent in error to Bodmin Road instead of Bodmin and had been in the luggage room living on the stationmaster's rations for nearly five days.

The moment it arrived it caught the spirit of the place to perfection—nerves, bloody-mindedness, frustration, every-thing. Overjoyed at the sight of its master on the first day, the following afternoon it bit him. Then, having located the rabbit enclosure, it cleared the wire fencing when nobody else was about and turned all lupine and atavistic—bill for new rabbits two-seventeen-six. And the following Thursday—the Security Officer's half-day—it ran away completely. Reports of sheep-maiming in the Barnstaple district was the only clue that we ever had as to the route that it had taken. Then, mysterious as always, M.I. recalled the Security Officer himself. His next destination, he said, was Top Secret, and with the aid of an A.B.C. we all worked out a good cross-country route to Harwell.

The very day he left, there was one little incident that was even more screwy than the centrifuge affair. Of all things, the hot air steriliser went wrong. And the steriliser easily the most reliable piece of kitchen equipment in the whole laboratory. It is set permanently at about 160 degrees Centigrade, and is, so to speak, the high grade washing-up machine of the whole department.

But either our steriliser wasn't working properly or we had

discovered a new strain of bugs with strong Phoenix affinities. The thermostat seemed all right too. And what made it so completely baffling was that the twin thermometers mounted in the top both showed 160 degrees as plainly as the blocks in a nursery alphabet.

We thought that Dr. Smith had put his pudgy forefinger on it when he suggested midnight power cuts as the source of the trouble. We were all wrong, however, Dr. Smith included. And again it was Gillett who spotted the real cause. Someone or something—we had most of us reached the stage where we were quite ready to believe in Cornish piskies—had reset the thermostat right down to the 110's. In normal circumstances, that could have been forgotten and forgiven. Any oaf can push the bar of a rheostat back a bit far—that's why thermometers are fitted. But what no one could swallow was the fact that *both* thermometers were not only faulty, but faulty in an identical way. With their little fannies shivering at about 112 degrees, their faces were flushed with a hectic 160. It was hanky-panky all right. And, if it hadn't been for Gillett with his natural flair for factory supervision, we might all have wasted weeks trying to exorcise the jim-jams. As it was, Gillett made a sudden grab at the thermometers. And while Whitehall was waiting, teacup in hand, to hear the latest on the germ-war front, the Bodmin Institute was down to elementary calibration.

When he had finished his little experiment, Gillett sat back wearing a smirk that for once I was ready to forgive him. He had the two thermometers held at arm's length between his thumb and forefinger, and he was gloating over them.

"Absolutely useless," he said. "Both utterly absurd. There, gentlemen, you have a notable example of British post-war workmanship."

And as he finished speaking, he gave a rather theatrical little flourish and dropped the pair of thermometers into the enamel waste-bin at his feet.

The demure one was watching him. In her eyes I saw love, admiration, worship, idolatry, and something else that I could not quite place—fear, possibly. I'd been right, too, about the demure one's eyes: they were remarkably fine, and not something to be concealed.

But, as soon as she saw me looking at her, the lids came down again and the display was over. She was just playing mousie-mousie again.

I found myself next to Gillett at dinner-time. And I had taken one or two extra gins before coming through. That may have been what made me a bit more forthcoming than I usually am when I have a side-face portrait for companion.

"Pity you busted up those two thermometers," I said. "You ought to have sent them to our local M.P. He could have asked a question in the House."

Gillett smiled. He liked playing the part of the honest, worldly-wise administrator, and this opening was all that he could ever have wished for.

"When I find something wrong," he said, "I like to put it right and get on."

It must, I reflected, be rather wonderful to be as perfect as Gillett. There was a natural simplicity about him that put me in mind of things like the Parthenon and the Beethoven Quartets.

I excused myself for a moment in between the shepherd's pie and the prunes and custard, and persuaded the club bar to open up and serve me another double. I was quick about it, too. By the time I slid back into my seat, Gillett had only got as far as "sailor" with his prune stones, and I don't think that he had even missed me.

"It's my belief there's been a bit of hanky-panky going on," I said suddenly. "Thermometers don't get like that. Somebody faked 'em."

Gillett smiled. It was that slow superior smile of his, as bland and reticent as the bloom on old silver.

"So that has occurred to you, has it? "he asked.

"You mean . . . " I began.

But Gillett shook his head ever so slightly.

"Not quite so loud," he said.

This rather offended me because, up to that moment, I hadn't thought that I was exactly shouting. But in the next breath he explained himself.

"There might be someone at this very table," he went on, speaking under his breath by now, "who would give quite a lot to know whether he's suspected. That's why we've all got to be so careful."

"Mum's the word," I said loyally.

It wasn't until I said it that I noticed that everyone at the table turned in my direction after I had spoken. Perhaps Gillett was right. I may after all have been bawling just the teeniest-weeniest bit this evening.

But Gillett was equal to the occasion. He got up in his elegant, rather languid way and linked his arm through mine.

"Come on," he said. "We shall be late."

As soon as we had got outside he let go of me again.

"I don't care to discuss it in there," he said. "Not with Kimbell and Swanton about. Or with Mann for that matter."

My mind was now working like a prosecuting counsel's. The instant Gillett stopped I made one of those electrifying pounces that would have knocked any defence half silly.

"So you've reduced it to one of those three, have you?" I asked.

But, honestly, I don't think that I've ever seen anyone more shocked.

"I've done nothing of the kind," he replied. "I merely mentioned the three who happened to be sitting nearest to us. My very earnest advice to you is not to start accusing people without evidence."

2

Meanwhile, despite the hitches, the lab. side of the work was still progressing pretty smoothly at the speed Nature had intended, and then some. It was not the slightest use, therefore, for a lot of porcelain figures from the Whitehall collection to begin ringing up the Old Man urging him to hurry.

Anyhow, the Old Man took no notice of their appeals. That was because, thanks to the M-substance, things had just started to move a bit faster down Mellon's end of the room. He was getting de-sporulation faster than he should have been. And if you have never worked inside a research laboratory you may find it difficult to understand the excitement that comes over the team when they really think they are on to something. About the nearest thing to it must be the emotion running through an Italian village when the priests tell them that their own local miracle has been recognised by the College in Rome.

Chapter VII

1

Then something really queer occurred up at the Institute. And by sheer bad luck I found myself mixed up in it.

Daylight robbery was at the bottom of it. Somebody outside evidently knew quite a lot about us. And just as evidently the same somebody knew exactly what it was that he was looking for. It was lunch-time when the unknown visitor turned up. And because he was complete with a visitor's pass—one of the "Valid for one visit only" kind—the doorkeeper let him in just as soon as he could get the padlock undone. The two of them, the commissionaire and the thug, had even chatted pleasantly together, it seemed, on the way across to the main block.

What's more, the visitor knew enough to ask how Dr. Clewes had been keeping, and that put all doubts at rest. When the doorkeeper finally went off in search of the Director, he left the stranger sitting on the settee in the front hall. And because we were all busy getting down to the fish pie that the Phoenician was slinging out at us, our visitor had the whole place to himself.

He must have been pretty well briefed in the geography of the Institute. He only had about five minutes to himself, but during that time he found his way not only up to the labs, but also up to the bench where young Mellon had been working. Inside that five minutes he managed to swipe a whole row of the most promising-looking Agar-slopes and let himself out through the front door again.

As it happened, the slopes weren't worth anything. But it was sufficient that someone had taken them. And what made it all so maddening was that Mellon was working on something else at the time, and didn't miss them until quite late in the afternoon. We'd almost forgotten about the vanished visitor by then, and the door-keeper couldn't even give a proper description of him. The only clue that he'd left behind him was his security pass. That was what brought me into it. Because on examination it turned out to be the one that I should have given in the first day I got there. The name K. W. Judson had been carefully typed where mine had been, and there was some rather dainty forgery around the date-line.

In the result, neither I nor the doorkeeper came out of it at all well. He was told that he shouldn't ever have admitted me without that pass. And I got it straight—the Old Man was even quite vehement about it—that a man of my education, whatever that meant, ought to have known enough not to leave uncancelled security passes lying about.

He was right there, of course. And all that I could do was to keep my head hanging down in the shame position. But it was interesting, too. It showed that I hadn't been mistaken in thinking that somebody had gone through my luggage the first day I had got there.

2

It was round about this time—about six weeks after I had turned

46

up in Bodmin—that I picked up a car cheap.

Considering that it was a 1926 model and that it was 1952 when I bought it, there was no reason why it should have been anything but cheap. But, in any case, it was just the kind of car that I have never been able to resist. Even if I hadn't needed it, I would still have had it. The appeal that it made was distinctly maniac. The bonnet was long enough for it to have two leather straps across it. The windscreens could be folded flat. The back-quarters were boat-shaped and finished off rather nicely in what looked like undertaker's mahogany. The exhaust pipe was curved upwards, ending in a wide flat flare like the business end of a vacuum cleaner. And the mudguards were minute crescents mounted direct on to the axle brackets.

The whole chassis was about sixteen feet long from the back light to the headlamps—they didn't fix bumpers in those days—and there was no hood. Indeed, come to think of it, that side of things was extraordinarily incomplete. There was also no pass light, no reversing light, no spares (I found that out later), no heater, no radio, no traffic indicator, and no door—you simply had to scale up the side and clamber over. But at forty-five pounds it was mine. And I've never seen a larger speedometer on any car : it was as large as a soup plate and calibrated in red from the hundred mark upwards.

I'm very fond of country motoring. My idea of a good time when I'm all healthy and extrovert and the little black demon is hushed up inside me, is to do about two hundred and fifty miles or so through the best country that I can find, and do it as quickly as I can. I regard the countryside of England as second to none in the world. I'm so enthusiastic that I would willingly die for it—and probably shall do one day. And I couldn't tell you what lies two feet on the other side of any hedge I've ever driven past.

Obsessional motoring is what my kind is called. And extraordinarily pleasant and invigorating, I've always found it.

I was just coming back from a quick breather and was on the last lap, trying to make the speedometer show red on the Bodmin flat, when I saw the red-gold girl in front of me. She was walking. That was my cue. I cut out and put the brakes on as hard as I could, even clinging on to the beer handle outside to see if that would do anything. And it did. In the result, I shot past at only about fifty-five, and a hundred yards or so up the road there I was, stationary and waiting for her.

"Can I give you a lift anywhere?" I asked.

The "anywhere" was put in just to make the whole thing sound as casual and informal as possible. But it was obvious enough where she was bound for. The way she was pointing, she would have to have said "Exeter" or "Salisbury" if it hadn't been the Institute.

I'd pulled over on to the grass verge in anticipation of this moment, and my cigarette case was open before I had begun speaking. "Shall we smoke a cigarette before we go on?" I asked.

It didn't help me much, however.

"I don't smoke, thank you," she said. "But why don't you have one?"

That wasn't quite the same thing. If only one person smokes there is the rather oriental flavour of a hashish addict holding up the caravan.

"Been walking far?" I asked her.

"Only just up to the Tor and back."

"I love walking," I lied to her. "I'm crazy about it."

"Have you done much of it?"

I shook my head sadly.

"Too lonely," I said. "No one to talk to."

There was no response. So I tried again.

"How do you like it down here?" I asked.

She paused.

"I think the work's important, don't you?

"Terribly," I said.

She was speaking like the lady member of a B.B.C. Forum by now, and there was the distinctive ring of the house captain and senior prefect in her voice as she was talking.

"There are plenty of other things that I'd rather be doing," she went on; "but now isn't the time for them, that's all."

"The very reason why I came here myself," I told her. "Couldn't have put it better, if I'd tried."

Out there in the wind my cigarette was smoking faster than I liked. I wanted this conversation to go on for a long time yet. So I kept up the flow of small-talk.

"I've been noticing you in the common room," I said. "You don't say much while the others are talking, do you? Is that because they bore you?"

"Some of them do," she said. "All Commies are very much the same."

"Meaning Kimbell and his boy-friend."

"And Dr. Mann," she said quickly. "He's just as bad really. When he first arrived he was always trying to get me to sign Peace Petitions, and that sort of thing. He'll be on to you next."

"He has been," I said.

"Well, you be careful," Hilda replied very seriously. "It's not for us to judge him, because he may be perfectly sincere. We can't expect to have the monopoly of good faith on our side. On the other hand, if we really believe in anything ourselves we've got to fight for it. And, if the Communists are wrong, any Peace Petitions that they get up are likely to be wrong, too."

49

My cigarette was finished by now. And to tell the truth, I hadn't been enjoying myself. The whole conversation was just a bit more rarefied than I had expected, and I felt rather like a rock-climber who has got up all right but can't find his way down again. Another ten minutes or so, and I should be calling out for the oxygen pack.

So this time I tried another approach altogether. It was not startlingly original. But I had reason to be grateful to it because it had helped me out often enough in the past.

"Do you mind if I call you Hilda?" I asked.

The question seemed to surprise her. Genuinely did surprise her, I think.

"Why ever should I mind?" she asked. "We're all working together on the same job, aren't we?"

I didn't want to fall into the trap and begin answering questions the way our great doctor always did, so I said nothing. I just sat there looking at her. And, speaking as one who has put some serious research into the matter, I would say that she had the best cheek-bones and eyelashes that I have ever seen on a girl. They took me right back to my schooldays when I used to go to sleep thinking of Norma Shearer.

I knew that so long as I had her near me and could see her and speak to her there was one side of me that I needn't worry about. Sublimation is what the psychologists call the state. That is how I was feeling at that moment, and that is what makes it so damn silly that I should suddenly have turned to her, and said: "May I kiss you?"

I knew perfectly well as soon as I'd said it that I'd done the wrong thing. And I had the uncomfortable feeling that Hilda was going to do the right one. She did.

"Better not," she told me quite nicely. "We've got to go on

working alongside each other and I'm sure we want to avoid a lot of awkward complications. So perhaps we ought to be getting back, don't you think?"

It occurred to me afterwards that perhaps it hadn't really been so bad for her as I thought at the time. After all, a girl as good looking as Hilda must have been through the same routine several times before. And I don't believe that a woman is ever anything but secretly pleased by the fact that someone has wanted to kiss her. But, at any rate, I felt flat enough at the time.

"I'm sorry," I replied. "I can't think what came over me."

We drove back to the Institute in the best tradition of English silence and, when we got there, I was so distant I said: "Allow me," when I gave her my hand to help her out.

As it happened, young Mellon was just returning from somewhere at the time, and I noticed the respectful expression on his face when he saw the two of us together. I rather think that he must have made one or two tries himself in the same direction when he first arrived here.

And I didn't need anyone to tell me that he must have failed, too.

Chapter VIII

1

But, Even if Hilda had shown willing, there still wouldn't have been much time for fancy motoring. That was because young Mellon had been doing better than ever on de-sporulation. And someone else had been doing even better than young Mellon. That someone else was Gillett. And as the work proceeded he gradually emerged as senior midwife. Despite all indications to the contrary, there must have been something or other propping up that profile from behind. And the fact that Bodmin was able to confirm a new, streamlined birth process for *B. anthracis* was really Gillett's own personal triumph.

He was certainly the Institute's blue-eyed boy when the Old Man called us all together. And Gillett knew it. He was therefore careful to keep his profile turned towards us throughout. That may have been because he suspected that, full-face, the old hatchet stock came out a bit too strongly.

The Old Man weighed in straight away. He crossed over to the safe, fiddled with his keys and finally produced a test-tube rack with the tubes all nicely stoppered down with cotton-wool and sealed off with metholin.

"This is what we might call our Exhibit A," he said proudly. "So far as we know these are the only anthrax cultures grown with the aid of M-substance in the country. Their multiplication rate is something between five and six times above normal. They may be the only cultures of that kind in the world. We don't know. And it is no part of our duty to find out. We are merely scientific workers."

The "merely" really meant that he could not think of any higher occupation for Man. And, with that, he put the rack down on the table in front of us, and then turned to face his audience again.

"And now I'm sure you'd all like Dr. Gillett to say a few words," he remarked sweetly.

We all clapped politely. Then we sat back for Gillett to give us his electoral address. And I must say that he did it beautifully. Almost too beautifully. First he thanked the demure one for the part that she had played in it, and there would have been tears in our eyes if he had lingered for a moment longer on the theme of love-in-harness. Next he paid a tribute to Dr. Mann which was probably perfectly justified. He thanked Rogers, the ex-lab. boy, and brought in Bansted in the same breath. He mentioned Hilda, who murmured: "No, that's too much." He even went out of his way to salute Kimbell and Swanton, which you could see upset them because they both loathed him. He referred to young Mellon. And he offered me a personal crumb of his admiration— for not having dropped something that he had once handed me, I think it was. Then he looked very carefully round the room, and said: "I don't think I've left out anyone, have I?"

He had. He had left out the great Dr. Smith, and the omission was obvious and deliberate. I felt rather inclined to admire him for it. Or at least I might have admired him if I had liked him better. But, at any rate, it didn't surprise me. All research workers above a certain level are a pretty jealous lot of queens. And just to make sure that he wasn't given time to correct himself in case the omission had been accidental. I started up the clapping.

That was the end of the prayer meeting. The Old Man put the test-tube rack back into the safe, locked it carefully and restored the key to his key-ring.

Dr. Mann simply sat there staring at the door of the safe long after the key had been put away again. He reminded me of a picture in the old nursery at home of a hungry schoolboy sitting outside the larder door.

2

Elevenses that morning were rather more lively than usual. I wished afterwards that I could have kept a recording of the whole conversation because there were one or two rather useful point-ers left carelessly lying around amid the general litter. I was the first to arrive. And I had my own good reason for that. It was simply an attempt to get to my coffee while it was still in the black state. The Phoenician had a healthy country girl's prejudice against black coffee, and at eleven hundred hours precisely she used to go up and down the line with her milk jug like someone doing the honours in a dairy show. When I snatched my cup away from her I saw the expression in her eyes of brute nature stupefied: it was as though a favourite bull-calf had just told its mother that it had gone on to the water-waggon.

Then Dr. Mann came in. He did not look well. I had noticed that earlier. There was a sort of frozen waxiness to his complex-ion, and his eyes were staring. I think that he was already saying something when he came into the room. And if he was, he must have been talking to himself because there was certainly no one else there. As soon as he saw me he came over, and all that I got was the tail-end of something.

" . . . it must not happen. It must *not* happen," he said slowly and with increasing emphasis. "There must surely be some way of stopping it, no?"

"Only by taking the milk jug right away from her," I told him.

Dr. Mann did not seem to have heard me, however. Or, if he had heard, he had not understood.

"It is not even sufficient to think that the Russians possess it also," he said. "They do not know the extent of our knowledge. Therefore, they may be tempted to think of us as ignorant. And, if they do think so, they may be tempted to make use of this weapon believing us to be unprepared, no?"

"That would seem to be about the general picture," I agreed with him.

"But that is what must not happen," he said again. "And there is only one way of stopping it. Only one."

"Which way's that?" I asked.

The strain of telling me was almost too much for him. He was trembling as he stood there, and he was shaking his little egg-shaped head so violently from side to side that I knew that the chick was due to be delivered almost any moment now. But when it came it had a rather old-world appearance. It was Easter-all-the-year-round for that kind of chick.

"By publishing our results internationally," he said.

"Then there would be no more danger from it. International results would neutralise themselves. There would be no more spying, no more counter-spying, no more fear in the minds of men. It would be the end of war if results were published.

"But suppose the other fellow was a bit absent-minded and forgot?" I asked.

"The choice," said Dr. Mann solemnly, "is between possible failure and inevitable disaster. I would sacrifice my life to see it happen."

"I get your point," I told him. "But I still don't think that it would be a good risk on Lloyd's."

"Lloyd's, plees?" he asked.

I did not enlighten him. I must have taken part in precisely that conversation at least a couple of hundred times before. And when I had been younger I had, God forgive me, started about half of them. In fact, it is the basic attitude of every serious scientist, this sharing of results. There is also a higher mystique to it. Pure knowledge knowing boundaries of neither race nor creed, and that sort of thing. And Dr. Mann was just getting ready for that part.

But by now we had been joined by the two King Street emigrés. And the level of the conversation took a sharp slant downwards.

" . . . there is only one country in the world in which such knowledge would be really safe," Kimbell was saying. "And that's the . . ."

"U.S.S.R.," Swanton put in almost automatically.

These two boys had done their double act for so long that I had begun to doubt whether they ever knew exactly which had said what in their particular line of cross-talk.

"Imagine a weapon like this in Truman's hands," Kimbell went on, without even noticing that he had been interrupted. "Can you see a free Europe if he possessed it? It all fits so perfectly into the old peace-through-fear formula."

Rogers, meanwhile, had gone one better. He had Bansted with him, and the pair of them were extraordinarily reminiscent of my old employer.

"And in time of peace just think of the commercial possibilities," he pointed out. "There'd be tremendous possibilities in all sorts of fields for the first firm that gets working on it."

There was a lot more from him in the same vein, and you could watch the mind of the ex-lab. boy working. I think that he was already seeing himself as the head of a retail chemists' chain with branches in all seaside towns, complete with tearooms and lending libraries in every one of them.

But it was left to the great Dr. Smith to score the absolute top-high somewhere down at the wrong end of the scale.

"Always assuming that there is something in it, and, personally, I am expressing no opinions either way"—he could really hardly have said less after the way in which Gillett had snubbed him—"let us only pray that we keep it to ourselves. I have reason, good reason, to believe that the Americans are only passing on a fraction of the atomic knowledge that they possess. If we can offer a threat every bit as terrible as theirs, we may be able to sit down at Lake Success as equal partners, and not as poor relations."

This was Hilda's turn.

"Hear, hear," she said, looking more pre-Raphaelite than ever. "Only we should use it as a bargaining instrument rather than as a threat. We must always remember that the alliance of the English-speaking peoples is the most important thing in the long run. It's simply that we mustn't let the Americans trample on us."

When she had finished, I made a vow that as soon as we were married—and I made my mind up on that point—I would get her interested in bee-keeping or babies or something, and off international politics altogether. That is, if I was in time.

The way she was heading, she was due for the British Information Services to fix her up for a trans-Atlantic coast-to-coast goodwill mission tour almost any moment now.

Chapter IX

It was the Old Man's idea that we should all take a short breather. And from my point of view, I knew at once that it would be fatal. With a nature like mine that has a spot of mildew somewhere near the centre there is only one thing that has ever really suited it—and that is a job of work that doesn't allow of any let-up.

A sudden compulsory half-hol. in the middle of term was easily the worst of all. I could feel my defences going down like cardboard as I read the Old Man's release note. In a queer way that rather worries me on these occasions, while one half of me was thinking hard of madder music and stronger wine, the other half kept saying: "Achtung! Achtung! Hier ist alles verboten." What's more, there was the complete me, the real me, asking myself in a dopey, helpless sort of fashion which me was going to come out on top. And from long and intimate acquaintance with such situations I would confidently have said that it was evens.

If you have finally decided to paint the town red there are better places than Bodmin to choose for doing it. The whole of Cornwall for that matter is pretty much of a write-off. You need somewhere with plenty of pubs, and a bit of life going on before you get there.

I consulted my A.A. map, and the nearest that I could get to the prescription was Plymouth. Sailors on leave appear to have quite a lot in common with me when I'm in one of my problem-child moods, and we rub along rather nicely together. Plymouth, then, was the answer. And, as soon as I had decided, I changed into my check sports shirt as more in keeping with what lay before me. I'd bought a rather nice check cap in Jermyn Street to go with the sports shirt, and out came that, too. It was all rather childish and silly. But one part of me has always insisted on the dressing-up process.

It was a nice little run in the car, and I did it in twelve minutes under schedule, which meant some pretty mean driving on the way. This did not surprise me. It was the mean me who was at the wheel that afternoon. And I was able to get everything worked out in my mind while the West Country kept up a fairly steady sixty past the side panels. The plan that I evolved was simple and self-explanatory. It was to start high and work downwards. The object was to get full value for money and avoid all unpleasantnesses. If I were to start trying to get back into the Grand or the Royal or the Palace in the state in which I intended to be later on that evening I should probably be chucked out. And I'm bad at being chucked out of anywhere.

It was six o'clock when I arrived in Plymouth, and I went straight to what appeared to be the best hotel that the Luftwaffe had left standing. The saloon, marked 'Residents Only,' was a comfortable spot with a good fire, and I knocked back three doubles at a speed that made the barman first of all look respectful, and then anxious. But he need not have worried. All that I had got out of it was a new sense of inner power and well-being. And euphoria always suits me.

Then I remembered my car. There were two reasons against leaving it in the street outside the hotel. The first was that I still didn't know exactly how the evening was going to plan out, and I didn't want to run the risk of having to leave it there with the lights on all night. And the second was that I had just noticed that the licence was a shade off-colour and on the overdue side. So I tipped the porter and arranged with him for me to leave it round the back where I could get it if I wanted it. That is, if I could still drive.

By now, completely free and without even a car to tie us down, we strolled off down the High Street together, me and my little black devil. For a man with my background three drinks is nothing, repeat nothing. It merely helps me to look the future in the face a bit straighter. It would be the next two or three that would decide things. I knew that. And I knew that even then it would be entirely in the laps of the distillers. Because, when I'm drinking alone, I never know for certain whether I'm going to end up morose or frisky. There isn't ever anything for it, therefore, but to go on with the series and find out the empiric way.

So far, I was still the sort of customer that all decent-class hotels pray to see coming up their front steps. This time I chose the best of the second best and continued with the treatment. I was rather dainty about it, I remember. And, in between the sips, I ate a few peanuts and potato crisps from a dish on the bar counter. Up to that moment, indeed, I even considered changing my plans rather and dining in the hotel with a bottle of Burgundy all to myself and a glass of brandy and a cigar afterwards, possibly finishing up with a seat in the two-and-fours at the local flick-house.

But the memory of other provincial hotel dining-rooms, out of season and with only one or two old ladies ranged round the walls like treasures out of Pompeii, was a bit too much for me. They are a separate race, these hotel old ladies, with their lace chokers and their artificial pearls and the little saucer of scraps for the dog, and they have a way of looking at a man that makes him feel hairy and dissolute even when he's only thinking about his income tax.

But already something was happening inside me. There had been a distinct click as that last drink had gone down. And I now wanted something a bit more exciting than a hotel dining-room.

At moments like this, instinct is a wonderful guide and coun- sellor. Put me down in any foreign capital, blindfold me and turn me round three times, and I could still make off in a bee-line for the dive quarter. For example, even though I had never been in Plymouth before, I knew that on leaving the hotel I had to turn left and then left again to get to the Barbican. And I was feeling marvellous. I was humming cheerfully to myself as I walked along. And when I saw a match-box lying on the pavement I took a running kick at it. Nothing very sozzled in that. If I had been put in front of a police surgeon I could have graduated with honours in all subjects.

I was now spreading my drinking very carefully. Only two singles in any one pub was the rule—and no doubling backwards and forwards between the Public and the Saloon pretending that they were really two different pubs.

The last two pubs that I had been into were no better than cold, rather coffiny little compartments with barmaids who were evidently cousins of the original bearded lady of Bodmin. But what was important was that compared with the first few drinks that I had taken, every extra single now counted about four. And the signs of it were coming thick and fast by now. It wasn't simply that I was feeling sorry for myself. I can manage that often enough when I'm stone sober. What was much more to the point was that I was becoming fumbly. I had to chase one wet sixpence up and down the bar before I could get my fingers under it.

It was my fourth pub, rather a large noisy one, this time. And I wasn't quite so steady on my feet by now. When I had finally pocketed my change, I went and sat down in one of the little alcoves at the side. There was a sailor from H.M.S. Something-or-other and a girl already sitting in the opposite corner. The sailor was a hot-looking young man with a complexion like sausage-meat, and the girl was quite slim and rather pale. She had a lock of fair, soft-looking hair that kept falling across her forehead every time she bent forward, and her hands were the long delicate sort with the veins showing.

When the sailor got up and excused himself, the girl smiled across at me. She was rather a pretty girl and I smiled back. That decided her, and she moved up nearer.

"I wouldn't say 'no' to another drink," she told me.

It was only the West Country in her voice that saved it: other-wise, it would have been just the kind of wheedling, cheap stuff that sets my teeth on edge. But, as it was, I smiled back all right.

"If you hadn't asked, I was just going to suggest it," I told her. "That's what I was going to do—suggest it."

I had now reached the careful and repetitive stage. With me, that's one of the surest signs of all.

"Well, make it a gin and lime, will you?" she asked.

"Gin and lime it shall be," I said. "If you hadn't told me I'd have ordered a gin and lime just the same. That's what I'd have ordered—a gin and lime."

It was a bit difficult getting out of the alcove. I'm a large man and the table jutted out over the seat rather awkwardly. But it was getting back again that was the really tricky part. I remember that I was all tangled up with her legs by the time I was settled in again. But the drinks were all right—I can't remember when I've ever spilt a drink that I've been carrying.

We were getting on quite nicely together by now. The girl had just told me that her name was Pat, and I had said that I could have guessed it if she had only given me the first letter. Then the sailor came back. At first, everything was all right. He even asked if he could borrow my matches.

It was the drink that I'd bought his girl that caused the trouble. If she'd wanted another one, he said, she should have asked him. His face had reddened up a bit by now. And it occurred to me that perhaps he wasn't a very nice sailor. But I still knew enough not to interfere and just sat tight, looking at my finger-nails.

Then he began to get rough. He picked up the free drink and emptied it on to the floor beside him. And, in doing so, he upset mine as well. And I still think that it was to my credit that I should have taken it all so calmly. I behaved in correct U.N.O. fashion, and merely tabled a vote of censure before getting down to anything like counter-violence.

"Are you aware, sir," I asked, intoning as precisely as if I were in a church dramatic society, "that you have spilt my drink?"

It was obvious from the way the sailor took the remark that he was aware. He thrust his face close up to mine.

"Washermatterwivyou?" he demanded.

Having done so, he turned back to the girl beside him. And putting out a great red hand, he began pulling her about. That decided me. I saw then that I would have to intervene in an effort to resist aggression.

"Unless you stop mo-lest-ing that girl," I heard myself saying slowly and rather beautifully, "I shall be forced to knock you down."

The gallant, or Old Virginian school, is one of the phases through which I always pass on these occasions. And this was merely me passing through it. The sailor, however, did not appear to be unduly cowed. Instead of replying, he caught hold of me by the lapels of my coat and began banging my head against the panelling behind me. I was a bit dizzy by the time I managed to struggle to my feet, but I still could see straight enough to hit him. As a matter of fact, I hit him rather hard. He fell back on to somebody else's table, and then the whole place became like Marseilles on VE night. There was broken glass everywhere. He came crunching through it as he made his way back towards me. Then, when I saw that he really meant business, I went into a clinch with him. That was what put us both on the floor together. And it was then that the girl started screaming.

I don't remember much more of that part. Because by now the sailor was propping me up in the crook of his left arm while he was hitting me with his right. Smash. Smash. Smash. I felt the first one, and merely counted the other two. Then I must have passed right out. When I came to again the girl was mopping at me with a handkerchief—my handkerchief, it turned out to be— and the landlord was saying: "Oo started it?"

It was only the evidence of the girl that saved me.

"This gentleman was just sitting by himself," she said. "I know, because I saw him. Then Jim came along and socked him. I feel ever so ashamed of Jim, really, I do."

We left shortly after that, and the girl put her arm through mine. What I needed, she said, was taking care of. And she strongly recommended me to have one more just to settle my nerves. So we went into another pub, and sat quietly holding hands. We didn't stop long, however, because we could see the top of Jim's head over one of the partitions. He was going over the whole episode, and was describing exactly what would happen to me if he ever saw me again. We neither of us liked the sound of it. And when we had got outside again, the girl suggested that as it was so late I had better go back with her.

Chapter X

1

It was still quite early when I woke up next morning. And I have noticed that when I have been well and truly soused the night before I always wake up an hour or so earlier than usual—which means that I don't miss even a single moment of the hangover.

In the circumstances, I behaved with considerable dignity and self-restraint. Knowing that my little friend of last night was watching me from behind the bedclothes, I assumed an air of easy and tranquillising nonchalance. Going over to her mirror, I first of all examined the eye that the sailor had bunged up for me. Then I put on last night's collar and combed my hair down.

The mistake that my companion made was in sitting up on one elbow to say good-bye. She had the sort of good looks that get better as the evening grows later. Seen in the dawnlight, there was the disconcerting appearance of something that had just been dredged up from the bottom of the Sound. I was glad that I had spent the night in the armchair.

I caught the first Torpoint ferry of the day. And I was back in Bodmin by nine. But the actual homecoming wasn't exactly what I had expected. Naturally I didn't go up to the front gate. Instead, I swung in at the side entrance and garaged the car in the coach-house where I always kept it. I was just heaving my legs out over the coachwork when somebody stepped forward. It was a policeman, and just behind him was standing an inspector.

"Good morning, officers," I said, speaking a trifle on the loud side, as I always do when I am trying to appear bluff and hearty. "You're quite right. It is out of date. But the new one's in the post. Very smart of you to detect it. I'm afraid this licence business must give you an awful lot of extra work."

The constable looked a bit taken aback and confused at that. He began passing his tongue backwards and forwards across his lips as though they didn't work properly when dry. But the Inspector was a different kind of animal altogether. If I had caught his eye a little earlier I might even have dropped my voice instead of raising it. It was a cold, ice-like eye.

"Dr. Hudson?" he asked.

I nodded.

"Would you mind, sir, accompanying me to the Director's office?" he asked.

It was one of those polite commands that are all the more commanding for being so polite.

But I was doing some pretty quick thinking.

"Anything wrong, officer?" I said.

And the reply was the usual one.

"Just a few questions we'd like to ask you, sir."

Nothing very revealing in that. But also nothing very reassuring. Nothing very reassuring either in the fact that he asked the constable to stand by the car and not leave it until he had come back again. Inside me, I felt a cold patch developing.

And, as soon as I saw the Director, I knew that something really serious must have occurred. He was sitting at his table, hairy and miserable, with his chin supported in his hands. He looked like the Forsaken Merman. And I can't say that his face brightened up when he saw mine. Not that this surprised me. I hadn't brightened up myself when I had seen my own face.

Then I noticed something else. The whole Institute seemed to be exuding policemen this morning. There was one standing over in the corner just behind me.

The Inspector got down to work straight away.

"Would you mind telling us where you spent last night?" he asked.

That was awkward. I had come down to Bodmin to make a fresh start. And I had seen enough to know that the Director was the kind of keen family man who might not like the idea of having his assistants temporarily occupying top rooms in Plymouth.

So I started lying.

"As a matter of fact, I slept in the car," I said.

"Why did you do that?"

"I'd drunk rather too much cider," I said. "When I'd had the second half-pint I decided it was safer not to risk anything. So I just parked the car and dossed down."

"Where was that?"

"In a lane."

"Whereabouts?"

"Oh, about thirty miles from here. Say thirty-five. I didn't measure it."

"Can you name anywhere it was near?"

I paused.

"It was between Okehampton and Exeter," I said finally. "On

68

the left as you go up."

At that moment I accidentally caught the Inspector's eye, and then avoided it again.

"Okehampton and Exeter are about twenty-five miles away from each other," he told me.

"You don't say," I answered.

"Well, can you be a bit more exact?"

I shook my head.

"Sorry," I said. "If I'd known you'd be interested I'd have looked it up for you."

"Well, can you describe the spot?"

"Oh, yes," I said confidently, "I can do that. There was a sort of hedge on one side and a gate on the other. I'd know it at once because there was a haystack just a bit farther on. And a tree. I'm practically certain there was a tree."

"It must have been cold in the car, wasn't it?"

"Nice of you to ask," I said. "As a matter of fact, it was."

"Did it rain?"

"I was asleep," I answered.

"There isn't any hood on your car, is there, sir?"

"No," I said. "That's another thing."

"Were you wet?"

"Very," I said. "The dew's terrible in these parts. Especially at night. I wonder nobody's done anything about it."

"Were you alone?"

"All the time."

"See anyone you knew?"

"Didn't even see anyone I didn't know. I've told you: I was asleep."

"How did you hurt your eye?"

"Fell against the windscreen."

"Can you remember the name of the public house you went into?"

I paused.

"Well, I can't be sure," I said. "But no doubt you can check it. I think it was The George. Or it may have been the Duke of Something. Or possibly The Chequers. There are such a lot of pubs, aren't there? It wouldn't surprise me if you said it was The Crown."

The Inspector drew in a deep breath as though he needed one.

"Are you ready to sign what you just told me?" he asked.

"Pencil, please," I answered.

2

It wasn't until I had joined the others in the common room that I learnt what all the fuss was about. And, when I did learn, I didn't like it. During yesterday evening somebody had opened up the Old Man's safe and made off with the one slope that counted for anything. In short, Gillett's culture was missing.

There were some strangely glassy-looking eyes all round me. But that may have been because nobody was allowed either to enter the building or leave it. The entering part didn't matter. But the not-leaving-it bit was different. It doesn't take more than about five minutes for a normal healthy man to develop a sense of claustrophobia. And some of the people weren't exactly what I would call healthy and normal to begin with. There was little Dr. Mann, for instance. He was behaving as though he had still got the missing culture hidden on him somewhere.

"Now, it is terrible," he said. "Like a prison camp."

"Well, let's hope they soon find it," I said. "There won't be any let-up till they've got it back again."

But that didn't suit him either.

"It will only be good if they never find it," he replied. "Never. Never."

"Don't say it so loud," I advised him. "If you do they may take you up on suspicion."

Dr. Mann turned several shades paler. His face went turnip colour. This was most disturbing, but it was turnip-shaped already.

"Why me?" he asked. "Please say that you do not mean me. It could not be me. I can account for myself all the time, no? It is very frightening when there are police."

It was Hilda who tried to soothe him. But she wasn't looking her best this morning. She was pale, and had shadows under her eyes. A person who's just had an entirely sleepless night might look rather that way.

"But our police aren't frightening, really they're not," she said. "They only want to find out everything."

The Dioscuri apparently thought differently, however. Swanton was the first to speak.

"Why not call it a Police State and be done with it?" he demanded of no one in particular. "It's much better calling things by their proper names."

Kimbell ran his fingers through his hair-fuzz, and nodded approvingly.

"Our friend here"—he indicated Dr. Mann, who recoiled visibly as soon as he saw that stained finger-nail pointing at him—"will soon be able to see the wonderful British police force at close quarters. They'll be arresting me next for playing chess with a foreigner. Then we can all compare notes." He turned to me as he was speaking. "Have you been done yet?" he asked.

71

I nodded.

"Rubber truncheons, pins under the nails, and all the rest of it," I told him. "But they didn't get anything out of me."

It occurred to me afterwards that perhaps rubber truncheons and torture-chambers weren't really so very funny to the Dr. Manns of this world. But it was too late now. The door had just opened and the Director's secretary stood there.

"Dr. Mann," she said. "Would you mind going over to see the Director, please?"

It was impossible to get down to any really serious work while the Gestapo stuff was still going on in the Institute. In the result, we packed up and spent the next few hours of Government time simply talking things over. Hilda and the demure one had both withdrawn. We were thus just one big unhappy stag party. And there were one or two quite interesting side-lights on human nature by the time we had finished.

For a start, young Mellon was obviously feeling rather pre-occupied about something.

"Say," he asked at last, "are those guys thorough? D'you reckon they check up on what you tell them?"

"The English police force," I said slowly, "is the mother of all the police forces in the world. If you think you've made the least slip in anything that you may have said to them I should correct it now before it's too late. They're always ready to make allowances for carelessness. But deliberate lying—never."

Mellon began fingering his gold lighter-cum-cigarette case. It was a very comprehensive piece of Fifth Avenue jewellery, and looked as though there might be a portable wireless built into it somewhere.

"Aw, hell," he said. "It isn't that. I told 'em all right. It's just that I don't want the dame's husband drawn in. We haven't ever been introduced socially you see."

Dr. Smith raised his eyebrows.

"You'd much better call your lawyers," he advised. "But, in any case, the Embassy will probably stand by you. They can always plead diplomatic privilege if it comes to it."

"But not matrimonial." It was Bansted who had spoken. He looked more than ever like a bank manager to-day. "I happened to run into an old friend of my wife's yesterday," he went on. "Purely accidental, of course. Hadn't seen her for years. But it could look bad, all the same. I know just how Mellon's feeling."

As he said it he gave a little laugh that sounded like the jingle of handcuffs. And I took up from there.

"Were you seen together?" I asked.

He nodded.

"It was over at the Royal Crescent at Newquay," he replied. "I booked a table for eight-thirty. Name of Jones. Her idea, not mine. All most unfortunate. You see, she's waiting for her decree to be made absolute."

"Bad luck," I told him. "Anyone see you?"

Bansted paused.

"Not exactly," he said. "But the waiter's bound to remember us. I upset the claret. He had to put a clean napkin over the tablecloth."

"That's tough," I replied. "But I shouldn't worry. It's a test tube, not a woman they're looking for."

I was careful to conceal the admiration in my voice as I said it. It seemed to me that he had sewn up his alibi very neatly. Upsetting a glass of claret shows the hand of real experience, and I wondered how often he had used that old dodge before.

But Dr. Smith was speaking again. And, when he had finished, he revealed that he was better at almost anything else than being consoling.

"Do you really think so?" he asked. "I should have imagined that if something were missing the first thing that the police would look for would be an accomplice."

"But why advertise the meeting place?" Swanton demanded.

I think that he was playing his part quite straight at this moment. I liked him best when he was applying his mind to problems where the *Daily Worker* hadn't told him the answer already.

Dr. Smith merely re-raised those eyebrows of his.

"That will be for Bansted to explain," he said.

Then Rogers began to wriggle as though he too wanted to make his confession. Altogether it was becoming more and more like the Oxford Group every moment.

"As a matter of fact," he said, "I was with a woman myself last night." He paused rather obviously for effect. "Only in my case, it's different. She happens to be my wife."

"Then what have you got to worry about?" I asked.

"We aren't living together," Rogers replied. "I suppose that much is obvious. Or I shouldn't be here. As a matter of fact, she came down here to discuss a separation."

Bansted coughed.

"Isn't this rather personal?" he asked. "I mean, you don't have to tell us if you don't feel like it."

Rogers frowned for a moment.

"Not so personal as all that," he said slowly. "You see, it was something to do with politics we parted over. She's been mixed up in it all her life. She's secretary of an Anglo-Russian Fellowship Group at this moment. It may look a bit fishy, you know, having her down here on the night the thing was stolen."

"Distinctly so," Dr. Smith agreed. "Did you tell the police?"

"Only in general terms," Rogers replied. "I didn't want to blacken her character more than it's already blackened." He was silent for a moment. "Extraordinary thing politics," he said. "She's a very brilliant woman, my wife. Ph.D. and M.Sc, and all that."

His voice curtsied almost visibly as he spoke of the degrees.

"Better go back and tell them the rest of it," Dr. Smith urged him. "Save time all round later on."

There was a kind of gloomy virtuousness about our Dr. Smith that I found increasingly irritating this morning.

"Come to that," I said, "where did you spend the evening?"

Dr. Smith smiled rather wanly.

"In bed," he answered. "I was tired and gave myself the whole day in bed. What's more, I feel much better for it."

"Anyone come to see you?" I asked.

"No," he said. "I particularly gave orders that I wasn't to be disturbed. I looked after myself entirely."

"So we've only got your word for it that you were there at all?"

Dr. Smith smiled again.

"Precisely," he said. "And it will be rather interesting to see whether the Inspector appreciates the significance of that fact. There is no corroboration whatever."

He regarded his finger-nails for a moment.

"Come to that," he went on, "Kimbell's and Swanton's alibi is no better. A reciprocal alibi is really no alibi at all."

"Meaning what?"

Kimbell swung round on him as though up to now his word had always been taken for his bond.

"Meaning that you and Swanton went for a walk on the

moors," Dr. Smith said quietly. "It would have been possible for the two of you to have made an assignation with a third party, who again was either not seen or not noticed by anyone else. Someone in a car, for instance. There are roads across the moor, you know."

"And Russia has vast fleets of helicopters," Swanton reminded him.

But by now Kimbell was frowning at Swanton, and I got the impression that he didn't want to figure in the conversation much longer.

"In any case, we aren't the only ones," he said. "What about Gillett, for instance?"

"I understand," Bansted replied, "that Gillett spent the whole day with his fiancée. Una had a cold and they didn't go out at all. The Director himself vouches for both of them."

"And Hilda?" It was Kimbell's Manchester voice that asked the question.

"Church bazaar at St. Clynt's. She was in charge of it. Whole village saw her there."

It was Rogers who supplied this piece of information, and he had the knowing air of someone who had been asking a few questions on his account.

Then Dr. Smith turned his smile on me.

"And how did Dr. Hudson spend *his* time?" he asked.

I did not reply immediately. But when I did I gave the answer loud and clear.

"Mackerel fishing," I said. "I was out all night. Alone. I only saw one submarine. It wanted to know the way to Murmansk and I told it. That's all that occurred. Nobody's got anything on me."

Chapter XI

1

I've never seen anyone in worse shape than Dr. Mann when he came back from the Director's office.

"This is the end of me," he said as he sat himself back down in his chair. "I am finished."

Dr. Smith turned his round smooth face towards him.

"What happened?" he asked. There was no noticeable sympathy in the voice, merely a cold scientific curiosity.

"Third degree, by the look of it," Swanton answered for him. "The police are all swine when it comes to it. If they weren't swine they wouldn't be police."

Whenever Swanton was excited by anything his voice always rose a semi-tone or two. He was now positively fluting at us. It was the corncrake note of Kimbell that put in the rest of the chord.

"Precisely," he said. "And if they can see that there's a tender spot naturally they jump on it. They probably prefer someone who's been mauled over once or twice before."

"No doubt. No doubt," Dr. Smith answered, with a little wave of the hand. "But perhaps Dr. Mann himself could tell us."

Dr. Mann, however, could not speak immediately. He was crying; actually crying.

"Plees," he said. "It was not like that. Not at all. They were very kind to me. Good, also. They offered me a chair and a cigarette."

Kimbell and Swanton both gave a gesture of despair as they heard him. If Dr. Mann had said that he had been strapped on to a triangle with an electric iron held against his big toes they would have felt that they were getting somewhere.

But Dr. Mann was still talking.

"Everything I said they have believed," he went on. "Everything. The Inspector shook hands with me. But now I see that I have made one mistake. It will betray me. I am finished."

"What was the mistake?" I asked.

That, however, was what Dr. Mann was telling nobody. He shook his head fiercely.

"No," he said. "I am too suspect. I cannot tell. A man who has dug his own grave must lie in it. I must be alone and think. It is all very terrible."

Then he started weeping again.

2

I've already hinted that in the ordinary way I can do without highly-emotionalised Central Europeans. There is something about adult cry-baby stuff that dehydrates all my own tear-glands. But I could not help feeling sorry for little Dr. Mann. He was so utterly defenceless. Two different experiences, the first with the S.S. and the second with N.K.V.D. had stripped all the outer skin clean off him. I knew that he was all bare flesh and nerve endings.

He didn't come down to dinner at all. Kimbell and Swanton both agreed that despite the nice things he had said about the Inspector he must have been worked over pretty thoroughly. When I left them they were getting all ready to compose a letter to the Council for Civil Liberties. It was Kimbell who volunteered to type it. And I took note of the fact that he was a typewriting enthusiast.

For my part, I thought that I would go across to the annexe to see whether Dr. Mann would like anything. A Guinness, for example. I had one myself in the bar first and then took the other one over to him on the off-chance. And I had to hammer on the door panel to get him to open up. When he did come, he looked blotchier and more distraught than ever.

"No, go away, please," he said as soon as he caught sight of me. "It is unwise for you to be seen with me. I tell you, I am finished."

I put the Guinness down on the corner of the washstand. And as I did so I noticed that his razor was open on the toilet shelf. He was the old-fashioned sort of shaver, and used an open razor of the kind that looked as though it had come from a cavalry regiment. I took one more look at him, and finally shut up the razor and slipped it absent-mindedly into my pocket.

But I could not get him to drink the Guinness. All that he wanted to do, he said, was to be left alone so that he could think. And for that his head must be clear; quite clear. No alcohol, plees, he kept saying.

So just to show friendly I sat down on the end of the bed and cleared up the Guinness myself. All the time, Dr. Mann had his eyes fixed on me. I told myself that he was trying to appear grateful for my kindness and compassion in calling on him at all. But he succeeded only in looking impatient. And, finally, with a pat on the back that nearly broke his spine, I withdrew quietly and left him to his Sturm und Drang and Weltschmerz, and all the rest of it.

I may have been a bit worried myself, I suppose. At any rate, I couldn't sleep properly: the dormital only made me feel faintly sick. And by the time 2 a.m. came along, I thought that I might slip along the corridor to see how Dr. Mann was progressing. For all I knew he might have a spare razor hidden away somewhere. So I folded myself up in my thick Jaeger, slid into my bedroom slippers and slopped along the corridor to cubicle B.

There was no answer when I knocked. And no sound from inside the room either. But the door wasn't locked, and I went straight in and switched the light on. Then I breathed more easily. The bed was crumpled, but not bloodstained.

Because I hadn't got much else to do, I put the light out and lay down on the bed and waited. Waited for quite a long time, in fact. It was nearly three-thirty when I heard some faint pussy-pussy footsteps in the corridor. And then, a moment later, the door handle turned, very quietly.

The bed was behind the door, which meant that Dr. Mann did not see me immediately when he turned on the light. But I could see him all right. He had on a raincoat, and a ridiculous little Tyrolean hat that was tied down over his ears by a muffler. On his feet were ordinary gym-shoes, muddy all over and soaking wet. And something must have happened to his hand. It was cut right across the knuckles, and the blood had come through the handkerchief that he had wrapped round them.

When he saw me lying there grinning at him with my head up against the bottom rail and my feet on his pillow, he put his hands up to his face for a moment. But he didn't scream or faint or attack me or anything. Instead, he came over and with a wet little hand, the uninjured one, he clasped mine.

"*Plees, plees*" he said piteously. "I can explain everything. Everything. But not now. You must not have seen me. If you see me, I am sentenced."

"I haven't seen anyone," I told him. "But I should just burn that handkerchief, if I were you. It doesn't look sterile."

Dr. Mann sank down into the wicker-chair and stared at his poor damaged hand.

"If I am still alive, I can explain everything," he said again.

"I wouldn't be surprised," I told him, and with that I went back to bed.

Next morning I heard that the village post office had been burgled, and last night's collection from the Institute had been found strewn over the floor. All the envelopes had been ripped up, some of them so carelessly that the contents were just in strips and slithers.

Chapter XII

1

The Ice-Eyed Inspector was really working on his right level when it came to the post office job. The whole thing by now is probably a Hendon College classic. For a start, the Inspector interviewed everyone within a two-miles radius—all fifty of them, including the seven who were bedridden. Police stock went up several points in consequence. Then the Inspector got the sub-postmistress on to checking up all her dubious accounts—Old Age Pension forms with smudged signatures, Savings Books with badly written sevens that might really have been nines, missing postal orders and that sort of thing. And while she, poor old soul, was trying to behave as though she really understood what the innumerable little forms and columns of figures were all about, the Inspector was doing his fingerprint and footmark stuff all over the house and garden.

Judging by the questions that he asked us later on that day up at the Institute, it must have been good growing weather. The post office was apparently dimpled all over with finger-smudges, and there was a simply magnificent footprint, the footprint of a lady's rubber plimsoll, right under the broken window.

The lady's footprint interested me a great deal. Dr. Mann had very small feet, rather like castors on a comfortably built armchair. And he had certainly been wearing gym-shoes when he came back. I didn't wonder that he was jittery,

I discovered afterwards that there was another piece of evidence that had confirmed the police in their belief that they were looking for a woman. The evidence was a small embroidered handkerchief with traces of what seemed to be scent still on it. Only it wasn't scent at all, really. It was NASOL, one of W.D.P.'s products, with which Dr. Mann had been trying to fight back a common cold. And the handkerchief had been intended for his elderly female relative in the East Zone. It was simply that Dr. Mann had run through his own stock that had made him take his old Grossmutter's along with him.

But by then I had decided that perhaps the Inspector's I.Q. wasn't so very high after all. And that was because he was so ingenuous about his reasons for wanting a blood specimen from each one of us.

"The county pathologist will be over in the morning, sir," he said. "It won't take a moment and it's quite painless."

"But don't tell me that there was blood all over the money orders and things," I exclaimed, clasping my two hands together. "Good gracious, how terrible! Why, they'll have to cancel them."

"There were traces of blood," he admitted.

"And if you find a trace of blood can you really say who it came from?" I asked.

I was leaning right forward by now like a gallery first-nighter. The Inspector nodded.

"There are groups. We work that way," he said with the simple pride of a Cornishman speaking of something where Cornwall was so obviously leading the rest of the world. "Then if the blood in the stain and the blood in the specimen are found to belong to different groups we know that we're on the wrong track. It's more a method of eliminating the innocent than finding the guilty party, if you follow me, sir."

"It's difficult," I said. "But I think I do. And are you sure it's really painless—getting the blood, I mean?"

"Just a pin-prick."

"You don't actually *see* the blood, do you?"

The Inspector brought out his iced-gimlet look again.

"It isn't the size of a dewdrop," he said pityingly.

"Well, thank you, Inspector," I replied. "You've explained it very nicely. I want to help you all I can, and I'm quite ready to consider it. I'll speak to my doctor this evening. If he thinks I can give that much with safety you're welcome."

But I don't think that the Inspector was really an understanding kind of man. Either that or he was in a hurry. This time it wasn't simply the ice squirt that he gave me. It was the whole berg, hurled hard and hammered home.

2

By now, however, the Inspector was already on his way out. M.I.5 had decided to take over from him. Their own men, a colonel and a couple of captains, had come straight down from London the day the missing culture was reported.

The two captains didn't amount to very much. They were mere note-takers and coffee-carriers. But I must say that I was more favourably impressed by the head of the mission. He was a chain-smoker like myself, and he had bags under his eyes that would have roused the suspicions of any Customs officer.

Wilton, his name was, and I found out afterwards that he had been in the Egyptian drug-control racket for over twenty years. He was a B.Sc. London. But somewhere in the Courts of the Pashas, he had acquired a kind of unconcealed boredom that made him indistinguishable from the genuine Cambridge article. And thank God, when it came to cloak-and-dagger stuff in a research laboratory, he spoke our language.

The Director had made over his breakfast-room for temporary Gestapo headquarters. And Wilton sent across almost straight away to say that he would like to see me. But compared to the ice-eyed Inspector, Wilton might never have conducted the interrogation of a witness before. He simply stretched his long, thin legs in front of the fireguard, wriggled his shoulders like a camel settling itself, and said: "Well, tell me all about yourself."

I grinned. "There isn't much to tell beside what's in the dossier," I said.

"Isn't there?" he asked.

While he was speaking he lit a fresh cigarette from the stub of his old one, and dropped the butt into an open ashtray without even troubling to stamp it out. There was a whole lifetime of excessive smoking in that single gesture. But he didn't press the point. Didn't even give the impression of being the sort of man to press anything.

"Where do you suppose the stuff's gone?" he asked at last.

I paused.

"Russia, I suppose."

"And do you think it got there?"

"One of us must have sent it."

"Any idea which one?"

I shook my head.

"Not a clue," I told him.

"That's my trouble, too," he said.

85

While he was speaking, he uncrossed those long legs of his. And now that he was standing I could see how tall he was. He wasn't camel-type any longer. It was definitely somewhere in the giraffe series that he belonged.

"Have a drink," he asked.

Considering that it was only makeshift, he had got the place remarkably well equipped in no time. There was a bottle of Scotch and two of Gordon's in the corner cupboard, that up to last week had contained nothing more exciting than a few pieces of Crown Derby and old Rockingham.

When I said, "Gin," he poured me out a glass that even I looked at respectfully. And I found myself hoping for his sake that M.I.5 took a generous view of his expense accounts. Then we both had the other half. We didn't say very much while we were drinking. And Wilton spent most of the time simply staring out of the window.

"Mind if I go on asking you a few questions?" he inquired, still with the same general air of vagueness.

It occurred to me then that, perhaps the Egyptian sun had got at the poor fellow. Either that or he'd taken to sampling some of the choicer drugs that he had confiscated. Because in the real sense of the word, he hadn't so far asked me anything. We'd just been gossiping.

"Carry right on," I invited him.

"If the stuff's gone to Russia, I suppose that means a sympathiser here in Bodmin, doesn't it?" he said.

He seemed to be thinking aloud. And the thought didn't strike me as particularly brilliant either.

"That's how I see it," I agreed with him.

"Noticed any signs of Communist activity since you came here?"

I shook my head.

"Not a hint."

It was a silly question, anyhow: Communists aren't all that dumb.

"Happen to know if any of the people you're working with are Commies?"

Again I shook my head.

"Nobody tells me anything," I answered.

"Or ex-Commies?"

"Not so far as I know."

He continued to stare out of the window as though sunlight and white clouds were something new to him. And I wondered if the cross-examination was now over.

"That was an awful lot of tripe you told the Inspector," he said at last. "What made you?"

"Just shyness," I said.

"D'you often go into Plymouth?"

"Who says I was in Plymouth?"

Wilton had closed his eyes by now. From the peaceful expression on his face he might have been ready to doze off at any moment."

"You were, weren't you?"

This time I was the one who paused.

"As a matter of fact, I was," I said simply.

There was another pause.

"Would you like me to make a fresh statement?" I asked.

Wilton blew his lips out.

"Not worth it," he said. "Besides you probably don't remember the details by now."

We didn't seem to me to be getting along very fast. And the same thought must have crossed Wilton's mind. He straightened himself like one of those Angle-Poise lamps returning to the upright, and got up.

"I'd much rather you forgot about it and helped me to find a Commie or an ex-Commie here on the staff of the Institute," he went on. "That's your job."

"But why me?" I asked.

"Only because I thought you might be able to help me," he replied. "But don't lose any sleep over it. If you can't, somebody else will. The facts are bound to turn up sooner or later."

With that, he shook hands with me. And I noticed then what a limp, feeble sort of handshake the man had. My own grip seemed rather bad form by comparison. But I didn't like the turn the conversation had just taken. And he seemed rather to be harping on it.

My trouble was that I had joined the Communist Party right back in 1926. And I didn't want to have anybody nosing his way around me.

Chapter XIII

1

I wasted a lot of time wondering how much Wilton really knew. And, in the end, I decided that it couldn't be very much. Otherwise, he would have pounced. Not that I was alone in wondering. There seemed to be an unconscionable amount of speculation going on up at the Institute.

Alone among us, it was our great Dr. Smith who showed brave by publishing his conclusions.

"Looked at dispassionately," he said with irritating slowness, "it might appear that some person or persons"—here he stared hard at Kimbell and Swanton while he was speaking—"had an interest in preventing, or at least delaying, any positive outcome of the experiments. Now that the work is over, the accidents have ceased entirely, and the law of averages can apply again. That is a characteristic of all sabotage."

"Thank God for that," Bansted said devoutly, before either Kimbell or Swanton could get their little forked tongues into the forward position. But a split second later Kimbell cut in like a radio comedian.

"So it was sabotage, was it?" he asked. "Have you told the

Sunday Express about it?"

"Sabotage, or rather the fear of it," observed Swanton, taking the cue up perfectly, "only occurs during a decline. Any society that is expanding never gives a thought to it. But once the whole bloody thing starts crumbling then the word begins to crop up. Look at the papers. Ammunition train blows up—sabotage. Naval turbine breaks down—sabotage. You never even hear the word 'strike' nowadays; it's *industrial* sabotage every time."

By now Kimbell was talking again.

"As for these accidents having stopped," he asked, "isn't it a bit early to speak? How about your theory, if something happened to-morrow? Gremlins do sometimes return, you know."

And to-morrow was precisely when the next accident did occur. One of us, Gillett's own girl-friend Una, very nearly went up to heaven in gauge oo pieces.

I don't expect laymen to know what an anaerobic jar is. But if you're working on the anaerobes you have to simulate their normal living conditions, and exclude the oxygen. To do this you take a large glass jar, seal it hermetically and begin pumping the air out. Then when most of it has gone you add a little hydrogen to taste.

So far, it's mere nursery stuff. But just to make sure that all the oxygen has really gone and that you're giving the anaerobes a sporting chance, you begin heating the mixture. This brings on condensation and leaves room for more hydrogen. By the time you're through, it's a thoroughly hydrogen-happy little jar that you have with you. But the heating bit can be tricky. There is an element of palladium black right inside the jar to lay on the heat. Naturally the little capsule is all wired off, like the Davy safety lamp that miners use. That's because hydrogen when mixed with even the remains of oxygen and brought into contact with a naked flame makes one big Brock's benefit. And it's easy enough to monkey about with the element to make it lethal.

It was the demure one who was working the jar. And the two of us were the only people who were in the lab. at the time. Young Mellon, who had just located a new ash-blonde in the St. Austell area, had slipped off rather early to reconnoitre, and Gillett had taken Bansted out to gloat over a pregnant guinea-pig. I was aware somewhere at the back of my mind of the hum of an electric motor which told me that the demure one was using the vacuum pump on the anaerobic jar, and I heard the faint clink of metal on metal as she fitted the spanner into the hydrogen cylinder. Nothing on earth could have been more normal so far.

But it didn't stop that way for long. The demure one bent down for a second to pick up a pencil or something that she had dropped, and at the same instant the jar exploded. There was a bright white flash like a pocket atom-bomb, a bang like Judgment Day, and no more anaerobic jar.

And no more demure one—that was my first thought. I made my way as quickly as I could across the litter of busted plates and smashed-up bottles, and found her. She was lying in a heap on the floor right up against the side of the opposite bench. There was blood on her forehead where one of the little slivers of glass had cut it, and her legs were twitching. She might have been dead or she might not. I couldn't say.

I bent down to pick her up. And, while I was still holding her, Gillett came bursting in.

"What happened?" he asked.

"Oh, nothing," I told him. "It's just the way friend Kimbell said it would be."

"Is she all right?"

I nodded.

"You'd better have her," I said.

And, with that, I passed her over from my arms into his. Then I paused. Gillett was so pale that I thought for a moment that he was going to faint, too.

2

Then something happened that made the whole thing seem odder still. What's more, the oddity came from quite the most unexpected quarter. It came from Hilda. And when she asked me if I would go for a walk with her on the moor, I knew that there was really something up.

She was an uncompromisingly open-air kind of girl, and she walked rather faster than I did. If I had attempted even to hold her hand I should have had to start running just to make sure that I didn't have to let go of her again. Then, about a mile from the Institute, Hilda got to the point.

"I want you to do something for me," she said.

"Agreed," I told her.

"I want you to help me to get Una away from here."

That stumped me. If she had asked me to persuade Bansted to shave off his moustache I felt that I should have had about the same chances of success.

"Why me?" I asked.

"Because I can't," Hilda replied, with the astonishing substitute for logic that women have been using for years, and usually get away with.

"But, still, why me?" I asked her. "I've hardly spoken to the girl."

92

"Because you're about the only person here that I trust," she told me.

That really meant something, coming from her.

"Could be," I answered. "But I still don't see how to set about it. I'm not the kidnapping kind."

"Don't be silly." she said.

I wished that Hilda hadn't got quite that governess sort of note in her voice. It didn't go with her eyelashes. But it went with everything else apparently.

"Listen to me," she went on. "I want you to talk to Gillett and say that after what Una has been through you feel that she should go away somewhere. And I want you to be tactful about it. If he thinks that you're trying to get her away from here for good of course he'll oppose it. Make it sound only like a few days. That's all I want you to do."

"And then?"

"I'll do everything else there is to do."

"Meaning what?"

Hilda's mouth tightened.

"Meaning that when she's gone she's never coming back again," she said. "Never."

"So," I answered non-committally.

Perhaps too non-committally. Because it didn't seem to satisfy her. She suddenly thrust her hand out and laid it on my arm. I was surprised to find how strong her grip was.

"It's your job to get Una away from here," she said fiercely. "Just that. Afterwards, it's my business."

When I got back to the Institute it was already after six o'clock. I went straight along to the bar to drink things over. If Hilda had been the first girl to tell me that I was the only living male whom she could trust, I might have been bowled right out by it. But members of the other sex had been telling me that kind of thing for as long as I could remember. I think that it must be something to do with my appearance —the hacked-out ruggedness and the crowning disfigurement of the scar. There is an ineradicable Puritan belief among the English that the ugly must necessarily be good.

And I was still suspicious. Gillett was so easily the Institute's best-looker that I could understand any girl, even Hilda, wanting to get him back again all for her own. The only thing was that I didn't see why I should help.

I still had other plans for Hilda.

Chapter XIV

I think that it must have been the presence of M.I.5 that led our local Inspector to redouble his own efforts. Perhaps he was hoping for a transfer from the rick-fire and cattle-maiming side. Whatever it was, he certainly dashed about a bit. And he was just on the point of arresting a tubercular tramp somewhere over in Wadebridge and charging him with the post office burglary, when he suddenly found the shop that had sold a pair of the right-sized plimsolls.

That changed everything. The two young captains started behaving as though the trial were to-morrow, and went stamping about the Institute with bundles of papers under their arms and an aloof, mysterious expression on their faces like children playing Red Indians. And I can tell you that it caused a bit of a sensation inside the Institute when we heard that poor little Dr. Mann had been asked by the Inspector to attend an identity parade.

The only person to remain calm and apparently disinterested was Colonel Wilton. He ordered—and, what was more remarkable, actually got—another half-case of Scotch and six of gin, and invited me across to help him get through it.

I didn't enjoy it quite so much as I should have done. And there were two quite different reasons for this. The first was that Wilton would keep harking back to Party members and ex-members, which gave me a distinctly coolish feeling in the pit of my stomach every time he mentioned them. And the second was that I couldn't help feeling pretty badly about Dr. Mann. He was taking things worse even than I would have expected. It didn't even seem to comfort him any when I told him that I had agreed to stand in as an extra in the identity line just to keep the numbers up and see fair play. And I still had a sort of haunting feeling that he might feel like borrowing somebody else's razor rather than go through the ordeal of looking a lot of policemen in the eye.

The identity parade took place at 9.30 a.m. sharp. I drove myself down just to show off the new licence on the windscreen. And when I got there I found myself let in for a bit of a surprise. Two surprises, in fact. The first was that the whole ruddy Institute was assembled. Apparently at the last moment, the Inspector had gone round explaining that the more people who turned up, the better Dr. Mann's chances were likely to be. Wilton explained to me afterwards that the only thing that the girl in the shoe-shop could remember about the person to whom she had sold the plimsolls was, that he was foreign-looking and somehow didn't seem to belong. And it was simply to avoid standing Dr. Mann up amid a lot of sheepish and bewildered cowhands, that the police had roped in the most convenient colony of obvious misfits that they could lay their hands on.

The shoe-shop assistant was a tired, drooping sort of girl, rather like a limp black plimsoll herself. And she spoiled the whole effect by pointing out Dr. Mann as she came in through the doorway. And that made the rest of us feel rather foolish. We were left standing there like a lot of nightmare Ziegfeld girls playing to a stone-cold house.

But the Inspector asked us if we would mind not breaking off for a moment. And that was where surprise Number Two came in. Because the next instant he came back again with my little fair-haired friend from Plymouth. She looked pretty ghastly in the hard morning light of the courtyard—that dredged-up appearance came out more strongly than ever. But I must say that she behaved magnificently. True to the finest traditions of her profession, she went down the whole line without batting an eyelid. And then, balancing herself on her five-inch heels, she said that she had never set eyes on any one of us before.

I was still admiring her poise and integrity, when something considerably less pleasant passed through my mind. For, with none but the noblest of intentions, she had destroyed a perfectly good alibi. And I might find myself needing one almost any moment now.

It called for imagination, lying, perjury and a supreme display of honest, manly indignation before I was able to get Dr. Mann out of the nasty jam that he had got himself into.

And it wasn't easy. The Inspector was still in the first flush of his triumph. I learnt afterwards that Dr. Mann's was the first decent footprint that the Inspector hadn't accidentally tramped on while he was still looking for it. There had, too, been some rather cunning undercover business going on at the Institute. Apparently he had bribed the Phœnician to procure one of Dr. Mann's ordinary walking shoes for purposes of comparison. And he was all ready, when the moment came, to produce it in court as a proof of size. That decided me. I told him that Dr. Mann had spent the key-hours, midnight until 2 a.m., sitting in my bedroom telling me all about life in the Third Reich. Even when I swore to it he still disbelieved me. He had something there. But I was so sure that the little German was too jumpy to steal anything that it still seemed worth trying.

So I turned to Wilton instead. He was much more reasonable. And when I added by way of a brilliant afterthought that I remembered all about that evening because Dr. Mann had cut his hand opening the metal cap on a soda-water bottle, that seemed to clinch matters. The clue of the cut hand had been our ace card that the Inspector had been keeping up his sleeve ready to slam down at the last moment.

I don't know how M.I.5 works in relation to a County Police Force. It may be that if there is trouble at a board meeting, M.I.5 has the casting vote. At any rate, we heard no more about the arrest of Dr. Mann. And his gratitude in consequence became downright embarrassing. It was like having a pet poodle jumping all over me.

"Can I ever thank you enough, no?" he asked me, his pale round eyes protruding so far that they seemed to be pushing against the back of his spectacle lenses.

"Not another word. You've done it," I told him.

"But somehow I must repay," he went on. "I am considering ways." He paused and seemed to be trying to make up his mind between a year's subscription to *Punch* or introducing me to his sister. Then he rounded on me suddenly. "And why did you do it, plees?" he asked. "It was too wonderful. Saying that I was with you that night."

"Why, good gracious," I answered. "It's the truth, isn't it? My memory's getting simply terrible these days."

Dr. Mann understood that one.

"You are right," he said. "It is important to be discreet. "Not even to you should I speak of it. I am discreet again. No one shall ever know about me."

I was still thinking about Dr. Mann's last remark when I came on the third of those typed messages. By now, I had grown so thoroughly familiar with this means of communication that I used to make a kind of regular scraping movement along the pillow before getting into bed. And this time my fingers encountered one of the familiar little slips.

But this time the wording was easily the most disturbing of the lot. There in capitals I read the words: THOU SHALT NOT BEAR FALSE WITNESS, COMRADE.

I didn't like the look of that at all. Someone—and I still had no idea who—was rather too intimately familiar with the facts. Also, he seemed to have an uncanny reading of my character.

At least, he knew enough to figure out that if he had merely referred to the Commandment by the code number, I probably wouldn't even have known what he was talking about.

Chapter XV

1

It was Hilda who kept me from getting neurotic about the screwy messages. She had a distinctly one-track mind. And she kept on at me about getting Una away from the Institute. She was so earnest about it indeed that I didn't like to tell her that I still hadn't quite made up my mind.

And then on the evening of the third day, I did manage to touch lightly on the subject. I happened to be in the bar alone when Gillett himself came in. And it couldn't have been easier or more natural. He was wearing a slightly drawn expression that I think he must have known suited him rather, or I am sure that he wouldn't have worn it at all. And I had taken just enough drink not to mind what I said. So I went right in at my very heartiest.

"Have a drink, old chap," I said. "You look as though you could do with one."

We weren't really on old chap terms, or anything like it. And telling Gillett that he looked as though he needed a drink was about as risky as telling him that his profile had slipped.

"Just a small one," he said. "I've still got some work to do."

That gave me just the kind of lead I'd been playing for.

"Pack it up, chum," I advised him. "It isn't worth it. And it isn't fair to Una either."

I saw his eyebrows go up a shade when I called the demure one "Una." As a matter of fact, I was a bit surprised myself.

"And there's another thing," I said. "Why don't you get her away from here? She ought to go right off somewhere just to get over it. She must have swallowed an awful lot of glass when that jar went off."

Gillett passed his hand across his forehead. It was perfect the way he did it. He knew all the right gestures, and could easily have got himself a gold medal at the R.A.D.A. any time. There was even the surprise pay-off. It certainly caught me unprepared.

"I wish to God she would," he answered. "Perhaps you'd speak to her. She won't listen to me."

"Two more pink gins," I told the barman hurriedly. "And make them large ones."

I was getting really interested by now. The only trouble was that the pattern seemed about as subtle as an expanse of black-and-white squared tiling. Hilda wanted me to get Una out of the way so that she could have Gillett to herself again. And Gillett was evidently hankering after pretty much the same arrangement. I wanted to see what else I could learn, so I began shifting my ground a bit.

"Well, after all, she probably knows best," I said. "I just thought that it would be good for her."

"So it would," Gillett answered. "Damn good." He dropped his voice a little even though Charley, our barman, was the only other person in the bar. "I don't like some of the things that have been going on here. Have you ever known an anaerobic jar explode like that?"

"No," I answered truthfully.

He paused.

"Nor have I. And I still have a feeling that there's something pretty queer still going on around here. As a matter of fact, it's rather more than a feeling. I think I've stumbled on to something."

"That goes for me, too," I said, again truthfully,·

"And that's why I'd like to get Una quite out of it," he went on. "This Institute isn't the place for a woman. At least not just at present, it isn't."

If he had said that it wasn't the place for two women I should have been perfectly ready to agree with him. But, as it was, I didn't want to give the impression of being one of the nervous kind. I was calm and casual in the way that six gins can make anyone calm and casual.

"Aren't you dramatising things a bit, old man?" I asked.

"I don't think so," he said.

Then he brought out the same gesture again. Hand drawn slowly across the forehead and eyes half-closed while he was doing it.

The only trouble was that he had become so good at it that he was in danger of convincing even himself.

2

All that took place on a Wednesday. And by the following Friday, the Inspector had something more than size five plimsolls to worry about. He very nearly had a murder—Gillett's murder—to investigate. Someone up on the moor had been practising with a firearm and had apparently happened to let it off when Gillett had been passing right in front of the sights.

102

It was only bad marksmanship, or possibly the blinding effect of Gillett's profile when viewed through the little aperture that had saved him. But it certainly left him shaken. For once he forgot to look his best when he told us about it. "Too damn near for my liking," was what he said. And having said it, he kept repeating it.

What he didn't know was that it had been too damn near for my liking, too. The report had seemed to come from just over the other side of a small hillock where I happened to be resting. I was assistant-on-duty in the lab. at the time, and had just slipped out for a breather. But I couldn't very well say anything. It would only have worried the Director if he had thought that the discipline on the routine side of the Institute was getting shaky.

There were, however, two other witnesses to the shot. Dr. Mann was one of them. But he, poor fellow, hardly counted because he was always hearing Vi's and distant explosions and things that didn't reach anybody else's ears, and he wouldn't have been credited even if he'd been the one who was fired at. The other witness, however, was Bansted, our Bisley man. And he insisted that it was a Luger or something of the kind that he had heard. The report, he said, had come from somewhere not more than half a mile from where he had been himself, and must have been a close-range job. That sounded reasonable enough because the afternoon had been distinctly misty, with visibility of not much more than about a hundred yards. But that in turn showed that the shot couldn't have been all that casual. Someone must have been just sitting there waiting for it.

That was Gillett's view of the situation. And it was Hilda's view too. But what didn't make sense was that it was still apparently Una that she was most worried about. Or was she? I couldn't get rid of the uncomfortable feeling that she didn't care two hoots for Una, whereas she would have died cheerfully for Gillett whenever he asked her. But if that was so, she was certainly a pretty convincing kind of actress. And she would insist that somehow or other the shooting had increased the danger that Una was already in.

"Increased the danger?" I asked quite innocently. "You didn't say anything about danger before."

"Oh, but it's so obvious. It's so obvious," Hilda went on. "If you can't see it, there's nothing I can do about it. I only want you to get her away from here. That's all that you've got to do. And you've got to do it quickly."

She was becoming about as near to hysterical as she was ever likely to be. Her colour was higher by now. And she was indulging in the short, sharp kind of breathing which is one of the first really tell-tale signs in a woman. Then very abruptly she came right up to me.

"You can kiss me now if you like," she said. "Only you've got to do what I ask you."

That kiss gave me back just nothing at all. It was her cheek that she offered me, and not her lips. And, in any case, I don't like being offered a kiss as a reward for good conduct. This particular one reminded me of a jujube handed out by an exasperated mother as a last desperate attempt to get poppet to do something.

In any case, there was far too much going on for there to be any possibility of my having a *tête-à-tête* with the demure one. Gillett was guarding her like a mother-lynx with kittens. And it was suddenly Bansted who had become the centre of everything.

I must say that it certainly did look a bit fishy. Because it had suddenly come to light that when he had left the Institute on the afternoon of the shooting he had taken his rifle with him.

As soon as he heard, the Inspector was ready to whip out his book of blank arrest-warrants, or whatever the exact procedure is. The only trouble was that it was Dr. Mann who was the sole source of the information. And, on principle, the Inspector didn't believe a single word that Dr. Mann said. Also, Bansted wasn't exactly the staring, glassy-eyed kind of assassin. And the other sort don't normally march off to the chopping-up with the axe slung over their shoulder.

What, on the other hand, was rather bad was that Bansted should have forgotten to mention that he had ever had a little thing like a rifle in his raincoat pocket. An umbrella is the sort of thing that anyone could overlook. But to forget about a rifle spells carelessness. And Bansted wasn't in the least naturally careless.

Chapter XVI

I had already arrived at some preliminary conclusions about Wilton. But for the sake of our friendship, I was careful to keep all conclusions of that kind entirely private. For the plain fact was that Wilton was past it. No doubt in his youth he had been a wizard at unravelling things. The mere name of Wilton Pasha may once have hung like a three-generation curse over every dope-peddler in the Nile delta. But in this, his Bodmin period, the wizardry had all too obviously departed. What deductions he did make were mostly pretty fumble-fingered and unsubtle.

Like the one about Hilda and me, for instance. Simply because he knew that I had once given her a lift in my car, Wilton seemed to assume that I would be buying a ring as soon as my first pool combination came out right.

"She's the religious type, isn't she?" he asked.

"That certainly is what first brought us together," I replied.

"Ever say much about it?"

I shook my head.

"There are some things you can't put into words," I explained. "Perhaps music comes nearest to it."

Wilton filled up my glass for me.

"More tonic?"

I shook my head.

"Gets on well with the Vicar, doesn't she?" Wilton asked.

I locked my two forefingers together.

"Like that," I told him. "Been a second father to her."

"Know why she left the Vicarage?"

This was where it was beginning to get difficult. Because I didn't know that she had left. I'd only had one real conversation with Hilda so far. And neither of us had thought to bring either the Vicar or the Vicarage into ft. But if Wilton wanted to talk about parish politics it was all right with me.

"It was the sermons," I said. "Always used to go through them out loud in the room next to hers. Took all the freshness out of it on Sundays."

"Keen churchgoer, isn't she?" he asked.

"Morning, afternoon *and* evening," I replied. "That's more than you can say for some people."

I'd got him on the raw there. And he knew it. But he tried to pass it off.

"Must be a good sort the Vicar," he said vaguely.

"Fine type," I agreed. "Grand men, these old country parsons. Son of the manse myself, you know."

"I thought you'd get on well together," Wilton replied. "That's why I asked him over."

"You haven't," I exclaimed. "How delightful." I paused long enough to light a cigarette. "I wonder if he'll recognise me, though," I added. "I always make a point of sitting right at the back. Less conspicuous, you know."

"Much," said Wilton, and left it at that.

It was the tinkle of a bicycle bell that announced that the village padre had at last toiled up here. And as I sat back waiting for him to come in, I could picture the machine—green, probably, with a wicker basket in front and a great felt cushion strapped on to the top of the saddle.

Then the door opened and the breathless old thing tottered in. He must have been somewhere in the early thirties. At first glance he was all flashing teeth and horn-rim spectacles. Teeth particularly. His two front ones came down on to his lower lip as though a small white butterfly were resting there. And it was obvious that he was the keyed-up sort. He spoke in short, staccato sentences like a telegram, and added a little laugh in place of the full stops.

"Evening," he began. "Got your message, ha-ha. Came straight away. Something absolutely red-hot, ha-ha. . . . "

He saw me standing there. Then, realising that he had just been indiscreet in the presence of a total stranger, he blushed deep red like a schoolgirl. If he'd had long plaits he would probably have begun chewing at them in sheer embarrassment.

"Sorry," he started up again. "No idea anybody here, ha-ha."

Wilton sat him down, and made him take his goloshes off. Apparently he'd seen quite a bit of him before. Because he knew all about his habits.

"Cider?" he asked.

"Oh, rather."

"Smoke?"

"Never use them."

Except for indicating the gin bottle with his thumb, Wilton seemed to have forgotten all about me. His back was turned full in my direction by now, and he was concentrating on the parson.

"What's the position?" he asked.

There was a little wriggle of excitement as though the parson had been saving himself up for this bit, then the reply came.

"Worse," he said. "Much worse, ha-ha. Last three Sundays not a sign. Not even Communion. Resigned from Sunday School, too. Said the work was too much. All very mysterious, ha-ha."

"Spoken to her?" Wilton asked.

I could tell from the tone of his voice that his eyes were probably closed. Wilton always did most of his questioning in a state that was only just this side of sleep.

"Tried to yesterday," the Vicar answered. "Not satisfactory. Both on bicycles. Wouldn't wait for me."

Wilton stretched himself. It was the creaking sound that made me look at him. And those creaks were always telltale. Whenever Wilton stretched himself it meant that he was getting bored and wanted to change the subject.

"Oh, well," he said, "thanks for telling me. They all get a bit run down, you know. She'll probably be all right again when she's had a holiday."

But the Vicar wasn't going to be brushed off like that.

"More to it than that, ha-ha," he replied, going faster than ever now, as though he were delivering the telegram as well as sending it. "Real evidence this time. Only came this morning. On my way up here when you rang. Look at this."

Out of the inside pocket of his jacket he produced a thick roll of something done up in a newspaper wrapper. The stamps, I saw, were foreign ones.

"Postman tried to push it through the letter-box," he went on. "Too big. Got stuck, ha-ha. Wrapper torn all down one side, ha-ha. Look what it says."

That was really too tempting. I couldn't resist the Vicar's exhibit. So I came over. And I must admit that it was interesting.

Through the long slit in the wrapper the name of the journal showed plainly enough. *L' Action Communiste* was what it was.

"Ever had any like these before?" Wilton asked through a yawn.

"Rather," the Vicar answered. "Every week. Ever since October. No idea what they were. Burned them if I'd known, ha-ha."

"Better leave 'em with me," Wilton told him.

But that brought out another side of the Vicar's nature.

"That all right?" he asked anxiously. "Her property, you know. Rights of the individual. Interception of letters criminal offence. Don't like being a party to it. . . . "

"More cider?" Wilton asked.

Chapter XVII

I was still thinking about that batch of Communist literature and wishing that the Vicar hadn't gone in for counter-espionage himself, when suddenly the whole emphasis shifted. And this time it was Kimbell who came up from nowhere right into the centre of the picture.

It was the postal censorship that was behind it all. Wilton had opened quite an efficient slitting-and-steaming department in a back room in Bodmin just opposite the Co-op., and Swanton claimed indignantly that there were now big subhuman thumbprints all over his weekly copy of the *New Statesman*.

Then the vigilance team really did turn something up. One of the chaps, who happened to be able to read, discovered that someone from the Bodmin Institute was in daily, or rather every-other daily, correspondence with an address in Vienna's Russian zone. The missing days, he found out from his colleague at the other end of the counter, were filled in by the replies that came through in the other direction as regularly as clockwork. And when they saw that the two-way exchange was in code, they wanted to have Kimbell arrested on the spot.

Wilton invited me over the same evening. He had one of the

dwarf captains still with him. He was a nice boy with a fine fresh complexion, as though he used wire-wool instead of a safety-razor. And he must have had a rather pleasant sense of humour because he called me "sir" right from the start.

There was a chessboard set out on the table and the Captain was standing over it, looking as pleased with himself as though he had just invented the game.

"It's the same as draughts, sir," he was saying to Wilton as I came in. "There are sixty-four squares altogether. Thirty-two white ones, and thirty-two black. I've just counted."

But I couldn't let that one pass.

"Better count 'em again," I told him. "I think you've left one out."

Then, before the Captain could answer Wilton beckoned me over. That is to say that he stood where he was with his back turned towards me and made a sort of scooping movement in the air with his left arm.

"You play chess?" he asked.

"I did once," I said. "Man who taught me took up bridge almost immediately afterwards."

"Ever heard of an 'E'?"

"Name again, please," I said.

"An 'E.'"

I shook my head.

"Game must have changed since my time," I told him. "I'm not surprised. It seemed to me pretty much exhausted twenty years ago."

Wilton did his usual straightening act. Shoulders and arms and knees and things kept appearing in the most unexpected places.

"I suppose you know why we're doing all this?" he asked.

That stumped me. Of course I knew. The whole Institute knew. But what I didn't know was whether anyone except Kimbell was *supposed* to know.

"There's going to be a tournament," I suggested.

"Kimbell said he'd told you."

I eased up at that.

"Why so he did," I answered. "I shall be forgetting my own name next."

"And what did he tell you?"

That stumped me.

"About correspondence chess, I think it was," I answered. "Can't stand it myself. Takes all the tang and fury out of the game."

"And you believed him?"

"I'd believe anyone."

"Then it might interest you to know that with Continental or any other notation this game still can't be played. It says here"— Wilton waved the paper in his hand—"to move some of the pieces into squares that just aren't there."

I reflected for a moment. This certainly did seem to raise some interesting possibilities.

"And it isn't draughts either," Wilton went on, in his slow quietish drawl.

"Or backgammon," I volunteered, wanting to show helpful. "No dice."

There was a pause. Quite a long pause. Wilton seemed to have a natural knack for reading other people's minds. Because the next moment he asked the apple-cheeked Captain if he could find some more tonic water.

As soon as he had gone, I turned to Wilton.

"Why are you telling me all this?" I asked.

"I'm still hoping you'll be able to help me," he said.

"But I don't know anything about chess."

Wilton was lighting a fresh cigarette from the stub of the old one. He was rather slow about it, I thought. And when he had finished he moved over to the window and began looking at the clouds again.

"Chess isn't the only game," he said.

Chapter XVIII

Evidently after I had left him, Wilton must immediately have made things over to the Inspector. Or, at least, that was how I worked things out. Because less than four hours after I had downed my last gin tonic, the police swooped. It was the trampling of a lot of heavy feet in the annexe corridor that woke me up. Only it wasn't Kimbell that they were arresting. It was Dr. Mann.

The first thing that I heard really distinctly were the words:

"Plees, plees, I am innocent."

Next came a low rumble that could only have been an English copper explaining about what could be used as evidence and what could not, and then Dr. Mann's voice again:

"Let me go. I can explain everything."

I had a kind of proprietary interest in any explaining that little Dr. Mann might be thinking of doing, and I made a quick grab for my Jaeger.

When I opened the bedroom door it was not a pretty sight. Two large plain-clothes men, complete with an Inspector in uniform, were dragging Dr. Mann along between them. And they hadn't even given him time to put a collar on. He looked as though he were half-way to the scaffold already.

Moreover, at the sight of me he began struggling. Of course, with all that weight against him, he didn't stand a chance. But it was obvious that the one thing he wanted was to come to me for protection.

"What's going on here?" I asked.

But the Inspector saw the flaw in that approach.

"You keep right out of this, sir," he said. "We don't want the whole Institute disturbed."

It was the tone of voice as much as anything else that annoyed me. So I turned bloody-minded.

"I only wanted to be quite sure it wasn't a kidnapping," I said, raising my voice so that most of North Cornwall could hear. "What with stolen cultures and explosions and rifle shots, what *is* going on round here?"

But I could have saved myself the trouble. Because next moment Dr. Mann started screaming. I had never heard someone scream before when he wasn't being hurt. And it was horrible. One of the policemen said something that sounded like "these bloody foreigners " and tried to clap his hand over Dr. Mann's mouth. But the Inspector knew enough to stop that. The way things were going, bruises might be a key point for the defence.

As soon as Dr. Mann had used up all the air in his lungs I addressed him.

"Don't worry, old chap," I said. "You go along with the nice, kind gentlemen. We'll soon have you out again."

By now, other doors all the way down the corridor had opened. Kimbell was the first to appear and he went a delicate duck-egg green at the sight of the Inspector. Then he did something that was rather odd. He turned on his heel and went back

116

inside his room again. A moment later, I heard the sound of a key turning. It was left to Swanton to speak up for civil liberties.

"You're twisting the man's arm," he said to one of the policemen. "I shall call witnesses."

It was Bansted he turned to. But Bansted was standing there with a very different kind of expression on his face. It was obvious that if called upon he would step up smartly and go to the assistance of the law.

So Swanton had to go on single-handed.

"It's the half-Nelson," he said. And in his emotion his voice went up into treble clef as he said it. "You know that can dislocate a man's elbow. I shall report this."

That made the Inspector turn nasty.

"If I have any more trouble from you," he said, "I shall have to take you into custody for obstructing."

By now Swanton was quivering with the sort of frustration that makes a man want to do something damn silly just for the hell of it.

"Very well," he said, right up on top A by now. "Do it."

I thought that things had gone far enough by now. So I stepped forward. Gillett and Rogers and the others were out there on the landing by now. But it was my big moment.

"That's all right, officer," I said. "I'll be responsible for him. He won't give you any more trouble."

The Inspector looked at me rather queerly. From his point of view, it was rather like a puff-adder going bail for a black widow.

But taking advantage of the sudden calm, I acted quickly. Putting my arm round Swanton's waist—he was only junior Miss size—I yanked him into the cubicle behind me. He was so surprised that he came easily. But, having got him there, it wasn't by any means so easy to keep him. In the end, I had to stand with my back up against the door and my two hands ready in case he started anything. He was still pretty angry.

"You filthy swine," he said. "You're just a bloody nark yourself. I might have known it."

But here I shook my head sadly.

"Oh, sonny," I said. "If you only knew."

Then he did a silly thing. He tried to kick me. But it was his knee that he used and not his foot. And, because it hurt, I hit him.

Hit him hard and felt better for it.

Chapter XIX

1

Down at the police station next morning nobody would say anything.

"What about bail?" I asked. "I'm afraid I've never been mixed up in anything like this before."

The sergeant merely shook his head at me.

"All in good time, sir," he said. "Bail's a matter for the Court, bail is."

"And when do you expect the case to come up?" I persisted. "I take it that habeas corpus still obtains within the Duchy."

The sergeant, however, didn't seem to be any too anxious to commit the Duchy to anything.

"If you care to look in this afternoon, sir," he said, "the Inspector'll be back by then."

"That's nice of you," I said. "But I don't think I'll bother. We seem to have been seeing so much of each other."

Just as I was going out, I met Swanton. He had cycled down. There was a piece of sticking-plaster on the corner of his mouth where I had hit him, and I felt rather ashamed when I saw it.

"It's no use," I said. "They won't let you see him."

Swanton looked a bit dashed. I think that he had pictured himself thrusting files and hacksaw blades in through the grille of the cell door.

"And they won't say when he's going to be charged," I told him.

Swanton pulled the corners of his mouth down, and shook his head disapprovingly. Then he pushed past me.

"Where are you going," I asked.

"Just to see if you've been telling me the truth," he said. "Nothing personal about it."

Altogether I was getting quite fond of the boy.

"Pity you've got your bike," I replied. "I'd like to have offered you a lift."

I cut a pretty good figure at the breakfast table. That was because I was the only one who had actually been down to the station to inquire about our poor brother. Rogers was the first to say anything.

"I must say I'm not surprised," he remarked. "I always had my doubts about him. Nothing definite, you know. Just doubts."

This brought an approving nod from Bansted. He was in one of his more severe, must-reduce-your-overdraft moods this morning.

"Never did approve of having foreigners on this kind of a job," he said. "Stands to reason they haven't got the same loyalties."

Dr. Smith gave a slow, unhumorous sort of smile.

"I suppose you've overlooked the fact that our friend Mellon here is a foreigner," he said. "Does that mean that you don't approve of Mellon?"

Satisfied that he had said something to embarrass someone, he stuffed another piece of toast into his mouth and went on eating.

But nerves were a bit frayed all round. And it was Mellon and not Bansted who answered.

"Say, why are you always picking on me?" he asked. "Just because you're a bum lecturer over on our side you don't have any cause to wash other people's heads for them."

"And I object most strongly," Bansted replied. "I had no thought of Mellon when I was speaking. I don't regard Mellon as a foreigner. I was referring to Mann, and to Mann alone."

I could understand Bansted's feeling of bitterness towards Mann. After all, it had been Mann who had seen him go out on to the moors with that pop-gun of his.

But before anyone else could answer Mellon spoke up the way his father's people would have liked to hear him.

"Well, I'm sorry for Mann," he said sweetly. "You show me a refugee, and I'll show you someone who's taken a pretty tough hiding."

Then Gillett said something. He had been rather more silent than usual, I thought. It may have been that with a profile like that he couldn't risk spoiling things by talking with his mouth full.

"I'm glad for his sake that this is England," he remarked. "At least he can be assured of a fair trial."

But this last remark was too much for Kimbell. He got up so suddenly that he nearly overturned his chair.

"Of all the bloody rot," he said. "Do you imagine that a refugee ever gets a fair trial? Can you imagine any jury that wouldn't rather convict a foreigner? I can't, if you can."

And with that Kimbell left us. In the doorway he nearly collided with Swanton, who was just coming back from his early morning cycle ride. It only occurred to me later that it was highly significant that Kimbell and Swanton should have been going in opposite directions. They hadn't even stood shoulder to shoulder when Mann had been arrested.

But it could hardly have been that one of them had discovered something about the other. My guess was that they both knew everything already.

2

Dr. Mann was charged the following morning. And we couldn't any of us have been more astonished if it had been a bicycle that he was supposed to have pinched . . . "*that between the 20th and the 27th November he did steal 1,000,000 international units of penicillin and did unlawfully attempt to transmit them to a foreign country in contravention of* . . . " was how the charge read.

We all went down to the court house in a body to hear it read. And right up to the moment when the doors opened, Swanton was convinced that the case would be heard in camera. He clearly suspected trickery somewhere when we were all invited inside, and a policeman asked if we would like to have the window closed.

But as soon as little Dr. Mann appeared in the dock, we could all see what the poor fellow must have been through. He was completely tallow-coloured. And, from the circles under his eyes, he didn't look as though he had been having a particularly good sort of night. But it was the eyes themselves that were the most remarkable thing about him. There was a quality of—this is the only way I can put it—defiance about them.

But if the charge itself had come as a surprise, there was a bigger surprise waiting for us. And it was Gillett who sprang this one. He had been unusually restless for him ever since he had been in court. Twice he took out his Eversharp and got ready to scribble something down on the little loose-leaf jotter that he always carried. And twice he put it away again. But the third time he went right ahead. And when he had finished what he was writing, he beckoned to one of the policemen. Even in this small particular there was an air of distinction about Gillett. The way he called the policeman over was like a restaurant regular snapping his fingers at a rather slow waiter.

I watched the passage of the piece of paper. It went from the policeman to the Inspector, from the Inspector to Wilton, from Wilton to the magistrate's clerk, and from the magistrate's clerk to the magistrate. And, wherever the little piece of paper went, whispering broke out all round it.

Altogether it was obviously being a big morning for the bench. The magistrate was a bald, retired builder, who wore a stiff, white shirt front with the ends of the narrow black tie tucked in underneath the collar. He had the air of a puzzled double-bass player who is anxiously trying to discover where the horns have got to. Finally, he called Wilton over to him and they went through the score together. That settled it.

"The prisoner has applied for bail," the double-bass player announced at last, "and the court sees no reason to oppose it. Bail has accordingly been arranged in the sum of one hundred pounds and the prisoner is free to leave the court."

"Good," said Gillett. "I wasn't sure they'd allow it."

"You paying?"

Gillett smiled.

"Not exactly. He won't run away."

3

A man on bail is always in a rather curious position. He is like a person going about in quarantine for measles. Some people naturally sheer off him. Bansted, for example, could obviously see the spots every time Dr. Mann approached. And Rogers and the great Dr. Smith were both clearly looking out for any signs of scratching. Even Gillett took no steps to make life any easier for Dr. Mann. From his whole manner it was obvious that, having done the decent thing by arranging bail, that was where his intervention ended. And Mellon, who had just been reading the latest batch of magazines from America, was convinced that the entire British Commonwealth was being purely frivolous in the matter of counter-espionage. Martyr or not, Dr. Mann in his view, should have been kept in the cooler for safety's sake.

This meant that I saw rather a lot of Dr. Mann. He came bearing down on me full of inspissated Teutonic gloom.

"It is because you have all been so good to me that it is so terrible," he began.

There wasn't very much that I could say in answer to that. So I asked him to have a drink. But even that didn't work any longer. He shook his head at me and pursed his lips together.

"No. That would be wrong," he said. "I have no right to drink any more. In prison I shall have my drinks brought to me every day, no?"

I think that it was the first joke that Dr. Mann had ever attempted. But it wasn't very successful.

"So you did really pinch it?" I asked.

Dr. Mann went that pale tallow colour again.

"It was in order to save life," he said simply.

"Any luck?"

"Not now the police have stopped it," he replied, shaking his head again. "They are murderers only they are too stupid to understand. Stupid people are always the most cruel."

Any conversation carried on in generalisations inevitably gets me down. It is one of the bad continental habits like not covering up the works on their locomotives.

"How did you try to get it out?" I asked.

Dr. Mann spread his hands in the international gesture that is intended to convey that the speaker is holding nothing back.

"In the fountain pen for my mother," he said. "I removed the rubber sac and refilled it. If it had not been for the theft of the culture no one would ever have known. But then, of course, they examined everything. It was like Germany again."

"That's about the way the culture could have been got out, too, isn't it?" I asked casually. "A fountain pen's just about the right size."

Dr. Mann nodded.

"Exactly right," he said.

"Was that why you burgled the post office?"

Again Dr. Mann nodded.

"Which were you looking for," I asked, "the penicillin or the culture?"

"The penicillin," Dr. Mann answered. "The culture had gone long ago. But I was too late. And now there is nothing more that I can do. My sister's fiancé will surely die."

"What's the matter with him?" I asked.

Even though we were alone, Dr. Mann dropped his voice as he told me.

"That's certainly tough on your sister," I agreed with him.

Chapter XX

1

The next day I had my first opportunity of speaking to the demure one. She was back on the job again even though she shouldn't have been. And when she put down her last slide she gave a faint expiring groan. Gillett heard it and came over. But it was nothing, she said, just a headache. And she announced then that she was going to take a walk to get rid of it.

It was scarcely one of her brighter ideas because the mist had been hanging over the moor all day. And if she was going to have 'flu or something, she would just be speeding up the process. Gillett certainly tried hard enough to dissuade her. And I think it was the first time I'd ever heard him raise his voice to anyone.

"You're simply being absurd," he said. "Let me get you some aspirin."

But the demure one was obviously being obstinate too. And that seemed to annoy Gillett.

"Well, for goodness' sake, wait until I'm through with this and then I'll come with you," he said.

That, however, apparently wouldn't satisfy her either. She was already half-way to the door while Gillett was talking to her.

Gillett was still reasoning with her as he went by me.

"I don't like you going out there," he said. "Not alone. And with all this mist about. Not after what happened to me. I'd just rather you didn't."

I heard the word "silly" on the demure one's lips and something about "stop fussing." Then she went. Gillett stood there looking worried.

"I wish to God she *would* go away for a bit," he said, feelingly. "She isn't doing herself any good by stopping here. And I don't think it's safe for her. I'd feel a good deal happier if they had the moor patrolled properly."

Then I saw the other side of him. The shutters came down. He went straight on with his work just where he had left off. His hand on the focusing knob on the microscope was steady and rather distinguished looking. And when someone is staring down a mike you can't see whether he is still looking anxious or not.

2

I passed Dr. Mann, who was carrying a slide or something over to the Director's office, and caught up with the demure one about quarter of a mile from the Institute. She had taken the one decent track that led over the moor. And, even though the mist had thickened up considerably, I could see her a good hundred yards ahead of me.

"Carry your bag, miss," I said, as I drew alongside her.

She turned sharply when I spoke to her. That was because I was wearing my crepe-rubbers and must have given the effect of creeping up on her. I don't think that she had been expecting to meet anyone. And I'm pretty sure that she didn't want to either.

When she faced round I could see that she was crying. But I pretended not to notice.

"Mind if I walk with you?" I asked.

The demure one said that she didn't mind, and we walked on together. But even that didn't get me very far. Because I couldn't extract so much as a single word. She just kept her head deliberately turned away from me. And only the occasional sniffs that came in my direction indicated the kind of walk that she was having.

So I waded right in up to my armpits during the long silence.

"I've been noticing you," I said. "You haven't looked at all well lately."

I got back a muffled and rather resentful I'm-all-right-thank-you-please-don't-start-bothering-yourself-about-me kind of answer.

"But we're all worried about you," I said. "It's not good for a girl to get a lot of glass in her hair."

This time the reply was the same as before only more emphatic.

That meant that I might as well take a real plunge even if it meant getting my ears wet.

"Why not go away for a bit?" I asked. "Give yourself a break."

But there was evidently something about the whole idea that rankled. And a moment later I knew what it was.

"Did Hilda ask you to say that?" she demanded.

"Hilda among others," I replied quite truthfully. "It occurred to several of us."

"Well, I'm not going," she said. "I'm not going. And it's no use trying to make me."

She had turned towards me as she said it and she had stopped crying by now. The whole effect was a bit smudgy at the corners. But there was no further effort at avoiding me. I was looking right into her eyes as she said her piece for the third and last time.

"I'm not going, and that's definite," the words were.

But I wasn't really listening. Not with any attention that is. A girl's eyes usually look terrible when she's been crying. But the demure one's had somehow managed to survive the test. They were deeper violet than ever.

"Okay," I said. "I'll get a refund on the ticket."

The path here ran along the bottom of a little valley. And the mist really had begun to fill things up by now. It came sliding over the crest like liquid cotton-wool. I didn't care for the look of it.

"Gone far enough?" I asked. "Looks a bit sticky round the corner."

We stood there for a moment watching the mist. By now it wasn't merely rolling up on us from in front. There was an unpleasant pincer movement on either side as well. It was as though the mist were making a deliberate and intelligent attempt to cut us off. And as we turned somebody fired out of the mist just behind us.

It was so close that I could see the flash. I felt the girl beside me suddenly catch her breath and stumble.

As I grabbed her, I realised that this was the second time that I had held Una in my arms. But never for very long. Last time, Gillett had burst in on us. And at the present moment, I couldn't forget that somewhere in the mist-pockets on all sides of us, there was a lunatic prowling around with a revolver.

Chapter XXI

1

We must have been about six yards from the bull's-eye area when I bent over her to see what had happened. And when I got her raincoat open I didn't like the look of what I found. There was blood everywhere. A lot of it. From the shoulder downwards one side was already fairly soaking. And my application of first aid was probably exactly the sort of thing that the St. John's Ambulance was founded to prevent.

But blood can be rather dramatically misleading. That is, if you're not used to the sight of it. There usually appears to be more of it than there really is. I knew that much. My trouble, however, was that I couldn't find out where it was all coming from. Whenever I started feeling about anywhere my fingers came away sticky. And I saw then that there was nothing for it but to start undressing her. And here I wished that I had listened a bit more carefully when the A.R.P. lectures had been on.

I used the quick, simple method, and I ripped the seams open. I've always carried one of those flat, razor-blade affairs about with me. They come in very handy for cutting string and sharpening pencils, and I've even used them for the purpose of elementary dissection. This time I went down the sleeve of the Burberry like an east-end slasher. And then I slit about another six guineas' worth of fine woolwork by opening out the sleeve of the jumper and working upwards.

The bullet had gone clean through the brachial artery all right, and the blood was fairly pumping out. But arterial bleeding isn't all that difficult to stop. Even the very words out of the text-book came back to me: "The brachial artery if severed should be suppressed against the inner aspect of the humerus." And with the help of my pocket handkerchief and using my fountain pen as a lever to make the knot a bit tighter, that's how I suppressed it. It was good now for about ten minutes. After that anything might happen.

The whole time I was working I had a slightly jumpy feeling wondering where the next bullet was coming from. And when. The main thing that troubled me was thinking of what a waste it would all be if the dirty bastard out there in the mist suddenly decided to pump in another one just when I'd got everything tidy. And I was bound to admit that for the life of me I could not imagine why he didn't. We were a number one stationary target, and he could have hit us with a catapult.

So far, I haven't said a word about the patient. And this is always the highest tribute of which any doctor is capable. For the demure one hadn't fainted, or done anything silly like that. And, after the first little gasp when the bullet had actually hit her, she hadn't even cried out. She had just lain there, biting her lip. And like a sensible girl, she had kept her head turned away while the plumber got on with the job.

It must have been about three-quarters of a mile back to the Institute, and I carried her most of the way. But even quite a small person feels like Tessie O'Shea after about the first hundred yards. And it doesn't make things any easier when you're trying to hurry. She did give a little moan occasionally when I couldn't avoid jogging her. But that was the fault of the fog mostly. Visibility had now closed in to about fifteen feet, and I had to keep on stopping just to see which way I was carrying her.

I was feeling safer every moment now. But apparently Una wasn't. And now that it was all over, the effects of delayed shock were showing up text-book fashion. She was as cold as a dead bather. Also she was trembling. When she felt me pause for a moment and look round to see if we were being followed, she suddenly went all to pieces. Hitching her good arm round my neck as though she were trying to strangle me, she started whimpering. Not that I blamed her. No girl likes being shot at twice on one afternoon.

The Institute itself couldn't have been more than three or four hundred yards away by now. And that was good enough for me. I let out a shout. And, a moment later, I heard an answering call from somewhere out in front of me. I wasn't sorry. The way things were going, Una would find herself carrying me before we'd get much farther.

I must have been nervier than I realised. And I gave a jump like a scared kitten when a figure suddenly appeared out of the mist not more than ten or twelve feet away from me. But the effect was certainly weird enough to make anybody jump. That was because the figure was dressed all in white. It was like a ghost in an old-fashioned Christmas supplement. And, as it came, it flashed a light on us.

"You there? Where are you?" I heard the voice calling out again.

Then I recognised it. It was Gillett's voice. And he was still wearing his long white overall. Evidently he had come straight out of the lab. to look for us. And, as he was naturally an efficient sort of chap, he had brought the Institute's inspection lamp along with him.

"Christ! Where are you?" he said.

I liked Gillett best when he forgot to use his brown suède voice. There was not even a trace of it at this moment. He might have been a paper boy, the way he was yelling.

And I replied in the same kind.

"Follow your bloody nose," I said. "I've had enough of this."

"My God," Gillett exclaimed when he saw us. But even at that moment he still remembered to do the decent thing.

"You might give another yell," he said. "The whole Institute's out looking for her."

2

It was really Gillett's vindication, that revolver shot. Ever since Gillett had come back with the story about having been fired at, I wasn't the only person who hadn't believed him.

Quite a lot of people would have been delighted to see Gillett caught out when spooning up a handful. And Gillett was quite intelligent enough to realise this. He seemed, therefore, genuinely glad to know that people believed him once more. It's always rather nice to have your spotlessness recognised, but it's a rather high price to pay when you very nearly have your fiancée murdered in the proving process.

And Gillett was certainly becoming more human. When he wasn't over at the Clewes's finding out how Una was getting on, he was down in the bar with me. And naturally there wasn't very much that he could refuse me. Contrary to his whole nature, he sat there drinking level. Only of course I was having doubles.

Even without the drinks, however, I think that the events of the day had been just a bit too much even for him. He was wearing a dazed, rather dopey sort of look. And all that he wanted to do was to hear about the shooting over and over again.

That didn't suit me. I had already told the Inspector. And Wilton. And left to myself, I would rather have forgotten it for the next couple of hours.

"You're dead certain you didn't catch a glimpse of him?" he asked.

I yawned.

"He could come into this bar now and I shouldn't know it," I replied.

Gillett edged his chair up closer towards mine.

"Is that just a manner of speaking?" he asked, dropping his voice almost to a whisper and giving his head a little backward jerk as he said, "Or d'you mean anything special by it?"

I looked in the direction of his nod. There in the doorway Dr. Smith was standing. His small piggy eyes were narrowed up, and he was staring at us.

"The only one who didn't turn out to help us look," Gillett added, under his breath.

"Perhaps because he was there already," I said.

But at that moment I wasn't thinking about Dr. Smith. I was back on to Dr. Mann again. I had just remembered that he was the last person I had seen as I left the Institute. He had been walking, rather rapidly for him, in the direction of the Director's office.

But it wouldn't have been in the least difficult for him to double round the back and get on to the moor ahead of me.

That night I'd taken quite enough of the Institute's gin to be able to dispense with the dormital. And I regretted it. The kind of sleep that you get after gin isn't dreamless. They were the worst kind of dreams, too, with a wild and crazy logic that was horribly convincing. The one I liked least was the one in which Hilda confessed to me that it was she who had fired the shot.

"I'm sorry if I hurt her," Hilda had said quietly, in her prim, rather precise way. "I only wanted to kill her outright. I shall try to do better next time. There'll be a next time of course. That's because no one suspects me. I'm quite sure the Inspector would never think of looking for a woman."

Chapter XXII

My respect for Wilton had never been greater than at this moment. Everyone else was in a flap. The Inspector, assisted by half a dozen extra policemen from Plymouth, was going round the Institute interviewing everyone. Gillett and Bansted and Rogers had constituted themselves a special branch of the Bodmin Beagles and were combing the moor in search of spent cartridge cases and that kind of thing. But Wilton did precisely nothing. With the circles under his eyes showing up like half-crowns, he just locked himself away and remained invisible.

The only piece of violent and dramatic display from his whole department was when one of the cub captains suddenly shot off to Bodmin in the staff car, driving as though he would have used the siren if there had been one. But that turned out to be only because word had just reached Wilton that a fresh supply of Players had just arrived, and he wanted to snap up a couple of hundred while they were still going. He seemed extraordinarily unconcerned about attempted murder.

All the same, I wasn't too happy about Wilton's behaviour. When a man orders two hundred cigarettes and promptly shuts himself away from everyone it usually means that he is thinking about something. And I didn't like it any better when he suddenly asked me to drop over and see him.

What I wasn't prepared for this time as I went inside was to find that Wilton had other company there. And of all extraordinary choices he had picked on Dr. Smith for a drinking companion. Moreover, from all the signs, Dr. Smith had apparently just succeeded in being clever. The smirk that was on his face might have been applied with a builder's trowel.

" . . . Around the turn of the century," he was saying, "the best brains in the chess world grew tired of the limitations imposed by the conventional game. Any number of variants have been tried out at one time or another. But it was Capablanca who took things furthest. He introduced the Marshal and Chancellor. It proved too difficult. The Emperor game was more successful. With nine pieces aside and the Emperor himself combining the moves of Queen and Knight while leaving those pieces themselves with their full powers, the new combinations were practically limitless. Indeed . . . "

Dr. Smith was in full flood by now. Since the death of Macaulay the world can hardly have seen anything like it. The sheer bad taste was simply appalling.

"So there could be an 'E,'" I said, turning to Wilton. "And there could be squares that don't seem to exist on a chess-board. It must have been Emperor Chess or whatever it's called that Kimbell was playing."

Wilton, however, was still only uncoiling himself after the interruption. And even when he was right way up, with his various limbs in approximately their correct places, he still didn't reply immediately.

"As a matter of fact," he said, "Dr. Smith here doesn't know anything about the game that Kimbell's been playing."

"Sorry I spoke out of turn," I answered.

I wouldn't have upset Wilton for anything. Not just at present, that is. But Wilton wasn't all that easily upset.

"Let's ask Kimbell to come over," he suggested very casually. "You and I can have a drink, while he and Smith play chess together."

This proposal, however, brought the great Dr. Smith as near to open panic as I have ever seen him. He actually blushed.

"If you don't mind I'd rather not," he said. "You see, I don't actually play chess, I'm only interested in the mathematical theory. That's quite different. Also"—here he began pawing the ground a bit—"Kimbell and I haven't really got very much in common."

This didn't seem to put Wilton out in the slightest. Indeed, he hardly seemed to be listening. He was pouring out another drink for Smith while he was still speaking, and obviously couldn't care less who were Dr. Smith's little play-chums and who weren't.

"Oh, well," he said, "just say good evening to him and slip away quietly. No one'll notice."

I admired Wilton for the way he had got in that last bit.

But already I was busy admiring Wilton for something else. The suggestion that Kimbell should come over had evidently not been quite the afterthought that it had sounded. Because at that moment there was a knock at the door, and Kimbell and the Captain arrived with the bond of invisible handcuffs between them.

I have never seen anyone quite so ill at ease as Kimbell. He kept his eyes to the carpet, and shifted his weight from one foot to the other as though he had on a pair of very tight new shoes.

It was his palest duck-egg blue complexion that he was wearing this evening.

Simply judging from his appearance I'd have been ready to suspect him of anything. And I noticed that when Wilton thrust a glass into his hand he promptly put it down again. Evidently he wasn't going to risk getting talkative.

But what was even more marked was the episode of the cigarette case. It was a rather nice plain gold one that Wilton carried about with him. And he offered Kimbell a cigarette along with the drink. But Kimbell, who was naturally a thirty-to-fifty-a-day-man, refused it out of hand. I may have been imagining things, but I got the impression that he did not want to touch that plain gold cigarette case for fear of leaving fingerprints.

But Wilton was an expert as a society hostess in not noticing when one of the guests is behaving a bit queerly. He just went straight on in his tired, dreary-sounding voice as though the whole idea of counter-espionage was a frightful sort of bore that fortunately had its funny side.

"We had a warrant out for your arrest last week," he said. And he dropped his voice so low while he was speaking that Kimbell had to ask him to repeat what he had just said.

"Your arrest," Wilton repeated. "We had a warrant out."

Kimbell drew in his lower lip, and began biting at it. There was a long pause.

"Did you?" he asked. He sounded about as casual as a man who has just been told that the house is on fire.

"All because of those chess games of yours," Wilton went on.

Kimbell's particular shade of egg-shell went about two tones paler.

"How d'you mean?" he asked lamely.

Wilton was lighting another cigarette. And that always took a little time because he didn't seem to know about things like matches and petrol lighters. His idea of the sacred fire was a wisp of smouldering tobacco at one end of a sodden and discoloured butt about quarter of an inch long.

"It was all a mistake," he said. "Rather a silly one come to think of it. Only nobody in the department plays chess, you see. It was Smith here who solved it for us."

But Wilton's last remark seemed to have annoyed Kimbell. It was the first thing that had roused him in the slightest. You could now see more than a hint of a yolk beneath the shell.

"Have you been discussing my affairs with Smith?" he asked. Wilton nodded.

"Expert witness," he said. "Cleared things up in a moment."

"And is Hudson here supposed to be an expert in something?" he asked.

"He reached the eighty-first square before we did," Wilton answered. "De-coding could make nothing of it."

"De-coding?" Kimbell asked sharply.

"Naturally," Wilton answered. "If you can't read anything, you send it to De-coding. It's what they're there for. They've had a strip torn off them this time."

"And what are you doing about it now?" Kimbell asked.

"Playing the game right through," Wilton answered.

"We've got someone from headquarters staff to help us. Used to play second board at Hastings. He's rather good." Wilton paused. "I'm afraid I've got some rather bad news for you," he added.

"Bad news?" Kimbell asked. There was no attempt to keep the anxiety out of his voice.

Wilton nodded. "Received his report this morning," he said. "Takes a very poor view of your position. Advises you to resign. More dignified."

Chapter XXIII

1

The inspector hadn't been doing too well lately, and he knew it. All that his posse of policemen had discovered in their last search of the moor had been a perfectly good thermos flask, a watch glass and a lady's compact. The thermos remained untraced but was obviously unimportant anyway—very few murderers are the picnicking type. The watch glass belonged to Bansted and had come out of the case when he was on the moor looking for Una *after* the shot had been fired—he was able to prove that one. And the compact had Hilda's initials inside it. She identified it immediately and said thank you. I was probably the only person who thought twice about it. But that may have been because I was the only person to have had my dream.

So far as suspicion went there were two of us who were not entirely in the clear—Dr. Mann and myself. In Dr. Mann's case, it was rumour. The whole characteristic of rumour is that you can't pin-point it. It is atmospheric rather. And I was conscious of the way it was closing in on Dr. Mann. The evidence admittedly was so negative as not to amount to evidence at all—simply that things had been entirely quiet while Dr. Mann was away, and then had broken out again at their most sensational almost immediately after his return. By now it was pretty general knowledge that Dr. Mann really had pinched the penicillin. And, in minds like Bansted's and Rogers's, theft is one of the really awful things, like travelling first with a third-class ticket or seeing if the other end can hear you before you finally push button A. It meant that he was a bounder and outsider, as well as a foreigner. And if there had been rape or arson, let alone attempted murder, anywhere in the neighbour-hood it was clear that they would both of them have been ready to pin it on to him.

I, on the other hand, was the Inspector's suspect. And he was keeping me all to himself. Admittedly the ice-cold eye was getting a bit chipped round the edges. But it could still focus. And I must have retold my version of the shooting at least a dozen times. What made it so peculiarly trying was that I made no attempt at improvements, and told the plain truth every time. It seemed safer that way. Safer, but more boring.

2

Dr. Mann had been telling the truth, too. He really was having an interview with the Old Man at the time when the shot had been fired.

But that was only part of the truth about Dr. Mann, and he wanted me to have the whole and nothing but. In consequence, he began turning up at all hours whenever he couldn't sleep. It was like having an owl about the place. I used to lie there after lights out, thinking longingly of the dormital bottle and wonder-ing whether at any moment the familiar scratch and flutter would indicate that another visit was impending.

This evening, for instance, he would keep trying to tell me how poor his people were.

"There is my mother, my grandmother and my sister," he said. "There is only one room. That is not much, no?"

"It's close quarters," I agreed with him.

"And they can afford so little," he went on. "One meal a day. That is all they have."

"What time of day do they have it?" I asked.

I wasn't meaning to be callous. I really wanted to know. But Dr. Mann merely shrugged his shoulders.

"For everyone in Germany it is bad," he said. "People say that it is more bad for the old. I tell you that the old do not matter. For them it is nearly over. It is for the young ones that it is most bad of all."

"That's one way of looking at it," I agreed.

But by now Dr. Mann had tears in his eyes.

"What is to happen to my mother if my gifts to her are to cease? If I go to prison she will die."

"You're not there yet," I reminded him.

But Dr. Mann shook his head.

"I have no hope," he said. "I wish I were to be executed. Then I should not know what happens to my family."

He was really crying by now. And I wished that he would stop. But when he resumed he was calmer. He was reaching that Weltpolitik stage that all Germans so easily slide into. And it can be pretty anaesthetising, except presumably to other Germans.

"To understand Germany," he led up to it, "you must realise his position in the land mass of Europe. And his history. Also his imperial tradition. Likewise his birth-rate and his need for the colonies that he has lost."

I didn't say anything, and Dr. Mann continued like the voice of the old *Bundesrat* speaking.

"And in the nineteen-thirties," he said, "Germany was a moral waste land. He had lost his soul. All women sold themselves. Perversion was everywhere. The revolution was waiting."

"You mean the Nazi revolution?" I asked.

Dr. Mann jumped to his feet. He was trembling all over.

"Never," he said. "Never. There were always two ways. The Nazi way that called up the dragon that is in the heart of every German. And the Communist way. The way of order and human reason. I chose the Communist Party. I joined a *Betrtibs-Zelle* and a *Strassen-Zelle* when I was nineteen. My family disowned me."

"You don't say."

Somehow I had never imagined Dr. Mann in any role as active as that of a Communist. If he had been sent out at night to put up illegal posters, I felt pretty sure that he would have contrived to paste them on upside down. But, in any case, that meant that there were two of us for certain with a C.P. past and I wondered how much Wilton knew about that.

I was still wondering when Dr. Mann came up very close and started to whisper as though the N.K.V.D. and the Gestapo were both listening just outside the door.

"And there is another," he said. "Why else should someone among us change his name and use a poste restante address for secret communications?"

"Could be shyness," I suggested.

But Dr. Mann shook his head.

"He is not shy," he answered. "He is proud. Very proud."

"Meaning?"

144

"Meaning Dr. Smith."

There was a pause.

"Have you told the Inspector?" I asked.

Dr. Mann shook his head.

"It would serve no purpose," he said sadly. "I am no longer believed."

Chapter XXIV

Walking has always seemed to me to combine all the disadvantages of being too tiring with those of being too slow. If the same amount of pedal energy could take you along at about fifteen m.p.h. I would have nothing against it. But even at four miles an hour it is a useful way of keeping the body ticking over while the mind is doing its thinking. And it was precisely because I wanted to think without interruption that I took myself out on the moor that afternoon.

The path that I had taken led towards the more distant of the tors. But I hadn't the slightest intention of going as far. That would have meant walking about four or five miles across wet bog-land. And even if I'd been out there in search of exercise—which I wasn't—it still didn't look like the sort of afternoon for really serious walking. The mist wasn't exactly thick. But there was enough of it about to take the sparkle out of everything. The whole moor was one subdued general dampness. And I didn't trust the moor any longer.

It was when I stood still for a moment to light a cigarette that I discovered that I was being followed. I don't mean that there was anyone on all fours darting about among the bushes. The man who was coming up the path behind me was as unconcealed as a policeman on patrol. But not half so impressive. He was a short fat man in a dark mackintosh. And he was wearing one of those black snap-brim trilbys that were put on the market specially for literary journalists. The snap-brim wasn't being given its fair chance, however. That was because it had just started to rain, and the short fat man had pulled the brim down all round like a small black umbrella.

It wasn't until we were practically on top of each other that he looked up. And then he shied away as if he hadn't been wanting to meet anyone. Whatever the reason, he turned his face away again the instant he had looked up.

Not that there was anything very remarkable about the face. You see whole rows of faces just like that in every café between Dieppe and Naples. It is the continental common denominator countenance. It was simply *here* that it was remarkable. If I'd been a casting director going round the agents in search of a foreign spy second grade, I'd have agreed to any terms if I could have been sure of getting hold of the little dago in the black trilby.

It occurred to me later that it might have been cleverer to have done a bit of shadowing myself. But I'm not awfully bright all the time. Particularly when I'm thinking about something else. And it was mostly Una that I was thinking about. I was heavy enough with my own cares already. My country brogues were letting in the water like a pair of superior double-welted sponges. I'd had a slight headache all day because of a miscalculation at the bar on the previous evening when I had fooled around with the gin, and mixed two different brands. And I was wondering why nobody really seemed to like me. That question, I must admit, had passed through my mind several times before.

147

But it was only now that I suspected that I knew the answer. It could have been that I didn't like other people very much.

It was getting on for dusk by now. And the landscape might have been made to order to match my thoughts. During the last five minutes the moor had turned a deep lead colour that was about as bright and as cheerful as a coffin lining, and the path across it glistened slightly like the trail a snail lays. Even Maida Vale seemed preferable, and I wondered why I had ever come here.

Then as I breasted one of the little hills I saw two people standing on the path ahead of me. One of them was Hilda. She was wearing a light-coloured transparent sort of raincoat that I'd have recognised anywhere. I couldn't see the other person. But they were obviously in conversation about something. And they were holding hands. It was a man that she was with all right. He was clasping her right hand in his, and he'd got his left hand cupped over them both. If he had been using adhesive tape he could not have made more sure of her.

It was round about this point that they both noticed me. And, as soon as they saw that I was watching them, they sprang apart. Then I saw who the man was. And I wished I hadn't.

It was my little dago friend.

Chapter XXV

1

Then something happened that put Hilda's dago friend right out of my mind. A big something. And, in the result, a very unpleasant one.

It all started with another of those cryptic messages. Only this time the method of delivery was different. Instead of being left for me on my pillow-case, it came by test tube. Or, rather, it was in the test tube and I collected it.

There were five of us in the lab. at that time—Bansted, Rogers, Mellon, Gillett and myself. Bansted and Rogers were on my side. And Mellon was opposite. Gillett had a bench under the window just behind. Lunch was over, and altogether it promised to be one of those long, quiet, boring, unsatisfying afternoons that all research workers know so well. It was an afternoon that would end at about five-thirty, with eternity left behind somewhere around tea-time.

I was just coming away from the steriliser where I had been to collect another frame of test tubes when I saw that there was something inside one of them. It shouldn't have been there, and I held it up against the light to see what it was. It was obviously a screw of paper. But the one thing that simply didn't occur to me was that there would be any writing on it. Let alone that the writing would be intended for me.

I removed the stopper of cotton-wool and shook out the little paper spill. The steriliser had been set a bit on the high side, and the paper like the cotton-wool was slightly charred. But not so charred that the words did not stand out plainly. The letters were all in good bold capitals. There in best office typing I read the message: KEEP AWAY. THIS MEANS YOU. It made even less sense than usual. And I spread it out on the bench in front of me, and sat there staring at it.

There were several points about it that were odd. In the first place, all five of us went to the same oven for our sterilised tubes. And if that particular tube had really been intended for me the odds were precisely five to one against my ever getting it at all. Then there is a note of privacy and intimacy about a pillow-case that is distinctly lacking from a test tube that is going to be unstoppered in a busy laboratory. But that, I realised, could mean one of several things. It might be that I hadn't taken as much notice as somebody wanted me to take of the messages that I had already received. This last one could have been intended as a sort of in-thy-bed-or-at-thy-work-bench-I-am-beside-you reminder. If so, it struck me as rather artistic and well conceived. The only difficulty was that if it really did mean ME, I still didn't know what ME had to keep away from. There was a third possibility, viz., that someone, still for purposes that I couldn't understand, wanted me to sound the tocsin on a bell-jar and announce at the top of my voice that I was being persecuted—and that, in turn, might be to provide a brief but effective distraction while something a good deal more important was going on elsewhere. Possibility number four was that the instruction might not have been intended for me at all and that I had been guilty of the offence of opening somebody else's mail: for all I knew, the whole Institute might have been living under a snowstorm of these little bits of paper. It could all have been a game in which I was simply odd man out. . . .

Before I had reached the nth variant, however, I was cut short by young Mellon. He was exactly opposite to me, and not more than six feet away.

"Say, what is it—a date with a dame?" he asked.

It struck me then that if it were variant Number Three, the tocsin-and-persecution device that had been intended, I could hardly have responded better. And I don't like being made a stooge at any time. So I screwed up the little piece of paper and chucked it into the waste-bin at my feet.

"They're all after me," I said. "When I don't reply, they just go crazy. It's something to do with the hair line."

That seemed to satisfy Mellon who went back to his blood-counts again. And it satisfied me, too. I meant to recover the piece of paper later on because I wanted it to add to my collection.

2

It was just then that the Old Man sent for me. And even though he was such a mild whiskery old thing he didn't to be kept waiting. Moreover, as the hag secretary herself had come to collect me there was nothing for it but to go along. But I might have known it. There was nothing urgent or even important about the Old Man's summons. It was simply that he wanted to find out if I'd give a lantion lecture on *B. typhosus* to the student nurses in the local isolation hospital.

I could have done without that. Student nurses in the mass somehow lack the charm that they may or may not possess individually. But after my bad black over the one-day visa, I felt that I owed it to myself to show something of the charm side of my nature.

"May I really?" I asked eagerly. "If they don't mind something a bit elementary, I'd love to have a shot at it."

The Old Man was so pleased that I think, if the Government hadn't been cutting down on everything, he would have recommended me for an increment on the spot. I learnt afterwards that I had been number nine on his list of candidates, and the other eight had all risked their careers by refusing.

I waited long enough to inquire after Una. And immediately the Old Man gave one of his nervous starts that always reminded me of someone who has just reached the theatre and then finds that he has left the tickets at home.

"That reminds me," he said. "She was asking for you just now."

"For me?" I asked, keeping my voice as level-sounding as possible.

"Probably wants to say thank you," he went on. "After all, you did save her life, you know."

made the ordinary pooh-pounds. Then, so that you might have thought that I was simply talking in my sleep, I added: "Of course. I'd be delighted. It's only because I thought she needed rest that I haven't been bothering her."

Because Ma Clewes was out scouring the Bodmin market, it was he Clewes's maid who showed me up to Una's room. And because she was only the maid she withdrew as soon as she had knocked on the door. That, I considered, was very understanding of her. I registered her action for an extra shilling in the Christmas box. It occurred to me only afterwards that it might have been Una herself who had arranged it.

"I wanted to see you alone," was what she said.

I told her that I thought that was nice of her, and took the chair that was drawn up alongside the bed. I have never denied that there is a lot to be said for really dark hair when it is cut rather short. That is when it is the kind of hair that reflects the light and takes on other colours as well. Una's was that kind. And the pink bed-jacket was just right for it. Between the two of them, they showed her eyes up to perfection. And except for an occasional flicker that I kept waiting for because I liked it, the blinds weren't drawn at all. For most of the time I was looking full into a pair of eyes that were so dark that I had to keep on taking another look just to make sure whether they were really violet or only an astonishingly deep blue.

They didn't waver once. Not even when she said: "I want you to do something for me."

"What is it?" I asked.

"I'm getting up to-morrow," she went on. "And I shall be back in the lab. on Monday."

Frankly, I was a bit disappointed. There didn't seem to be much in this for me.

"Isn't that rather silly," I said, "coming back before you're really fit?"

"But that's why I've asked you," she replied. "I want you to keep an eye on things."

"What sort of things?"

Una's face was turned full towards me. It was the best view of her eyes that I had been able to get so far.

"Me mostly," she said. "I'd just like it if you'd stay somewhere near me."

This was distinctly better. But I still remembered my manners. "Isn't that Gillett's job?"

It is interesting the way certain things conform to a dull and rather obvious pattern. I knew Gillett's first name all right; and she knew that I knew. But I couldn't bring myself to say it. Not to her at least.

"Michael doesn't mind," she said. "It's his idea really, just as much as mine."

There was a sudden sweep of the lashes as she said it, and I knew that at this particular moment she wasn't exactly speaking the truth. But I've never been a stickler about small things like that. And, in any case, Una hadn't finished what she had to say.

"There are bound to be times when Michael isn't there," she went on. "And I'd feel safer to-morrow if I knew that there was someone else around."

"There'll be someone," I told her.

There was a pause. A long one. The interview had reached that awkward stage when all the bits and pieces begin falling apart. Una was quite as much aware of it as I was.

"Well," she said, "I suppose you'd better be going now. Otherwise, people will begin to wonder what's happening."

"Not unless they're psychic, they won't," I answered.

And bending over the bed, I kissed her. When it was over Una didn't attempt to say anything. If anyone was to speak, it was obviously my turn.

"Sorry, ma'am," I said, and left her.

Chapter XXVI

1

The last few minutes had made me forget all about that little screw of paper in the waste-bin. But there was something else that I was forgetting, too. Young Mellon had simply been left there with nothing but his blood-counts and his curiosity. Before I had been out of the room five minutes he had come round to my side of the bench and begun routing about among the junk. And the idea of cryptic messages was evidently something that stirred up quite a lot inside him. He couldn't have been more excited if he had found a blonde in the waste-bin.

In the result, he was giving quite a party. They were all there gathered round him—Bansted and Rogers and Gillett. And Mellon had just passed the piece of paper over to Gillett, who was examining it. Dr. Smith had come into the room since I left. But he was getting on with his own work despite the chatter. He was even being rather self-consciously isolationist, I thought.

Gillett appeared to be enjoying himself. He was in one of his aggressively efficient and fact-finding sort of moods.

"Shouldn't be difficult to establish the typewriter it was done on," he said, with an air of having been engaged on typewriter detection cases ever since he had qualified.

I pitied him. If it ever came to the point of accusation and counter-accusation between Gillett and the Director's secretary, I was prepared to back the secretary. Those teeth could make nonsense of any profile that came within snapping distance.

As soon as he saw me, Gillett came over.

"Can you make head or tail of this?" he asked.

I shook my head.

"Me no savee."

"Do you think it's specially meant for you?"

"Could be," I said. "But it still doesn't make sense."

"Then that would rather suggest that it isn't for you at all," Gillett went on. He broke off for a moment. "Have any of you chaps," he went on, "ever received anything of the same sort as this"—here he waved my little slip of paper rather tantalisingly under their noses—"yourselves?"

The technique of the questioning was very nearly perfect. Without the use of the word "chaps" it might have sounded just a shade too much like question time in the Army Education Corps. After all, Gillett wasn't actually in charge of us. It only seemed that way.

But apparently Bansted and Rogers both loved being asked questions. Or, at least, they appeared to like being able to say "no" to this one. It was only Mellon who wasn't so sure.

"I had a coupla post-cards from some dame I'd never heard of," he said, unable to keep the note of regret out of his voice. "She didn't give no address. Just asked why I'd cut the date with her. But that was last summer. Said she'd look me up here some time. Only she never came."

Gillett shook his head. It was obvious that he was in no mood for comforting young Mellon for his one lost opportunity.

"Sorry," he said. "She's not the one we're looking for."

As he said it, he turned and faced Dr. Smith. I may have been wrong. But it still seemed to me that Smith took an unnaturally long time to realise that he was being looked at.

"Smith," Gillett said finally in his clear hi-waiter kind of voice, "have you ever had one of these?"

Even then Dr. Smith did not reply immediately. He finished what he was doing, or what he was pretending to be doing, and looked up wearing his G.C.M.G.-O.M.-F.R.S. expression.

"One of what?" he asked.

It was only then that I realised what an excellent pokerface all really young babies naturally have. The chubby folds and unwrinkled forehead of Dr. Smith revealed absolutely nothing. But at least he condescended to walk over towards us.

"You have something to show me?" he asked, when he had finally got there.

Gillett, I noticed, didn't actually give him the piece of paper. He merely showed it to him. Not that Dr. Smith seemed to mind. Rocking backwards and forwards on his heels, he scarcely glanced at it.

"Isn't there being rather a lot of excitement about nothing?" he asked.

That annoyed Gillett. The events of the past few weeks had rubbed quite a lot of the gloss off him already. I'd been watching him change before my eyes from French polish to ordinary fumed oak. And the way things were going he'd be antique finish before we were through with him.

"You *call* this nothing?" he asked.

Dr. Smith allowed his eyelids to fall for a moment.

"Not exactly nothing," he corrected himself. "Merely nothing of importance. It could, for example, merely be a mistake. Or a hoax. Or it might be intended as a perfectly straightforward and honest warning. I have seen similar notices exposed over switch-rooms in the States. The wording is—er—distinctly American."

"Say, what exactly do you mean by that?" Mellon demanded.

Dr. Smith put up his round fat hands as if to protect himself.

"Merely what I have said," he replied. "I was not seeking to attach any particular significance to it. Indeed, I have hardly considered the matter. If our friend here" —Dr. Smith broke off long enough to indicate Gillett, and in this gesture he contrived somehow to make him look like the Institute's No. 1 scare-monger—"hadn't invited me, I wasn't proposing to give an opinion at all. It is not a habit of mine to give opinions when I am totally ignorant of the facts."

"Would it alter your view in any way if I told you that this wasn't the first that had been received?" Gillett asked.

He had himself completely under control by now, and was fighting hard to regain his own position. No one with that jaw-line could possibly afford to have himself publicly debunked by a colleague who looked like a Glaxo advertisement.

But Dr. Smith was fighting hard by now.

"It might, or it might not," Smith replied. "That would depend on the nature of the message. By whom received. And in what circumstances." He paused. "Have you been asked to keep out, too?"

This was Gillett's opportunity. And he took it.

"I don't think that there is any need to go into what the messages——"

"So you received more than one, did you?" Dr. Smith asked. "May we ask how many? Frequency could be almost as impor-tant as content."

"I am not saying how many I have received," Gillett replied.

"At least not here. Merely that an unknown correspondent has chosen an unusual means of getting in touch with me."

"Through a test tube?" Dr. Smith asked.

Gillett smiled.

"As a matter of fact, the particular message to which I am referring was left for me clipped under the blade-guard of my electric shaver."

"And have you still got the message?"

Gillett shook his head.

"I took it straight along to Wilton," he said, getting out of his chair as he was speaking. "And that is where this one is going, too."

This was my cue.

"Hi, mister," I said. "That's my message. How do you know I wasn't expecting it?"

He had got almost as far as the door when I caught up with him. And when we reached it I noticed a curious thing. The door was about six inches ajar. And disappearing down the corridor away from us was the figure of Dr. Mann. There was no other door at our end of the corridor, and something must have made Dr. Mann change his mind rather suddenly.

He was almost running.

2

Gillett had noticed it, too, and for a moment his eyes caught mine.

"Pardon me," I said, as I removed the piece of paper from between his fingers. "This is part of the Hudson bequest."

Gillett seemed reluctant to give it to me. But then he let go. It may have been simply that he didn't want the paper to get torn.

At any rate, we changed roles and I became bearer. We both understood the position perfectly. I was accompanying him to see whether he had really given Wilton any previous messages. And he was accompanying me to see whether I was going to hand over this one. From the mood of mutual confidence we might have been two Foreign Ministers walking into a Peace Conference together.

But so far as I could see everything was open and above board. Gillett barged in on Wilton without even knocking and waiting for the "Come in." As for Wilton, he was doing exactly what I had come to expect of him. That is precisely nothing. He was standing at the window looking at the clouds. From his interest in clouds he might have been thinking of drawing them, or writing a book about them, or even having a shot at making some of them. He didn't turn round when we entered. Just went on sky-gazing.

"Now Hudson's had one of them," Gillett said, without attempting to keep the note of jubilation out of his voice.

"He's got it here."

"One of what?" Wilton asked.

He swivelled his head round as he said it, and I showed him the screwed-up piece of paper. I could see now why he hadn't moved immediately when we came in. He was standing on only one leg like an Indian adjutant, and the other was hoisted up on to the window-sill. Getting himself facing in our direction was like resetting a pair of folding steps.

"What's it say this time?" he asked.

"It says 'KEEP OUT. THIS MEANS YOU,'" I told him.

"Does it make sense?"

"Not to me it doesn't."

"Where d'you find it?"

"Bunged down inside a test tube."

"Your test tube?"

"Could have been anybody's."

"Ever had one before?" he asked.

I paused. This seemed to me to be a good opportunity for doing a little Gillett-reducing on my own account.

"Yes, as a matter of fact, I have," I replied. "Three of them. But I didn't see why I should say so in front of everyone. In my view there's been too much talking already."

"Three, d'you say?" Gillett asked.

I got the impression that he didn't like being outbid in the matter of secret messages. Also, that he didn't entirely believe me.

"Three's the number, brother," I replied.

And taking out my notecase I unfolded all the earlier specimens. They were a bit creased by now, and looked rather as though I had been sleeping in them. But the typing still showed up black and clear against the obviously inferior-quality paper that the unknown typist had been using.

Wilton took the piece of paper and began to examine it. Not very professionally either. He merely tilted back the shade of the desk-lamp and held the paper up against the naked bulb.

"Mind," I warned him. "Don't scorch it."

But either Wilton hadn't heard me or he always looked at pieces of paper that way.

"It *is* German," he said at last. "There's a bit of the watermark in this piece."

Gillett stepped forward as though he were on parade-ground. But, after all, it was my piece of paper, and I cut in front of him.

"Me first," I said.

There wasn't very much to see. For a start, it was right down in the corner. All that I could make out was what might have been an eagle's head and a scroll with some writing on it. The trouble was that the scroll was half-cut off, and the letters " . . . HE PAP . . . IND . . . " didn't convey very much to me. Wilton must have seen the expression on my face.

"Deutsche Papier Industrie Gesellschaft," he explained.

That certainly seemed to fit well enough. My respect for Wilton went up again. It isn't everyone who can read about one-sixth of a foreign watermark.

But Wilton didn't seem particularly excited about his discovery.

"Not that it gets us very far," he said. "They used to make about three-quarters of all the paper in Europe."

"But not three-quarters of all the paper in Bodmin," Gillett observed.

Wilton smiled. It was not much of a smile. A mere slackening among the muscles. Practically a paralysis. And because it added to the general air of limpness Wilton looked rather sadder when he was smiling.

"It's still three-quarters of all the European paper," he said. "And there are letters coming through the whole time. There's Kimbell's chess. And Swanton's League of Free Scientists. And Bansted's been fixing up for a holiday in the Tyrol. And there's you." Here Wilton jerked a thumb in Gillett's direction. "You're going to Switzerland. There's paper like this pouring in all the time."

"Not in blank sheets," Gillett observed.

I noticed that he sounded rather defiant about it. And I wasn't altogether surprised. I wasn't ready to say that his theory, what-ever it was, had anything in it. But, at least, it was a theory. And he was trying hard to push it. It must have been pretty depressing for a man of Gillett's energy to have to deal with someone about as nimble and enthusiastic as a used bath-towel. But if Wilton thought that Gillett was going to leave it there, he had underestimated him.

So had I. We were both of us completely unprepared for the Gillett pocket-model H-bomb that he suddenly produced. He had stepped back and was facing us with a ram-the-enemy-if-your-guns-are-jammed kind of expression on his face. His hands were shoved down hard in the pockets of his jacket, and his feet were planted firmly in readiness for the head-on collision.

"If you won't take any action, I will," he said.

"What sort of action?"

Even now, Wilton seemed to be not much more than casually interested. He was scratching the part of his leg where the suspender should have been.

Gillett paused. It was quite obvious that the pause was purely for effect. But what he had to say justified it. He didn't want there to be the slightest misunderstanding anywhere.

"Action that will lead to the arrest of Dr. Mann on a charge of attempting to murder my fiancée," he said, clearly and distinctly.

Wilton looked up. There was no pause this time.

"I suppose you're aware that it's a serious charge you're making?" he asked.

"It's because it's a serious charge that I make it in front of a witness," he said. "I don't want there to be any backing out this time."

"And if I tell you you're wrong?"

"I shall go into Bodmin and lay in my information before the nearest J.P.," Gillett answered. "I'm bloody well sick of policemen."

163

It was certainly plain speaking. And Wilton seemed to understand it. He started creaking and came slowly to the upright
position.

"Well, what do you want me to do?" he asked wearily.

"I want you to come with me and collect the weapon that Dr.
Mann used when he fired first at me and then at Una."

"Is it far?" Wilton asked.

He had narrowed his eyes down and was looking hard at
Gillett. There was something characteristic about the attitude,
and I realised what it was. Whenever Wilton was really looking
hard at anyone it was never full-face. Always from the side.

"I suggest to you that it is hidden in Mann's room at this
moment," Gillett replied. "And I suggest that if it isn't taken
away from him he'll use it again. It isn't your life that's in danger,
remember. It's mine."

"And Una's," I put in.

But I don't think he heard me.

"Why should yours be?" Wilton went straight on.

"Because he knows I suspect him," Gillett replied.

"How does he know that?"

There was another of those little pauses. Though whether it
was for effect or not this time I couldn't say.

"I told him," Gillett answered.

Wilton paused with an unlit cigarette between his lips and the
stub of the old one raised half-way towards it.

"When?" he asked.

"To-day," Gillett said. "After coffee. I couldn't stand another
damn minute of it. He was sitting there like some bloody little
Buddha talking about international brotherhood and nation-
shall-speak-peace-unto-nation and all that rot, and I suddenly
had enough of it. There were just the two of us. And I told him

164

what kind of a swine I thought he was. . . . "

I suppose that if you conserve your energies the way Wilton always did, you have more to draw on in an emergency. But whatever the explanation, Wilton certainly had something there. He was off in a burst that any ostrich would have envied.

"Where are you going?" Gillett asked as soon as we had caught up again.

"See Dr. Mann," Wilton answered.

The speed with which things were happening seemed to have shaken Gillett a bit.

"Don't . . . don't you want a warrant or anything?" he asked. But by then Wilton had gone too far down the corridor to answer.

3

When we got to Dr. Mann's room it was empty. And tidy. I don't mean to say that the other rooms along that corridor weren't tidy, too. There was a cousin or something of the Phoenician who played the part of bedder; and wastepaper baskets and hair-tidies were all regularly emptied by nine-thirty. But there was a neatness about Dr. Mann's room that was a straight projection of his own precise and systematic soul. The safety razor with which he had replaced the cut-throat I had stolen, hung from two little nails that he had driven into the woodwork. And even his dressing-gown was on a hanger. It was just the sort of room that any housemaster hopes to find when he is taking round a new parent.

I could see that Wilton had searched a room before. And that wasn't surprising. There must have been a period when he had been forced to get down to things and not merely stand around cloud-gazing. He started with the chest-of drawers, and worked very efficiently from the bottom upwards so that he didn't have to waste a lot of time shutting the drawers before getting to work on the next one. But he was just wasting his time: I could see that as soon as he started. The only thing that was the slightest bit unusual was a cardboard box in one of the drawers. It contained three bars of milk chocolate, a tube of toothpaste, two lengths of elastic, some safety-pins, and a tin of Lyons' coffee. It was obviously the beginnings of another of Dr. Mann's gift parcels, and I remember wondering whether it would ever get there.

I caught Gillett's eye while Wilton was going through it. But he quickly looked away again. I don't think that at this particular moment any of us wanted to be reminded of the dependence of Dr. Mann's female relatives. But ordinary human feelings didn't seem to play a large part in Wilton's make-up. By now, he was already going through the clothes in the wardrobe. And he was working quickly and methodically, patting the pockets and the seams as he worked over them one by one. When he had finished, he turned to Gillett.

"Give me a hand with that trunk, will you?"

It was easily the most solid piece of furniture in the room. And it looked as though it had been in Dr. Mann's family for a long time. Members of the Hanseatic League must have transferred their valuables in trunks like this one. The lock alone would have needed a hammer and cold chisel to break it open. It came as something of an anticlimax, therefore, when Wilton put his fingers into the catch and the hasp flew open. Somehow I couldn't see any man hiding a revolver in a tin trunk without a key. And I was right, too. That trunk was as innocent as a case of new-laid eggs.

Wilton turned towards Gillett.

"Satisfied?" he asked.

I don't think that it was the wasted effort he minded so much as the stooping. For the last five minutes he had been bent over double. And at this moment he was reaching the upright in a series of jerks and creakings. But it wasn't at Wilton that I was looking. It was at Gillett. He was standing in the doorway, his hands still thrust into his jacket pockets and his jaw sticking out farther than he usually carried it. The air of cocksure jauntiness had completely gone, however. He didn't even look up when he answered.

"I suppose so," he said.

"Quite sure?"

Gillett nodded. This time he didn't even bother to say anything.

But Wilton had been put to a lot of trouble in the past few minutes. And it was obvious that he didn't like being put to trouble. There was a mean side to his nature, and it came out now.

"No afterthoughts?" he asked.

Still no reply. Just a sad, sullen headshake.

Wilton, however, had no intention of letting Gillett off as lightly as all that. He just stood there giving the screw an extra turn or two for good value.

"Absolutely and completely satisfied?" he asked again.

As with banns it was the third and last time of asking. And this time Gillett couldn't stick it any longer.

"I've said so, haven't I?" he replied.

Wilton grinned. It was a wide, unpleasant schoolboy grin with Wilton's two large ears on the outer ends.

"Well, I'm not," he said.

There was only one other article of furniture in the whole

room—the laundry basket. Wilton went across to it. Every cubicle had its own laundry basket. It was a wicker affair like the chair; and, also like the chair, it was painted rose bud pink.

I could have told him what he would find in it. At least, at the start I could. Out came two dirty shirts, one of them a bit patched round the tail in a rough, amateurish kind of way as though Dr. Mann had been doing his own needlework. Next there was a pair of socks, ditto, with some fancy cross-stitching round the toes and the heels. And a pyjama suit with trousers that didn't match the jacket. About averagely sordid was how I would have described that basketful.

I even had a feeling that I was being a bit disloyal to Dr. Mann, just standing there rubber-necking while a high-grade army nark went through the wash-bag. But Wilton might have been sorting soiled undies all his life. And when he came to the end began battering the poor basket on its head. The bottom fell clean away. But it was a false bottom. Cut the same shape as the basket, it fitted neatly round the sides and left a space of about four inches underneath it. And the first thing that came tumbling out of that space was an old Luger holster—empty.

This was Gillett's moment. His eyes were shining, and he uttered a deep, long-drawn-out "Ah" as he saw it.

But it was also my moment too. Because there was more than a revolver-case in that little cavity. There was a whole collection of pieces of very inferior-looking paper all neatly typed with letters in heavy black capitals. And the one that I was staring at had a sort of crazy logic that was all its own.

"RELAX NOW. THE BIRD HAS FLOWN," was what was written there.

Chapter XXVII

The mist at Bodmin had a highly developed sense of the dramatic. It knew exactly when to come down and when to keep away. And I could see the windows steaming up as I stood there. The small ventilation pane at the top had been left open, and long tendrils of the mist were already reaching into the little cubicle.

Wilton had already picked up the Luger case by the strap and had wrapped it up in the old pyjama jacket. As for the messages he didn't seem to be nearly as interested in them as I was. He simply scooped them up into a ball and shoved them all in his pocket. It was Gillett he turned to, not to me.

"Lock the door after us, there's a good fellow," he said.

It was noticeable that his manner towards Gillett had changed considerably during the last few minutes. Wilton was now trying all he could to rub out those nasty marks that the thumb-screws had left. And the change showed itself in the confidence that he placed in him.

"Better put the key on your key-ring," he added. "I don't want anyone else coming in here until I get back."

That left me free to go off with Wilton. But Wilton was doing his ostrich-racing act again, and it was as much as I could do to keep up with him. He was looking for Dr. Mann.

The first place that we went to was the lab. But that didn't help us very much. Nor did Kimbell. He was the only person in the lab. when we got there. And I thought he looked a bit startled.

"Last time I saw Mann he was going out somewhere," he told us.

"How d'you know?"

"He'd got his raincoat on."

"Was it like this?"

Wilton indicated the window. Visibility was practically nil by now. It was as though someone had hung up a wet bath-towel across the woodwork.

"Not so thick," Kimbell replied, and went on pretending to screw up a clamp that looked to me perfectly firm already.

"How long ago?"

"About half an hour. I was just coming in."

"See which way he went?"

"Over towards the kennels."

"Sure?"

Kimbell paused.

"Pretty sure," he said. "I didn't notice him particularly."

And giving the clamp an extra turn that I had known all the time it didn't need, he splintered the S-bend that it was holding. It was quite good acting, so far as it went. But it just didn't go far enough. A better actor would have asked if there was anything wrong.

Wilton had set his own pace, and I followed behind like a pet Corgi. I'd never known Wilton so energetic before—I think that Gillett's threat of the Bodmin J.P. must have scared him. And he was inclined to be irritable. The first thing that he did was to get

170

the Old Man to call the roll. But everyone had knocked off by now, and getting them together was work for a good pair of sheep dogs. It took twenty minutes before he'd got all of them assembled. All of them in the Institute, that is. Swanton wasn't there because he was keeping a date with a dentist in Bodmin. Hilda had left early saying that she wanted to get away while she could still see to drive. Dr. Mann we had known all the time wasn't there to show up. And Una was the one missing one.

It shook Gillett when he discovered this. He had kept his profile under strict orders for years. But he had nothing like the same degree over his complexion. It went suddenly pale when he heard. And he wanted to go out there at once and start searching. But Wilton stopped him.

"Got to be done properly," he said, his voice taking on that hard edge which I had heard only once before—the time one of the cub captains had put too much pressure on to a loaded soda siphon. "I don't want everyone getting lost."

He turned to the Old Man.

"Better ring up for an ambulance," he said. "I'm going out with them."

We were lined up in the hall by now, and Wilton addressed us.

"It's thick already, and it's getting thicker," he said. "That means it's going to be difficult. Don't forget to keep within calling distance. And if you don't get an answer yell harder."

He was right to be careful. For all the good it did going out into the courtyard, we might just as well have remained inside. The mist wasn't just the standard Grade A white stuff. It was a real mid-Atlantic sea-fog that had overshot itself. The other side of the courtyard was blotted out completely even though it was only about fifteen feet away. Even getting across to the gate was largely guesswork.

Suddenly there was the strange throbbing bleat of a police whistle. But it was only Wilton putting his scout troop through their battle training.

"If you hear that again," he said, "it'll be me. And it means 'Stop where you are.' Don't forget: when you hear that, stand still until I tell you what to do."

"Aye aye, sir," I answered.

"You and Gillett stay next to me," Wilton went on. "I may need you."

"At thy side, master," I promised for both of us.

If it had been thick in the courtyard, it was simply silly out there on the moor. Your own mother might have been a couple of feet away from you and you would never have known it. First, we combed the kennels but without catching a glimpse of anyone. And now we were moving forward in a long half-crescent. It was actually a straight line that Wilton had ordered. But the direction from which the shouts were coming to us showed that the two ends were already getting a bit ragged.

Wilton blew his whistle twice. Once was because Rogers had fallen into a ditch with water at the bottom of it and seemed to be having some difficulty in getting out again, and once because Bansted thought that he had heard something. It had been like voices, he said, and had come from somewhere on the left. Nobody took it very seriously. But at least Wilton decided to wheel round in that direction. Heads down so that we could see what was underneath our feet, we went plunging on through the mist and into the darkness.

Then everyone of us heard the sound that we'd been afraid of hearing. It came from farther on the left still, right from the very heart of the blackness. And there were two parts to the sound. The first was the high-pitched report of a Luger. And the second was a scream. Una's scream.

The scream itself was not so loud because it was mingled with the throb of Wilton's police whistle. But it was loud enough for Gillett to hear. And forgetting everything that he had been told about standing still, Gillett was off in that direction like a gazelle. But gazelles, like racing cyclists, need clear weather. And Gillett had to pass close beside Wilton. Too close it turned out. Because Wilton was just getting himself under way at that moment and his long legs were straddled out all round him. There seemed to be more of them than usual. And he was as evenly distributed as a camera tripod. Gillett accidentally got one foot entangled and went flying. I heard him land with a loud crunch of wet crushed heather. But by then Wilton was off on his own account. And I was following, even though I still couldn't see anything.

That was where Wilton's deployed formation came in useful. And, actually, it was Kimbell who was the first to get there. His loud, corncrake yell sent us swerving round still farther. In the ordinary way, mist does a lot of funny things to noises. It seems to twist them up into kinks in the middle before handing them on to the next patch. But Kimbell's pure Manchester proved superior. No power on earth could give that accent a kink that wasn't there already. It came through the mist as straight and sharp as a skewer. And I don't think that I have ever heard any voice quite so shrill or so urgent.

I wasn't surprised when I saw why. There was Una with her two hands covering up her eyes. And Kimbell was on his knees, bending over something on the ground. It was wearing Dr. Mann's German mackintosh. And it had Dr. Mann's little pink hand protruding from the sleeve. But where the two big flaps of the collar came together something was missing.

There was a gap where the top of his head should have been.

Chapter XXVIII

1

The inquest, the verdict and the funeral blotted out everything else. About the only consolation was that the coroner's
jury finally decided on "Suicide while the balance of mind was
disturbed, etc., etc." And here it was Una's evidence that avoided
the bleak mediævalism of burial at the cross-roads or wherever it
is that Cornwall chooses to inter her alien and unhallowed dead.

It seemed that she had been out on the moor walking by
herself when the mist had suddenly grown thicker. Then, just
when she had reached the stage of beginning to wonder whether
to turn left or right to get back to the Institute, she had bumped
into Dr. Mann. And immediately he had produced his revolver
and pointed it at her. Then he had said either "I shall kill you"
or "I am going to kill you." Una could not remember which.

And this seemed to me a pity because the two phrases aren't
really interchangeable. "I am going to kill you," is complete as it
stands. But even though "I shall kill you" has got everything that
the grammar book says a good sentence needs, there is still something unfinished about it. There is just the suggestion that given
time to develop it might go on: " . . . unless you do something or

other." That line of reasoning, however, contained its own kernel of lunacy. Because, even allowing for some slight deficiency in Dr. Mann's English syntax, the simple fact remained that either way he hadn't meant what he said. She hadn't done anything, and he still hadn't killed her.

Then there was something else that added chaos to confusion. And again it was only Una's word that we had for it.

"The hunt has been too long," she said, was the second remark that Dr. Mann had addressed to her. And, naturally not wanting to have her brachial artery severed twice during the same calendar month, Una had ducked down behind the nearest clump of heather as soon as she heard. But there, again, there was the same contradiction. A Luger bullet can penetrate a few tufts of West Country heather without getting noticeably held up on the way. And still Dr. Mann had not fired. That was all part of the higher nonsense of the whole affair. And it was only by putting everything into reverse with Dr. Mann as the hunted and not the hunter that the answer to that part even began to come out right.

It could have been a note of despair that he was uttering and not a threat. At least that would explain the suicide.

But it still left the other two shootings unaccounted for. And there the law of averages came in. Because, even trying my hardest, I still could not believe that there were several different people all armed with German Lugers wandering about Bodmin Moor and taking a pot-shot at people as soon as the weather turned a bit humid.

The person who was most cut up about the shooting was Rogers. This was understandable. It tends to impress it on your memory when you turn a man over to look at a face that isn't there. I knew, because I'd done it: But Rogers simply wouldn't stop talking about it.

"Mind you, I've met plenty of poor old Mann's type before," he kept saying. "My wife's friends were all that sort. Brilliant woman, my wife in her way." That was the signal. I gripped the sides of my chair waiting for what was to come. "Ph.D. and all that," he went on. "But there's no real solidity in the type. Just pink intellectuals. That's what I used to call her lot. Many's the time I've said that if they really felt that way the best thing they could do would be to blow their brains out." He paused. "But I didn't know what I was saying. When I turned back the collar of his coat . . . "

There was one other person who seemed to think that it was pretty horrible. That was Gillett. By the time he had picked himself up out of the wet heather he must have been about fourth on the scene. But from the fuss he was making he might have got there before Rogers.

"By God," he said, "it was ghastly. I keep on remembering it just when I'm going off to sleep."

That moved me deeply. There is so much unhappiness in this world already that I couldn't bear to think of more of it than is absolutely necessary.

"You've got nothing with which to reproach yourself, pal," I said. "It's none of it your fault. After all, you didn't actually kill him. You only drove him to it."

2

I kept on going over the Mann business all the way to St. Lothiel.

It was only twenty-two miles to the Isolation Hospital. And in the ordinary way half an hour would have been plenty to take

176

care of the built-up stretch through Bodmin, the cattle-crossing notices and the double horseshoe as you get down on to the St. Lothiel level. But some of the Institute gremlins had started colonising in the car engine. Of the eight cylinders, about six and a half were working as the original designer had intended, and my right arm had developed its own variant of tennis-elbow by having to wave on Austin Sevens and Morris Minors as soon as we came up against a rise in the road.

That meant that I had plenty of time to think. Too much, in fact. I won't go over the Una part of it. It had been difficult enough while it was still all party manners between Gillett and myself. But now that he knew my real feelings about him, it can't have made matters any easier for Una. Gillett wasn't the sort of man to sit by and watch his fiancée talking to the enemy.

It wasn't Una, however, who was worrying me. It was Hilda. She had somehow become separated from the rest of us. She didn't mix any longer. She was a figure suspended in space: a presence, rather than a real, live human being. If you spoke to her, you didn't always get an answer. And when you did get it, it was as though she had recalled herself from a long distance. Nowadays, she had to make a real effort to become one of us again.

I couldn't help remembering something that Wilton had once let slip during the course of one of our long gin evenings. "Nine times out often," he had remarked, "the Communist who is planted in a government department sets an example for quiet, unostentatious efficiency. He has to. Otherwise, he may lose the job. And if he loses it, he stops being useful. On the other hand, he can't afford to shine too much. Because then people begin noticing him. Which is just what he doesn't want. The quiet type without any friends, that's what we generally look for. And it's

177

just as likely to be a woman as a man. . . . "

I could still hear Wilton saying it as I went down to second to get over a nasty stretch of about one in two hundred. The description certainly fitted Hilda. And there was more to it than that. A girl doesn't suddenly start a Communist reading course and change her lodgings and stop going to church unless a bomb of some sort has gone off inside her. I didn't attach very much importance to the fact that her compact-case had been picked up at just about the spot where whoever it was must have stood to take the shot at Una. After all, Hilda was out on the moor in all kinds of weather. It was that dream of mine that was still worrying me. I hate doubts in the subconscious.

The matron had laid on tea for me before the lecture. And I feared her at sight. She was one of those hard, masterful women who make grown men feel small fragile creatures, who have to take an occasional teeny-weeny double brandy simply because otherwise they couldn't get through things. She had a way of pouring out the tea that reminded me of boiling lead going down on to the heads of a storming party. And I rather think that the Phœnician must have arranged to get a message along the Bodmin bush telegraph: "Doctorman likee char velly velly milky." It was the top of the milk, practically pure cream, she confided, as she slugged a great gobbet of the pale yellow stuff into the thick hospital teacup.

The nurses themselves might all have been illegitimate daughters of the matron by different fathers. They had the same wild vocational look about the eyes. Offer any one of them Danny Kaye at the Palladium and supper at Quaglino's afterwards, or a fresh case of cow-pox and a cup of County Council cocoa and she would have plunged unhesitatingly for the cow-pox and cocoa. I have never looked so closely on eight young female faces and felt so gloriously immune from all temptation. What was worse, they were fiendishly knowledgeable. I don't wonder. The only men they ever saw were spotty ones. And there was certainly nothing else in St. Lothiel to distract them. There wasn't anything for those poor girls to do but work. In consequence, they had all done their homework to perfection. And what they didn't know about *B. typhosus* I couldn't tell them. There was even one ghastly little orphan-like creature in the front row who prompted me in a lisp when I couldn't remember something on the symptoms side.

"Ithn't that becauth the bathiluth thirculathes in the blood-thream?" she had asked on one occasion when I was peculiarly far from centre. And if there had been a power-cut I could have kissed her then and there simply for reminding me of what I was supposed to be talking about.

When it was over—and to the mutual relief of all ten of us it came out about ten minutes on the short side—the matron asked if I would like another cup of tea. But, even if I had wanted it, I would still have refused. There was a distinctly nasty look in her eyes that had nothing to do with vocationalism. I had the impression that this time she would probably lace up the Cornish cream with a little native hemlock. The one thing that I wanted to do was get away. And as I clambered like a nuthatch up the wood-work into the driving seat I reminded myself that even medium bad lecturers must sometimes have a total flop just to keep their average from rocketing.

The real trouble, of course, had simply been that I wasn't thinking about what I was saying. When I should have been concentrating on MacConkey's medium and Peyers' patches, I was going over Hilda's peculiar behaviour pattern. And it kept

179

on coming as a surprise to me to see those hungry fanatical eyes all staring at me and praying that they could somehow keep awake long enough to learn something. The funny thing was that if I had gone back now I could have delivered a perfect discourse. Because somewhere in the shame of my departure I had completely forgotten about Hilda.

So completely, in fact, that there must have been a five-or ten-seconds' time lag before I realised that I was looking at the dwindling back number-plate of her car. But there it was all right—WWW972. And there, also, through the rear window of the little Singer I could see Hilda—though why on earth she should be out in this part of the country I couldn't imagine. And still less could I imagine when she took the Padstow branch when she came to it.

It was then that I decided to follow her. I still didn't like to think of Hilda's being mixed up in anything. But it certainly looked pretty fishy. She had told me herself that she hadn't any friends in that part of Cornwall. And less than a couple of hours ago I had heard her telling the Old Man that she was going off early so that she could get to bed because of her headache. The way she was driving she had got rid of that headache long ago.

And now that she was on the straight she put her foot down. The car that she was driving was a 1928 model with marked curvature of the main shaft and thrombosis in the petrol feed. It was the sort of car that only a woman could have driven without realising that the whole history of mechanics was against her. And if she had let me be nicer to her I would have taken the engine and the transmission right down just so that the souls of the original fitters could rest in some kind of peace. But so far as engines are concerned, there is a brutality in the female sex that

180

is equalled only by the Italian's love for the horse. She was perfectly content with everything as it was, she said. By now the little medallion of St. Christopher that the dealer had supplied with the car had a mysterious dark stain across it that might have been blood. Or sweat. Or tears.

At the moment, she was knocking a full forty out of the thing and the shaft must have been turning like a skipping rope. For my part, I was following flat out at about 38.5. It was like a Hollywood car chase in slow motion, and it would have sounded fastest over the radio. Both cars were acoustically very impressive, and old men and little frightened children crowded to cottage windows to see which way the tank convoy was going.

By sheer bad driving and cutting off the corners with a ruler, I kept her in sight all the way. And apparently she knew exactly where she was going. Padstow isn't an easy town. Nothing that is built on the side of a hill with a harbour at the bottom ever comes out that way. There was even one moment when I thought I'd lost her. But it was all right. It was simply that Hilda had made one of those astonishing right-angle turns of which no man has ever found the secret. At one moment she was roaring up the hill with a plume of oil like a destroyer smoke-screen pouring out behind. And, at the next, without any indicator or hand sign or brakes, she had parked herself about twenty-five yards up a side turning. By the time I had followed she was already getting out of the car and going towards a small dark house that was so ordinary looking and respectable that the local agents could have charged Moscow almost any premium that they cared to ask.

What was significant was that somebody had evidently been expecting her. The light in the little hall had come on already, and the door was open. Over her shoulder I could even see the head of the man who had come to the door to meet her. The gaslight shone full down on him as though he were an exhibit in the waxworks: I could see the thin, greasy hair that had been brushed right across to cover up the bald part. But it wasn't until he raised his face that I recognised him. Then I saw that he was the dago who had been walking with Hilda on the moor.

There wasn't the slightest possibility of mistaking him. Cornwall is full of dark, swarthy people with features like fish-hawks. In some villages you could stage a whole Old Testament pageant simply by getting the Parish Council together. But this was something else. There was nothing vulturine in that face. It was a flat, blank face with smooth gentle curves where there should have been angles and hard ridges. It takes wine and olive oil to make a face like that. Sharp cider and national mark margarine produce an effect that is quite different.

Then the door shut. And I was left out there in the darkness of the Padstow night with the wind coming up from the Bristol Channel with the keenness of a band-saw.

I didn't like the idea of the white and red-gold Hilda being shut up in that house with the black and olive foreigner. And it was only because I told myself that Wilton wouldn't approve, that I didn't go straight across and start kicking the door down. Not that I was really Wilton's man in all this. Not any longer. I was determined to have a nice long talk with Hilda before Wilton, with that tired, bored grin of his, could slip the handcuffs on to her. If necessary, I was prepared to spend the whole night out there on the pavement just to be certain of getting my word in first.

It was the approach of a stalwart of the Cornish Constabulary that interrupted me. A large man who seemed to take his breathing seriously the way some people take singing, he came up to me to see if I knew anything about an open sports car with no lights on that was parked slantwise across the junction of Prideaux and Park Streets.

"Quite impossible, officer," I said politely as I walked back with him. "It just couldn't be mine."

It was while I was explaining to him that the lights weren't really off and that it must have been simply that I had kicked the switch with my foot as I got out, that I heard a sound that I didn't want to hear. It was the sound of Hilda's car starting up. And while I was still trying to convince the policeman that summoning me would merely be penalising the wrong social bracket, Hilda shot past me.

Chapter XXIX

Wilton had suddenly taken to cultivating me again. Apparently he couldn't snap back the spring of a Gordon's stopper without my image automatically coming into his mind. And with every day that passed Wilton was becoming more embarrassingly intimate. We had passed through a number of successive stages. Complete stranger and complete stranger. Policeman and suspect. Friend and friend. Soak and soak. Father and son. Brother and brother. And finally Darby and Joan. Every time I came into the room I was more than half prepared to have him toss over a pair of socks that needed darning.

This evening, however, he was unusually moody and silent. About the only sound that came from his corner of the room was the steady sip-sip as the tonic-water went down, and a noise like a piece of firewood snapping when he felt the need for exercise and unfolded his legs, recrossing them left to right. Then I remembered that it was the wife's place to keep the home cheerful. So I said something.

"Not getting very far, are we?" I remarked.

"Far from what?" he asked.

That showed obtuseness on his part and meant that I had to rephrase things.

"Other way round," I explained. "Not much nearer a solution, I mean."

Wilton paused. In a sense, he'd been pausing ever since I had come in. From nine o'clock onwards it had been one long uninterrupted pause.

"I wouldn't say that," he replied at last.

Then he sat back again. But by now the liveliness of Wilton as a conversationalist had got me all keyed up.

"How d'you mean?" I asked.

"Well," said Wilton, "we know more than we did, don't we?"

"You may do," I said, remembering my role. "I don't. You never discuss your work with me nowadays."

But this was no use. To-night apparently nothing less than a direct question could coax an answer out of hubby. So I tried again.

"Are you satisfied about poor old Mann?" I asked.

I'd had Dr. Mann on my mind rather a lot lately. That was because of a scheme I'd had for keeping up the weekly food parcels for the Berlin relatives.

"Perfectly, thank you," Wilton answered, and began opening another packet of twenty.

"Meaning *you* think he did it?"

I couldn't quite keep the contempt out of my voice. But I could see the shape of things clearly enough. The Wiltons of this world have to produce results like everybody else. And when a red-hot suspect commits suicide while on bail it comes as a godsend for the "Case closed" side of things.

But Wilton had got the packet open by now, and was able to relax.

"Meaning that I'm sure he didn't," he said. "I've eliminated him."

"Come to that, he eliminated himself," I pointed out.

"Same thing."

"Not entirely," I said. "If he'd still been alive there's quite a lot he could have told you."

"Such as?"

Here I drew in a deep breath. I didn't mean to. It just came. And I was rather annoyed by it. Because it meant that I was even breathing in cliches by now.

"Oh, about Dr. Smith," I said, speaking casually, as though the betrayal of a fellow-worker or two meant nothing to me. "Mann had several very interesting notions about Dr. Smith. Found out that he'd been using the poste restante at Plymouth instead of having his letters sent to the Institute."

I knew that in all this I was qualifying for a Class A Cad's Diploma, Top Grade. But there was a reason for it. I wanted to keep Wilton busy and occupied for as long as possible in other directions while I continued quietly and undistracted with my Padstow researches. I still, however, hadn't found the right dose for re-energising Wilton.

"Mann was a bit of an authority on post offices, wasn't he?" was all he said.

I smiled.

"You mean that story about the burglary?" I said.

Wilton nodded. I found that rather depressing. It meant that all my efforts to make him talk hadn't been too successful. If we were back to sign language already, the original primal silence might ensue at any moment. But I wasn't to be beaten all that easily.

"Silly, wasn't it?" I said.

"Very," Wilton answered.

"Because, of course, he was in my room all the time."

"Why 'of course?' You didn't usually sleep together, did you?"

This was much better. At last Wilton was really making his own contribution to the conversation. Soon I would be able simply to sit back and listen. And that would have suited me far better.

"Oh, no," I said, with the sort of laugh that smoothes out difficulties at big business conferences. "Nothing like that. It was purely coincidence."

"It was more than coincidence," Wilton said. He had shifted himself so far back in his chair by now that he was lying in a practically straight line. His neck was supported on the back of the chair and his feet were propped up against the fender to stop him from slipping. If I hadn't known him I would have said that he was in the tertiary and final stages of tetanus. But apparently he was comfortable. "It was co-existence," he went on.

This shook me.

"Come again, please," I asked.

"Co-existence," he said. "You know. Astral separatism. Projection of the body through space. Corporeal ambivalence. It's well attested."

The pause was longer this time. It may have seemed longer to me than it did to Wilton. But it evidently seemed quite long enough for him too. Because he turned towards me, and I saw that he was one long wide grin. The fact that he had a cigarette between his lips meant that the grin was also a thin one. It was like a new moon in the middle of his face. But it was still a grin.

"Don'tcher follow?" he asked.

"Only a long way behind," I admitted.

"Well, you see," he said, "one half of him was in the post office going through the mail bags while the other half was with you. Therefore, one of them must have been astraloid. I only wondered if you noticed anything strange about him. If you'd touched him, you might have found that he felt cold. They do sometimes when they're in that state."

"But that's absurd," I said.

I wasn't particularly proud of the remark. I wanted time to think, however, and I had to say something.

Wilton, I noticed, seemed disappointed in me.

"Not necessarily," he replied. "There have been other cases. Psychical records are full of them. You have to consider all possibilities in my job. Even doppelgangers."

"Mann never had a double," I said.

Wilton exhaled a lot of smoke through his nostrils. Playing dragons was one of his more irritating habits. And it always happened when the other person was impatient about something.

"That's my view," he said.

"And you still think it was Mann who burgled that post office?"

"I know it was."

"How?"

By now the grin was wider than ever. It had long since passed the new moon phase. The whole of Wilton's head looked like a boiled egg with the top ready to come off.

"I was there too," he said. "In the corner cabinet. Watched him for about ten minutes through the keyhole."

"What were you doing there?" I asked.

"Wrong track altogether," Wilton admitted. "I was looking for the culture. Thought it might have been sent by post. Silly of me."

I drank the rest of my gin-tonic before answering. In the last few seconds things had taken a rather nasty turn.

"Then to put it bluntly," I asked, "you didn't believe my story about having Mann up in my room all the time."

The grin didn't waver.

"I wouldn't say that," he replied. "Why, in those days I scarcely knew you."

Chapter XXX

It must have been because I had been reading one of the magazines that young Mellon had left lying about in the common room that the idea came to me. The magazine had been sent to him from the States, and was one of those immensely knowledgeable and outspoken publications that make you feel while you're reading them that everyone except the writer, and possibly the editor, has up to now been living right on the outside of things.

What may have roused me was that this particular piece of outspokenness was directed against the British. The author was evidently a Californian counterpart of our great Dr. Smith. He had been over here, sampled us, found the flavour a bit stale and tasteless, and had returned to warn the rest of mankind against further nibbling. In his eyes the one thing in which we possessed a whole corner was picturesqueness. But there was a scarcely concealed threat behind it all that if the British didn't pull their socks up and manage things a bit better they would find a United Nations Commission taking the job of preservation over from them. And as for scientists engaged in work of military importance, it was the writer's view that the time had already come.

190

"According to the F.B.I, files," the article went on, "British investigation methods are only 43.7 per cent as effective as the American. And Britain's Harwell"—I don't think that the Pacific Coast expert had ever heard of Bodmin —"is now the international staging-post for Stalin's spies playing between Las Vegas and Russia's Kharkovsk."

I read that sentence twice. The first time with a kind of sultry resentment because I suspected the fellow of over calling his hand. And the second time with a great flash of understanding as though one of Pontecorvo's pills (that was the writer's phrase, not mine) had gone off right inside me. Perhaps "understanding" is too strong a word. Because at the moment it was nothing more than one big, howling suspicion. But it felt like understanding all right. And I have noticed before that there comes a point in all philosophical systems where the straight hunch is worth any amount of pure reason. Not the least of its advantages is that it is so much quicker.

I argued it out this way. The U.S.A. is the most violently anti-Communist country in the world. *Ergo* any American is non-suspect. Nowadays an American could come into Southampton with a hammer under one arm, and a sickle and two H-bombs under the other, and the Customs man would chalk him up to go through the barrier before he had even had time to complain about the coffee.

Young Mellon fitted perfectly into that picture. You couldn't see him without liking him. Inside the first five minutes, fully-grown disgruntled scientists and policemen succumbed before the open sunny charm of the campus and the drug-store. And women didn't even have to wait that long. If Mellon had accidentally sunk the duty destroyer in the Sound the Admiral wouldn't have thought twice about forgiving him.

And I saw now the uses to which Mellon had been putting his charm. It had been the master key and passport to everything. Every time his big blue Buick swept down the Institute's front drive, the older ones, with all passion spent, had sat about shaking their heads sadly over another impending West Country fall. It was significant, too, that whenever the Inspector saw Mellon going by he winked at him—that from an ice-cold eye showed what the Mellon myth could do. And I remembered it was Mellon who had spread the myth. While we had assumed that he was safely rounding up some houri in Okehampton, he *could* have been half-way to the Soviet Embassy.

That meant that I now had no fewer than three separate lines of inquiry. I still wanted to know more about Dr. Smith's poste restante activities in Plymouth. There was an investigation agent's job to be done watching the disarming little villa in Padstow. And now there was Mellon's Buick to be trailed. That didn't promise to be too easy. Even when all my eight cylinders had still been working, Mellon's Fireball acceleration had always left me somewhere on the wrong side of the level-crossing.

But I had learnt one thing from Wilton. That was to leave the other fellow to do the talking. And it occurred to me that if I just planted myself on a bar-stool adjacent to Mellon's and kept the conversation going with an occasional "You don't say!" or "My, my, isn't this a small world?" I might be able to find out quite as much as if I bought a T.T. racing-model Norton and went road-hogging after him.

Starting up the conversation wasn't difficult. After mine—some way after—Mellon's thirst was easily the biggest thing in the Institute. Whisky ruined by ice was his tipple. And because he was a nice friendly boy he liked to have someone beside him just to suggest the next round to him. He was there exactly where I expected him to be. And his "What'll you have?" before I had even got across to the bar made me just a wee bit cautious. It occurred to me that he may have been just as eager as I was to get the other one to do some talking.

The first thing that I noticed was that he was still intent on establishing his part. He turned the conversation to sex before I got myself properly settled on the high stool alongside him.

"Say, what are your divorce laws like around here?" he asked.

I shook my head before answering.

"Pretty stiff," I told him. "Adultery's usually punished by stoning. Both parties." I paused. "It's worse up Somerset way," I added.

But young Mellon was in no mood for spoiling his own effect by seeming to take things too lightly.

"Do they still hang you if you kill someone?" he asked.

"Only if they catch you," I reassured him.

"And what about *crime passionel?*" he went on.

Here I shook my head again.

"No use pleading that," I advised. "If you'd ever seen an English jury you'd know that they'd convict for the *passionel* part even without the *crime*. They're dead against it in our law courts."

Mellon still looked worried.

"Can ya get police protection if you ask for it?" he inquired.

"You've been having it," I replied.

"Then I guess I gotta find some other way."

It was my turn to stand this round.

"Who're you planning to kill?" I asked.

Mellon pushed his glass away from him. This itself was an unnatural gesture and showed that the internal stresses must have been considerable.

"Ya got me all wrong," he said. "I'm the guy that's on the spot."

"Meaning you're hot?" I asked.

"Meaning there's some god-damn fool of a husband who's after me," he corrected me.

I smiled. Only inwardly, I hope. Because I didn't want Mellon to know what I was really thinking.

"And what do you propose to do?" I asked.

I had my fingers crossed at this point.

"Get outer here," Mellon answered. "Get outer here before they have to carry me."

That meant that my fingers could uncross again.

"Where to?" I asked innocently. "He'll find you easily enough if he's really all that keen. It's only a small place, Bodmin."

Mellon was reaching out for his glass again. Evidently instinct had got the better of panic.

"Who said anything about Bodmin?" he demanded. "I mean Paris; Paris, France."

"Or Rome, Italy," I suggested.

"Could be," he agreed.

"Then why tell me?" I asked. "I might help to put him on to you."

Mellon finished the rest of the drink before answering and called for another as soon as he put the glass down.

"Because I'm going crackers," he answered. "How d'you like it yourself if ya just had to sit around here waiting for some crazy guy to come sneaking upter ya?"

"I see your point," I said. "Must make ya sorter restless."

Altogether it was one of the neatest pieces of sustained strategy that I had so far encountered. And the acting throughout had been admirable. There wasn't a single one of us in the

Institute who wouldn't have been prepared to go into the witness-box to swear character—Mellon had seen to that. And even if running away from danger wasn't quite in the best Illinois tradition I felt that Mellon would be able to laugh that one off all right by the time he got through to Moscow, Russia.

What was more, now that he had told me everything, he knew that he was perfectly safe. Simple, sun-soaked and boyish, young Mellon may have been. But I felt that since he had arrived here, he had made a pretty accurate reading of English character. He knew that if only you confide in an Englishman you can tell him the date and time of his own assassination with the absolute certainty that he'll turn up punctually and wait about if necessary.

The only thing that he didn't know was how much an Englishman can think to himself without saying anything.

Chapter XXXI

1

The following day I decided to apply something of the Mellon technique on my own account. What I wanted to do was to keep my Padstow appointment that evening. And what I didn't want was to have Wilton out looking for me.

"Ouch," I said very loudly for the third time since lunch.

"This wet weather plays hell with me. Thank goodness I'm seeing the chiropodist this evening."

The fact that I had shown the forethought to be wearing one of my big woolly bedroom slippers on the left foot added just that touch of drama that was needed. And by the time five-thirty arrived both Bansted and Rogers had come round to my side of the bench and advised me to take things easily for a bit. Rogers even had some kind of crack-pot radium-impregnated sock that he wanted me to wear inside the bedroom slippers. But I declined politely and hobbled off to my bedroom with all the dignity of a confirmed sufferer who doesn't want to have his pain snatched away from him quite that quickly. And five minutes afterwards, having changed into my brogues, I was going pit-a-pat down the back stairs and out across the courtyard towards the car.

There was no moon that night. And whatever stars there might have been were obscured by a layer of cloud that was still undecided whether to remain aloft or come down and blot out everything. Not that it need have troubled itself. As it was, the night could have put extra shadows into the original Egyptian plague of darkness and still have had some.

A younger man could probably have gone straight on without falling over anything. But there's nothing like a combination of alcohol and nicotine for cutting down on the eyesight. With my habits I'd have been disqualified years ago even from shunting engines. I just had to stand where I was waiting for the tired old pupils to adjust themselves. And it was while I was still waiting that I heard someone coming.

Judging by the sound, whoever it was must have been in a hurry. There was a kind of flick and scurry rather than a good solid crunch about the footsteps. And they were heading straight in my direction. Either I had a bat for a co-worker, or somebody was taking risks in the darkness.

It wasn't a bat. And apparently I wasn't the only person in Bodmin with a marked vitamin A deficiency. For the next moment I was bumped into. Bumped into hard by someone who was running. And that someone was carrying something small but heavy that went clattering across the courtyard.

But then came the unlikeliest part of all. Because it was a woman who had cannoned into me. And, as a sex, women don't usually go dashing about from place to place the way men do. There is some protective biological reason that usually makes them take far better care of themselves.

But this was a woman all right. And, when I heard the gasp she gave, I recognised it. I knew then that it was Una that I had grabbed hold of.

"Going somewhere?" I asked.

But she was evidently in no mood for being held. She still seemed pretty frantic about something.

"Help me find it," was what she said. "You've got to help me find it."

"Find what?" I asked.

It was obviously no use expecting to get a reasonable answer out of her in her present mood. She was already down on her knees searching. And I went down on all fours and began searching too. It seemed thoroughly silly, the pair of us playing bears out there in the darkness, especially as one of the bears didn't even know what it was looking for.

And the next moment I put my hand right on top of something. It was a leather case, half jammed down into what seemed to be a lady's handbag. And from as much as I could feel of it, it seemed to be a very ordinary pair of binoculars that Una had been carrying.

"Here it is," I said. "You can stop worrying."

But that was apparently the one thing that Una couldn't do.

"Mind," she said. "Don't point it at yourself. It's loaded."

I lowered the case and handbag gently into my raincoat pocket. Then I put my arm round Una.

"Come and tell me all about it," I said.

But she was too nervy.

"There's nothing to tell," she answered. "I just want you to get rid of it for me."

I still had my arm round her, and we were walking over in the direction of the car.

"Look here, lady, I said. "That doesn't make sense. You were trying to *find* it just now."

"I wanted to give it to you."

"But you didn't know I'd be here."

"Yes, I did. I saw you come out."

"And you came after me?"

"Yes."

"That makes a difference," I agreed. "But what am I supposed to do?"

"Throw it into the sea," she replied. "It's safest."

"Why, what's it done?"

"I can't tell you. I just want you to get rid of it."

"And if I don't?"

There was no argument about that one.

"You've got to."

"Leave it to me," I said.

Then I had an afterthought.

"That your handbag it's wrapped up in?" I asked.

"It's only an old one," she replied, in the way that makes all female reasoning seem as though it's being carried on according to a quite different set of regulations.

"But it's still yours," I pointed out. "Could be awkward, you know, if that got fished up in a lobster-pot."

"Oh, very well then, give it back to me."

She was so obviously impatient that I think she suspected me of simply raising difficulties. But she seemed relieved by one thing. She had got rid of the revolver, and that was all that mattered.

"Where d'you find it?" I asked.

"I can't tell you," she said.

"Never?"

"Never."

"Not even in a hundred years' time when we're both of us old and grey."

"Not even in a hundred years."

She turned away as she said it without even so much as a thank you or a sorry-to-be-such-a-nuisance.

"I've got to go back now or they'll be missing me," she said.

"Who's they?"

"Mrs. Clewes and the Old Man," she said. "They don't know I've ever had the revolver. I've been hiding it . . . "

But by then Una had gone. She was running again.

2

I got the car out, and about half a mile along the road I parked. The one thing that I had been thinking about was the bulge in my pocket. And I wanted to examine it. The holster looked to me extraordinarily like the one that I had seen come falling out of Dr. Mann's wash-basket. And this wasn't surprising. Because when I opened it and put the weapon on my knees, there was the word "Luger" stamped into the gun-block. Evidently there must have been quite a cache of Lugers up at the Institute.

A moment later I had to cover the Luger up with the corner of my raincoat. That was because there was a sudden glare of headlights from behind me as young Mellon whooshed past at about eighty. I let him disappear into the distance with the array of rear lamps on his Buick as bright and lustrous as a firework display. Then I concentrated on the Luger again. Something told me that before getting rid of it the most important thing was to discover whether it had been fired recently. I'm not, however, very much of a gunsmith. As a matter of fact, this was the first automatic I'd ever handled. I knew enough not to look down the barrel while pulling at the trigger to see if it worked properly. But that was all that I knew enough not to do. And when I removed the safety-catch to see if I could remove the clip I made the mistake of not removing my finger from the mischief point. That trigger, moreover, must have been on the light side. And my finger evidently wasn't. There was suddenly a noise as though a land-mine had gone off right under my nose, and for the moment I thought that I was blinded. But the business end of the Luger had been pointing up into the night sky, and this was one of the occasions when I was glad that there was no hood to my car.

I sat on there quietly thinking things over. I have a real affection for anything mechanical that works smoothly. And I had just proved that this Luger would have passed any gunnery sergeant's inspection. To throw the thing away as Una wanted me to do would have been nothing less than sinful. Besides, it wasn't really the manner of its disposal that concerned Una. All that she wanted was to get rid of it. Inside my pocket would be every bit as safe as lying on the sea-bed for the first low-tide to uncover. Women don't remember about natural phenomena like tides.

So, having settled that point, I began thinking about Una. I'd got two girls on my hands by now. But there was a big difference somewhere. One of them trusted me, and one didn't. While I was still wondering why, a voice spoke to me close at hand out of the darkness.

"That you, Hudson?"

I jumped as though the Luger had gone off again. The voice was familiar. It was Bansted's voice. He must have been walking along the grass verge, and I hadn't heard a hint of him until he was right on top of me.

"You going into Bodmin?" he asked. "Can I get a lift?"

"Sure," I said, transferring the Luger into my other pocket so that it wouldn't bump against us as we drove. "That is if I can get her to go. The timing's all to hell or something. She's been back-firing like a machine-gun all evening."

"I know," Bansted replied candidly, "I heard you. I thought for a moment *you'd* shot yourself."

That wasn't so good coming from Bansted. Because Bansted was our ballistics man. And he'd been hearing rather a lot of Lugers lately.

Chapter XXXII

Later that same evening I met Bansted again.

As it happened, I was in bed at the time. I'd been in bed for about half an hour, in fact. The light was out, and the dormital was beginning to simmer gently. I could feel a delicious, cotton-woolly drowsiness closing in on me. In another minute I should be clean off.

Then, cutting in suddenly from the world that I was trying to let slide, I heard the sound of my door-handle turning. It wasn't much of a sound. But it was enough to rouse me like a shot of strychnine. There wasn't a more wakeful man in the whole Institute by the time the catch had slid right back and the door began to open.

I don't mind admitting that I felt a shudder go right down my spine as I watched that door. It wasn't that I was frightened. Nerves of that sort have never troubled me. It was simply that it was so horribly like what I had grown accustomed to in the old days when Dr. Mann had still had his room farther down the passage. And as I struggled up from sleep like a diver surfacing I had one thought and one thought only in my mind. It was straight nightmare. I wondered in what state I would find the top of my visitor's head.

But the figure that came round the edge of that door wasn't in the least ghostly. It was wearing a very ordinary camel-hair dressing-gown and felt bedroom slippers. Except that it was behaving rather more quietly than I had ever known anyone in the annexe behave, it might simply have mistaken its little cubicle. But the fact that it didn't put the light on showed that it couldn't be that. And a moment later when it switched on one of those little fountain-pen torches of the kind that doctors carry I guessed that the poor thing must be up to something.

I played sleepy-cat while the beam came over in my direction. And then, after I had felt the beam tickling my closed eyelids and go away again, I counted ten and opened up. It was just as I had expected. The visitor was hovering like a big moth round the chest-of-drawers. In the reflected light of the torch I could see that he had the top drawer half-open already.

Now I may not be nervous, but I am fussy. I've always been that way. Going through the Customs I have never liked having my scanties pawed over. And I didn't even know that my new room-mate's hands were clean. So I decided to do something at once.

"Looking for the Eno's?" I asked.

As I asked it, I switched on the bedside lamp. And there was Bansted. I was a bit taken aback because I had thought I recognised the dressing-gown as Dr. Smith's. But I was evidently not nearly so taken aback as Bansted. After all, I was only sitting up on one elbow being polite. Whereas he had transferred the torch to his left hand and was pointing a revolver at me with his right.

"Don't move," he said.

"Why not?" I asked. "Anything wrong?"

It could have been that my reply annoyed him. Or he may

have been afraid that I would take a flying leap out of the bed and try to grapple with him. Whatever it was he began moving away from me.

"Give me that automatic you've got." he said.

"What automatic?" I asked.

"You know," Bansted told me.

I shook my head. But Bansted was still in earnest.

"If you don't hand over that automatic I shall c-call for help," he said.

"Okay. You call, I'll help," I promised.

And judging by the way things were going, I thought that he would pretty soon be in need of some kind of assistance. Burgling somebody else's room does rather take it out of you if you're not used to it. And I'd noticed that there was a distinct break in Bansted's voice the last time he had spoken to me.

"I'm not jok-ing."

The same little break again. This suited me. Because, above all things, I needed time. It seemed now as if Una had been very sensible in wanting to dispose of that Luger. And it did look as though the bottom of the sea would after all have been the best place for it.

"How d'you know I've got an automatic?" I asked.

"I saw you fire it?" he said.

"Where?"

"On the moor. Last night. In your car."

"Oh, that," I said, with a shrug of my shoulders. "That wasn't an automatic. I told you. That was a back-fire. You saw yourself how badly she was running."

For a moment, I thought that had settled it. The shrug of the shoulders had been a very good one, and the pyjama jacket had concealed nothing. But the next remark of Bansted's made things difficult again.

"You hadn't got the engine running," he said. "You were holding the automatic in your hand when it went off."

"Were you all that near?" I asked.

"I was," Bansted replied. "If you'd pulled in a bit sooner you'd have hit me."

"Pity I didn't," I told him.

"I wondered if you'd say that," Bansted answered with just that note in his voice that revealed the triumph he was feeling. "Now will you give it to me."

"Oh, very well, then."

I gave that same shrug of the shoulders again. But there was another reason for it this time. I've got Una's automatic under my pillow. And I had to wriggle to get at it.

"There it is," I said, pointing it full at him. "I think this must be the one you mean."

Even at the time the funny side struck me. But the fun escaped Bansted entirely. His eyebrows went up at the same moment as his jaw went down, and I saw him suddenly change to pistachio colour. Not that this was surprising. He'd seen me with a revolver in my hand before.

Considering the state he was in, he behaved very creditably.

"It's—it's no use, Hudson," he said. "If you do anything foolish you're for it. I took the precaution of telling Rogers what I was doing. If I'm not back inside ten minutes he's going to sound the alarm."

"You don't say," I answered. "Is he in this too?"

That interested me. Because I'd never been able to see how anyone single-handed could have got away with things so successfully. It was because of this that I had been keeping an eye on the Kimbell-Swanton combination. But a Bansted-Rogers unit was much more promising.

"He is," I heard Bansted saying. "Rogers and I are acting strictly in conjunction."

"Then let's have him in," I replied. "He's got a right to be here."

There wasn't much difficulty in getting hold of Rogers. After all, it was only about three-quarters of an inch of Office of Works boarding that separated us. With my free hand I banged hard on the dividing wall.

"That you, Rogers?" I asked. "Could you spare a moment. We need you. There's no one to say when to fire."

He very nearly came through the wall he was with us so soon. And he had evidently been sitting up in readiness for a summons of some sort. His hair wasn't rumpled, and he still had his collar and tie on. This wasn't bad considering that it was after one-thirty already.

"Would you like to go back for a firearm of some sort?" I asked. "I'm sure Bansted would lend you one."

Then I turned to Bansted.

"Be a good fellow and make this thing so that it doesn't go off," I said. "Then I'd like to have it back, please. Sentimental reasons, you understand."

I had to hold the Luger by its muzzle before Bansted would come forward to collect it. And even then I was aware that Rogers was right up on his toes just to make sure that I didn't crack his pal over the skull with the butt. A sigh went up from both of them as soon as the weapon was safely in Bansted's possession. Then, as so often happens with anyone who is deeply in your debt, he turned nasty.

"You probably think you've been very clever, don't you?" he asked.

"Only so so," I replied. "I've found out you've got a revolver of your own as well as a rifle. But that's about all. Is Rogers the typist?"

Both sides were now putting up a very good acting performance. I was doing the casual Wilton stuff. And Bansted and Rogers were behaving with a church-warden kind of dignity that was not bad for a bedroom thief and his accomplice. The typist remark, for instance, had been received with raised eyebrows and nothing else.

"I've had my eye on you for some time," Bansted went on.

"Don't," I said. "Please don't. I'm ready to offer friendship but nothing more. Besides, think of Rogers."

Bansted crossed his arms. This is usually one of the most effective attitudes. But a dressing-gown is not the right costume for it. He reminded me of a comic on the music halls.

"I think, Hudson," he said, "that you rather underestimate our intelligence. Rogers's and mine."

"Impossible," I said. "Tell me more."

He nodded his head.

"That's what I propose to do," he said. "In the first place, this was a quiet, hard-working Institute before you came."

"Go on."

"The day someone fired at Gillett you couldn't be traced, remember?"

"I knew where I was," I said. "All the time."

"And when you found you'd missed him," Bansted went on, "you tried to spread the story that he'd invented the whole shooting."

"That's one reading," I agreed.

"And when Una was fired at you were the only witness."

"What about Una?"

"I've come to the conclusion," said Bansted slowly, "that she's concealing something."

That was practically the first thing he'd said that made sense. Because I'd arrived at the same conclusion too. But I wanted to hear what else Bansted had to say.

"Did I shoot Mann too?" I asked.

"Mann shot himself," Bansted replied. "Probably because he knew you were after him. He was in your room most of the night. Rogers heard you . . . "

I turned towards Rogers.

"Don't say we kept you awake," I interrupted. "I know these walls are just plywood, but . . . "

Bansted, however, hadn't finished yet.

"And we have proof you were in Plymouth the night after the culture was stolen. We know how you got rid of it."

"How did I?" I asked.

"In a match-box. You gave it to a sailor."

I shook my head.

"They were just matches," I said. "Just ordinary Bryant and May's."

"So you admit the incident?"

It didn't seem worth while denying it.

"Where were you sitting, chum?" I asked.

"We'd just come in," Bansted told me. "Rogers and I. We didn't speak to you at the time because we thought you were drunk."

"So did I."

There was a pause.

"What do you propose to do about it?" I asked.

"It's out of our hands," Bansted replied. "Wilton knows all about it."

"Including the automatic?"

"No," said Bansted, and I could detect the note of contempt in his voice as he said it. "Rogers and I decided that there was the need for action. That's why we took matters into our own hands."

"May I have it back, please?" I asked.

Bansted seemed surprised. Even a bit shocked, I thought.

"After the trial," he replied severely.

With that he picked it up and lowered it gently into his pocket. His own revolver was lying on the dressing-table close by his right hand.

"But it's mine," I reminded him.

He paused.

"Safer where it is," he said.

"Not necessarily," I told him. "I can't aim with it. You can."

Because it was obviously no use arguing, I got up and went over to the door. Bansted kept me covered all the time. But he had finished his little bit of detective work. And I was only just beginning. For a start, I jerked the door wide open all in one go. It was just as I had expected. Or almost. There was someone there—Swanton. He wasn't actually down on one knee, peering through the keyhole. But he was pressed up so close against the panel that he nearly fell inside on top of me.

"I thought I heard voices," he said lamely.

He was staring hard at Bansted, who was trying hard to conceal his revolver.

"No one here," I said. "Must have been owls."

But while Swanton was still staring at Bansted I was having a good look at Swanton. And he was certainly worth looking at. He was wearing an oilskin and a sou'wester that made him look like a Boy Scout collecting for the local lifeboat. Below the bottom of the oilskin appeared a pair of Wellingtons. But what particularly interested me was that the clothes were entirely dry. And that showed that he hadn't yet been wherever it was that he was going.

"Can I lend you an umbrella?" I asked.

Chapter XXXIII

1

What was disturbing me was simply the fact that Bansted and Rogers had been talking to Wilton. That meant that I would have to work quickly. So, just to get things sorted out in my own mind, I began making a list. There is always satisfaction in making lists. It helps you to conceal from yourself the fact that you aren't getting anywhere. Civil servants call it establishing first and second priorities, and they simply love it. So, in best Whitehall fashion, I got down to work and drew up an agenda. I kept the notes pretty full and set down everything I knew.

Item 1. Hilda Sargent. Why had she suddenly walked out of the old country vicarage, and why had she decided to give religion the go-by? Any connection with the batch of Communist literature from abroad? And any connection with the foreign gentleman in the small house in Padstow? Also, going back a bit, why had she been so anxious to get rid of Una? Jealousy? Or something else? N.B. Knowledge of the moor first class and conceivably very useful to her.

Item 2. Una Marchant. How had she come by the Luger?

And had she really been looking for me when she handed it over? Also, why had she asked for protection? From what? And why me? Could it have been a blind? If so, what did she want to distract me from? If the latter, who was she working with?

Item 3. Michael Gillett. By natural laws, should have been accomplice of Item 2. Or Item 1? Were Item 1 and Item 3 still working together, and had Item 2 discovered something? Was alarm for Item 2's safety false or genuine? If so suspicious of Dr. Mann, why stand bail on theft charge? Was Mann original accomplice and had he ratted? Finally, why accomplice at all? Why not lone-wolf? But if lone-wolf, why unchecked mating instinct?

Item 4. Dr. Mann self-eliminated. But innocent or guilty? If latter, why worry? If former, who had organised the suicide? Item 3 on own admission, but trifle too obvious? Third possibility: guilty, but unwilling, i.e. started the job, got scared, backed out, blackmailed, driven *to felo de se*. By whom? Consider possibility of Item 8.

Item 5. Alfred Kimbell. Nice point here. Even if not the thief, at least openly in favour of the theft. Double bluff, or sheer bloody-mindedness? Known regular correspondent with Communist in the Russian Zone. Was sudden cessation due to nerves, or was business completed? Second nice point. Why no open support of Mann after penicillin incident? Distinct possibility of being missing element in Item 4. Hence order in my list, but remember remarks re Dr. Smith.

Item 6. Edgar Swanton. Known, published and publicised association with Item 5. Views identical. Friendship accidental or deliberate? Why abrupt bust up of relationship as beautiful as David/Jonathan, Wilde/Alfred Douglas, etc.? Inexplicable night-walking habits.

Item 7. Dr. Smith (the Great). Cagey as hell. Entirely non-committal on all subjects, except the U.S. Most completely isolated man in whole Institute. Genius for alienating people, natural or acquired? Why use poste restante facilities when resident Phœnician ready to drop all letters into breakfast porridge as part of daily Institute service?

Item 8. Young Mellon. Blonde-hunting genuine or phoney? Fastest car in North Cornwall, and unique knowledge of surrounding district. Top-grade U.S. connections. Remembering Dr. Mann's eagerness for U.S. visa, any connection with Item 4? Extreme innocence illusory?

Item 9. Charles Bansted. Too knowledgeable about guns. High Toryism, real or assumed? Air of quiet always-mind-my-own-business gentlemanliness well maintained through-out, but bedroom burglary bad break. Story about meeting old friend of the family in Newquay on night of theft, fishy but far-fetched. In any case, why mention?

Item 10. Harold Rogers. Declared associate of Item 9. Very interesting. Same *proclaimed* views. But what about wife's views? Same point as in (9). If suspicious, why refer? Double bluff as in (5) and in (6), or useful defence in case of exposure, or alibi?

That was the list as I drew it up. It looked pretty formidable and businesslike, and I wished that I could have asked the Director's secretary to type it out for me. It might have given her something other than me to think about. Also, it would have been easier to read. But that list was for reference, not preservation. And after I had been through it for the third time I took out my cigarette lighter and held it to one corner. There is something dramatic in such a gesture. And also something extremely satisfying. I felt like the British Minister in some minor Iron Curtain country when the postman has just called.

2

I spent the greater part of the day in avoiding Wilton and tidying things up so that I could be sure of making a punctual getaway at five-thirty. The same sense of extreme urgency had oppressed me ever since breakfast. Even at table I had found myself looking round at the subject matter of my list and wondering on which wrist the handcuffs were going to be fastened first. It added a certain poignancy to the whole scene every time I caught Bansted's eye to think that anyone already so suspect as myself should still be free among them.

So finally, it was with the sense of freedom of an escaping prisoner that I climbed into the open driving seat and got away. But it wasn't only myself that I was worrying about. What I was afraid of was that someone was going to do something silly like arresting Item 1 or Item 2 while I needed only another twenty-four hours or so to present a cast-iron case for looking lower down on the agenda.

"Speed, Hudson! Speed," I kept telling myself as I roared along.

That didn't mean, of course, that there wasn't time for a drink when I got to Padstow to begin spying on Hilda. Interfering with normal habits merely upsets the metabolism and spells panic, not efficiency.

The pub I chose was a small one. There was no particular reason for picking on it beyond the fact that the lay-back in the road was convenient, and I could leave my car there without being arrested before I had even got my legs properly over the side. Inside, everything was of the simplest—just plain wood benches with high backs like church pews. And for a moment my heart stopped dead: I was afraid that I had blundered into a

Beer Only Licence. But it was all right. The invention of gin had already come to their notice, and they had nothing against dishing the new-fangled stuff out in doubles.

It was while I was sipping it that I heard a voice I knew. Mellon's voice. He was just behind the pew back I had my head against. And even if I couldn't hear every word, I could hear enough to make any Cornish father or husband feel distinctly uneasy.

"Say, d'you know what it was about you?" he was asking.

A long gurgling silence from his companion indicated that either she didn't know or wouldn't have cared to put it into words.

"It was ya eyes," Mellon went on. "As soon as I saw the colour of them, I knew. This is the end of the rainbow, I said. Those eyes are what I've been looking for."

Either the lady to whom the remarks were arrested was unusually bashful, or she was just plain dumb. Probably the latter. All that Mellon got for his pains was another of those drawn-out liquid silences.

"Mind you, sister, it was ya hair I saw first," he went on.

"Not just the colour either. The way it curls, I mean. Reminded me of ma mother's just as soon as I saw it. . . . "

If it hadn't been for my house-watching appointment I'd have been ready to sit there all night, simply learning. And even as it was I couldn't resist turning round for a moment. And what I saw staggered me. It showed that Mellon must have exhausted everything else and was scraping round pretty near the bottom of the bucket by now. The woman who was with him wasn't even young. Or smart. Or pretty. She had a comfortable settled-in look, and it occurred to me that the offer of a nice cup of tea might have won her even quicker than all those compliments.

Altogether it was a terrible revelation of young Mellon's hunger, and it showed that North Cornwall was a strong sellers' market.

There is probably nothing in the world quite so boring as standing looking at the outside of a house. By the end of the first ten minutes your whole heart goes out to private investigation agents and King's Proctors. You feel that you could draw the damn thing with your left hand, or reconstruct it in your sleep brick by brick. And after half an hour has passed you would be ready to faint from sheer excitement if the milkman called. I stood forty-five minutes of uninterrupted elevation-gazing and then decided to walk about a bit. I knew that Hilda must be there because she had parked her car outside.

There was some sort of a chapel next door to the little villa. And what's more, there was a service going on inside it. I could see that because the lights were shining through the very inferior stained glass of the windows. In a superior anthropological way I'm a bit of a connoisseur of chapels. I collect them. There is something about a plain stucco front with "Prepare to Meet Thy God" over the front porch that irresistibly draws me inside to see precisely what preparations they have been making. Anglican churches interest me less because I was brought up in them. Roman Catholic churches on the other hand have a fascination all their own. They contain everything that my father disapproved of, and always preached against. But I've out-grown that. There is nothing of the Cromwellian or the Kensitite about me. I wouldn't have a thing changed. I go round, awed and silent like a tourist.

The chapel opposite turned out to be one of the Roman sort. Our Lady of Something, it was called. As I opened the creaky little baize-covered door, and smelt the incense, and saw the business-like little bookstall of propaganda leaflets, I began gaping.

There was a small side chapel with a spike-frame for the candles. In front of just the glossy kind of altar that shows what has happened to religious taste since the Middle Ages a woman was kneeling. I didn't take much notice of her. Because, by then, I'd become interested in the priest. I'd never seen a priest extracting himself from a confessional-box before. It seemed a tight fit, and I felt sorry for him.

Then, as the priest passed me, I saw his face. It was the dago. And, as I recognised him, I knew who the woman was who was kneeling in front of the candle in that lady chapel.

3

I waited for Hilda outside. In her car to be exact. She hadn't locked it, and it was warmer than just lounging about on the pavement. I think that the chief feeling I had was one of utter loneliness. If you took a tone deaf man into the Albert Hall he wouldn't feel any more a part of it simply because other people were hearing something. And I suppose that there can be religious-deaf people, too. There was a mystery going on behind that door, and I knew that for me it would remain a mystery.

When she came out, I tried to pass things off lightly and casually.

"Thought I'd give you a bit of a surprise," I said.

But I couldn't get the right note into my voice. And Hilda didn't seem to be in a very light or casual sort of mood herself.

"I was praying I'd see you," she said.

"Praying?" I repeated. "Do you mean hands together—that sort of praying?"

"That sort," she replied.

This was a bit of a stumper. I'd imagined up to that moment that I'd been an entirely free agent. Playing instrument of heaven was a new one to me, and it gave me the creeps. But I didn't want to show that I was put out in any way.

"I came as soon as I got the message," I said politely.

She was beside me in the car by now, and I could see how tired she was. There were two deep lines beside her mouth that hadn't been there before. Evidently this conversion business had taken quite a lot out of her.

"I want you to do something for me," she said.

"Not Una," I began. "She won't budge. She told me last time——"

"No. It's not Una," she said slowly. "It's worse than that. It's . . . "

The pause was so long that I turned round to see what was happening. She was crying. Not the sort of noisy boo-hoo stuff that never hurt anybody. But the silent, tear-you-to-pieces kind.

"Like my handkerchief?" I asked.

She took it without saying anything, and I just waited. When it seemed reasonable to reopen the conversation I tried again.

"You got as far as 'It's,'" I reminded her.

But she only shook her head.

"I shouldn't have asked you," she said. "It was silly."

This was the other Hilda speaking. She was now being unapproachable again.

"But I thought you said you prayed . . . " I began.

"I did," she replied.

Then she put her hand on my arm in that strange disturbing way she had.

"I've got to go through with this myself," she went on.

219

"I'm going to see Colonel Wilton as soon as I get back."

"What about?"

"If I told you that I'd have told you everything."

"You might at least give me a hint." Hilda paused.

"I don't think so," she said. "If I did I mightn't go through with it."

We drove home with Hilda leading, and that faulty rear lamp of hers blinking in my eyes all the way. She had apparently meant what she said, too. I discovered that as soon as we reached the Institute. The Phoenician was still slopping about in the kitchen, and I heard Hilda ask her to see if the Colonel could spare a few minutes.

I was still wondering if I oughtn't to have gone along and stopped her, when I reached my room and switched the light on. Then I paused. The room looked as though something pretty hearty in the way of an end of term rag had been taking place. The contents of all the drawers were on the floor. My clothes lay in a heap in front of the wardrobe, with my Jermyn Street cap with the lining torn open on top. Even the mattress had been turned upside down.

Evidently Bansted and Rogers had been having a real thorough look round this time. Either that or the original owner had been hunting about for his missing revolver.

Chapter XXXIV

1

It was only one week off Christmas by now. And every day the Institute was remorselessly assuming the festive look. Paper chains, ingeniously woven by Ma Clewes during the long winter evenings, now hung criss-crossed in the awful little common room. Someone had put up a big fluted lantern affair in the hall. And while Hilda and I had been talking quietly together in the parked Singer, the same someone had gone to work on the dining-room. This morning we now had pink and green and orange streamers radiating from the centre light bracket. The melancholia ward in a big county asylum as decorated by the night sister would have had just the same air of simple cottage gaiety.

I had just finished my breakfast when the door opened and Hilda came in. Her new digs were the bed without board kind, I remembered.

She must have noticed the look on my face when I saw her. And I suppose that a twelve-stone man transfixed with the marmalade spoon held aloft in full drip is a bit conspicuous. It was obvious, too, that she didn't want to attract any attention.

"Good morning," she said. "Did you get back all right last night?"

It was the extreme coolness of the question that staggered me. But I was recovering my poise by now.

"In the end I didn't go out," I said. "Too cold."

That brought young Mellon in.

"Then someone else had your car out," he said. "Saw it in Padstow last night."

I wasn't going to let that get me started.

"Gipsies," I said briefly. "They're terrible in these parts."

I was nearly at the end of my breakfast. The Phœnician had brewed the coffee in a fish-kettle this morning from the taste of it, and I decided that I would do without my fourth cup.

"Duty calls," I said vaguely as I slid my chair back.

I'd got about two paces down the corridor when Hilda came after me. That was silly. Because so far she hadn't even had her Danish egg. But it showed that her calm wasn't real, only assumed.

"I want you to forget everything I said to you last night," she told me.

I looked her straight in the eyes.

"You're making a mistake, lady," I said. "You just heard me say I stayed in all the evening."

That seemed to satisfy her. But it didn't satisfy me.

"Wilton say anything?" I asked.

She didn't tell me. Which in the circumstances, was rude. But I forgave her for it. She had her part to play like the rest of us. And from what she had said last night I guessed that it was a hard part. I only wished that I knew the cue-line.

I didn't get very much work done that morning for thinking

about it. Also, there were too many interruptions. The first of them was waiting in the front hall as I went through. He had managed somehow to get past the draw-bridge and the portcullis, and he now had the air of impatience that suggested that if there had been a gong in the hall he would have sounded it.

"You Mr. Mellon?" he asked.

He was a large man with a florid complexion. Up in Norfolk in the turkey world he would have been regarded as a very handsome stag. As it was, he looked as though he would be very well advised to stick to beer and avoid spirits. He was wearing flannels and a rather noisy ready-made sports coat. And in his hand he carried a riding-crop. This struck me as odd. Because even in a country district I would have expected to find him on a bicycle rather than on a horse. But that may have been only because I had the advantage of prior knowledge. Even without his helmet he was still undisguisable. He was the policeman who had tried to arrest me for obstruction up in Padstow.

"Be along in just one minute," I said. "You'll recognise him—the tall, dark, handsome one."

"Thank you," the man said, and touched his forehead with his hunting-crop.

I promptly forgot all about him, and was thinking of Hilda again when I reached the laboratory. But straight away the telephone rang, and I went across to answer it. It was a bit early for calls. I suspected a wrong number. And when I lifted the receiver I was sure.

"Professor Sonnenbaum?" a voice asked.

It was a foreign-sounding voice, and very faint. A long distance call obviously.

"No Professor Sonnenbaum here," I said. "Try the little café at the corner."

"Pardon?"

"Never mind. They probably won't be open yet."

There was a pause.

"Is that Bodmin Moor 21?"

"That's right."

"Professor Sonnenbaum, please."

At this rate we could go on like that all the morning.

"There is no Professor Sonnenbaum here," I said very slowly and distinctly. "He died way back in the eighties. Family went out to Canada, I think it was. No forwarding address. Sorry."

I was just hanging up when the voice spoke again.

"But that is Bodmin Moor 21?"

"There hasn't been time to change it yet," I admitted.

"Then can I speak to Professor Sonnen? . . . " The voice broke off and seemed to be consulting someone. I could hear the mutter of conversation above the muzz of the longdistance line. "Dr. Smith, I mean," the voice corrected itself. "Dr. Sebastian Smith."

I paused. "If I go off and fetch him, will you promise not to change your mind again?"

"Pardon?"

"Doesn't matter," I said.

And then a really clever idea came to me.

"This is Dr. Smith's batman speaking," I said in a hard, clipped sort of voice that was new to both of us. "The doctor is out beagling. He's not expected back until dinnertime. May I have your number, please. He'll call you."

But I don't think that the person at the other end can have understood. Perhaps the line wasn't good enough. Or he was new at spying, and hadn't yet got as far as field-sports in his vocabulary.

"Thank you, it does not matter," the voice said.

With that there was a click, and it was all over. I saw then how much cleverer it would have been to call Dr. Smith, and remain at my bench quietly eavesdropping. But I couldn't do that. I hate underhandedness.

And at that moment the door opened and Dr. Smith himself came in. It was still only about nine-five, and he seemed taken aback to see anyone there. But he recovered himself admirably.

"Was that the phone?" he asked.

I looked him full in the eyes.

"Telephone Maintenance," I said. "Just checking up on the lines. Didn't leave any message."

The second interruption occurred at about nine thirty-five. This time it was Mellon's turn. When I had last seen him he was still looking like a displaced person on the Claridge quota—perfectly laundered soft white shirt, a dove-grey suit without a ripple in it and one of those extraordinary bow-ties with points instead of square corners. But there was now a bruise over his right eye and the front buttons of his shirt were all missing. The feathers of his dove-grey suit had a rather ruffled look and he kept holding one of his monogrammed handkerchiefs to his nose. But he can't have been doing too badly. At least he had the hunting-crop.

"Fallen over something?" I asked.

He didn't, however, seem to want to talk about it.

"Jeez Christ," he said. "Don't they have no family feelings in these parts?"

I paused.

"You've caught the spirit of the place," I said. He paused.

"Do you reckon there's a decent libel attorney anywhere in these parts?" he asked at last.

I thought for a moment. Then I answered him.

"There's a firm in Okehampton," I said. "On the right just before you come to the dairy. It's over a corn-chandler's. Looks all right to me. They've got the whole of the second floor."

Mellon was not impressed. He began flicking about with the hunting-crop.

"I'm going up to London," he said. "I want to get this thing fixed properly. I can't have some crazy guy going round here telling people I'm a traitor."

"A what?" I asked.

"You heard," Mellon answered.

2

From ten o'clock until ten-five I worked uninterrupted. Flat out. Giving the job all I had. Obsessionally. Then there came a message from Wilton. Really he was behaving in a most peculiar manner just lately. Like a kept woman. Cold at one moment. And all tingly and oncoming at the next. If the message had said that he had decided to sell the pearls or publish the correspondence I could not have been more astonished. It asked if I would play golf with him.

The cub-Captain didn't seem to know why I had been invited. Merely that golf was the latest whim of his strange master. Wilton had been practising putting all yesterday evening on the study carpet, the cub-Captain told me. And in consequence he was, I gathered, about as near the top of his form by now as he was ever likely to be.

"Of course, I'd simply love to come," I said. "Anywhere with Wilton. At any time. He knows that. It's just my work that's stopping me."

The cub-Captain had all the manners of a good bell-hop.

From the way he was standing, he might have been waiting for me to slip sixpence into his little paw.

"The Colonel mentioned he felt sure that the Director would excuse you, if you asked him," he said.

That looked rather as though things had been pretty much arranged already.

The cub-Captain was shifting from one foot to the other, and looked embarrassed.

"What shall I say, sir?" he asked.

"Leave it all to me," I said. "I'm just boiling some water. And I don't trust anybody to do my job for me. When I've drunk it, I'll come."

"Very good, sir."

He went off so pleased at having found me reasonable that I don't think that he even remembered about the tip. There was a distinct lilting movement in his walk as he moved away from me.

I thought all the same that I might as well mention things to the Old Man. And again I had the impression that he had been conditioned for something of the kind. He was walking up and down his room when I found him, and he looked hairier and more prawnlike than ever.

"Ah, Hudson," he said, somewhat jumpily as I came in.

"Good morning, sir," I began, in a bland, easy manner to put him thoroughly at his ease before hurling my odd little brickbat full at him. "It's a beautiful morning and Colonel Wilton has very kindly suggested . . . "

The method of my approach seemed to have relieved Dr. Clewes considerably.

"Oh, capital," he said. "I wasn't sure you played."

That was all he said. But behind it there was just a hint that it hadn't come as an entire surprise to him. And I still didn't want him to write me off as the sports absentee type.

"Wilton and I often chat things over together," I explained. "I expect there's some aspect of his work that he wants to discuss with me."

"Possibly," said Dr. Clewes, and began fumbling with his desk papers.

Chapter XXXV

It was the first really decent morning since I'd been to Cornwall. The air was clear, like gin. And the colours of the hills were at their loveliest. I felt on the top of the world suddenly, getting away from the Institute and all its troubles. If Wilton had been a woman I would probably have proposed to him.

The only flaw in the whole arrangement was that he had brought the pair of cub-Captains along with him. And when I suggested that it might be friendlier, just the two of us, he shook his head.

"They won't bother you," he said. "Simply trail along behind."

I wanted to do everything I could to make the outing a success. So I raised no further objections.

"Oh, very well," I said. "I'll have the dark one. If I'd known, I'd have made the bag a bit lighter for him."

In his youth Wilton may have been quite a good golfer. He had the right movement. But the limbs seemed in danger of falling off. With the first drive I expected to see arm, wrist-watch and shoulder go sailing away after the ball. It wasn't a bad shot, however. About eighty yards overall and bang down the middle of the fairway. Not bad, merely feeble. And I decided to show him what clean-living and sound basic instruction could do. But I had my wrong shoes on. No studs. And I must have been a bit sharp with my right shoulder. In the result I sliced my first shot. The ball went off practically at right angles and nearly killed the smaller of the two captains. Long after the follow-through he was still crouching there as though he were back in a battle school.

And, as it turned out, I was a bit too strong with the niblick this morning. Otherwise, perfectly hit, the ball skied over Wilton's head and came to rest in some heather over in the Lizard direction. It took three to get out of the heart of the Highlands. And then came another of my really strong ones. It was the wind as much as the hook that time. I followed the ball with my eye as it described a wide half-circle. And then with a wave of the hand to Wilton I followed it on foot. It was difficult country where it had landed and it was pioneer axe and machete work all the way getting back. When I finally reached the green I realised that I hadn't seen Wilton for the best part of quarter of an hour.

The same thought must have occurred to Wilton. He waved the cub-Captains away and turned towards me.

"Let's walk the next one," he said.

"Suits me," I told him. "It's the view as much as anything else I always play for."

Both the cub-Captains had dropped about half a dozen paces behind by now. And Wilton casually linked arms with me. It is a habit that I dislike. But I couldn't very well say so. For a colonel to get his hand slapped before subordinates is terrible for discipline.

"I want to talk to you," he said.

"What about?" I asked.

"You," he said.

It was so short and curt that I didn't like the sound of it. I hated the whole thought of talking about me in that tone of voice.

"Soon get tired of that," I said, with a shrug that I thought might dislodge Wilton's arm.

But it didn't.

"Depends on how long it takes," was all he said, giving my arm a squeeze as he said it.

"Just as you say," I replied. "Shall I begin, or will you?"

"I will."

The pause was so long that I began to think that Wilton had forgotten. I was just ready to start telling him about my night-fears as a child when Wilton spoke again. Then I wished that he had forgotten.

"I'm going to arrest you," he confided with his ear close up against mine.

"Sorry," I answered. "You've got my deaf side."

Wilton said it again. And I didn't like the sound of it. The tone of voice was still all wrong. I removed his arm quite forcibly.

"Serious?" I asked.

"Perfectly."

"And you're really going through with this?"

"Um."

It was merely the Wilton grunt and nod of the head this time. That made me furious.

"Well, you'll make a bloody fool of yourself if you do," I told him.

"There's always that risk," he agreed.

He was a difficult man to have a row with. One of his strongest suits was that he was quite uninsultable. We were still walking along side by side as though nothing had happened. And any moment I feared that he might try to take my arm again.

"Can I have a perfectly frank talk with you?" I asked.

"No holds barred."

"It's what I've been waiting for."

"I can probably tell you quite a bit you don't know," I began.

"That's why I asked you."

"Then you'll see what a mistake you're making."

"If I see, perhaps I shan't make it."

I really was thinking hard by now, because it was perfectly obvious that if I was run in like this, somebody else was going to get away with something. And I didn't see why that should happen. But the emotions were a bit complicated. Either I was putting country before self, or self before others. I wasn't quite sure which.

"For a start," I asked, "are you satisfied about all the rest of us?"

"Not a bit."

"Dr. Smith, for instance."

"What about him?"

"I don't believe it's even his right name," I blurted out.

"It isn't," Wilton replied. "He changed it. It's Sonnenbaum, really. Sonnenbaum's *Bacteriology for Advanced Students*. Got a new edition coming out. That's why he had all the proofs sent poste restante to Plymouth to avoid confusion. Very sensible."

This stumped me for a moment, and I thought of somebody else I didn't like.

"And Swanton?" I asked.

I put the question very deliberately because I thought it might be more effective that way. I didn't care for the offhand manner Wilton had when it came to dismissing things.

"Nothing wrong with him, is there?"

232

"Oh, no," I said. "Nothing actually wrong. Just a bit fond of late hours. Seems to prefer the moor at midnight for some reason."

"That all?"

"Well," I said. "You must admit it's queer."

"Not very," Wilton answered. "Not when you think of beetles."

"There is something in common," I admitted.

As a reply it struck me as rather ingenious. But this hardly seemed the moment for talking in innuendoes.

"There's a lot," Wilton said. "That is if you're a Coleopterist. Swanton is. Doing a census of some kind. Showed me his paper."

"And you allowed yourself to get taken in by it?"

"In my job you get taken in all the time."

I paused.

"I suppose you know all about his Let's-Make-Friends-with-Russia Society?" I asked.

The first answer was a grin. When the grin couldn't widen any farther, Wilton spoke through the middle of it.

"The Old Man's a member too," he said. "It was called something different when he joined."

"And you regard it as harmless?"

The grin faded.

"Not a bit," Wilton answered. "Just irrelevant."

I'd had enough of that.

"Then what about Kimbell?" I demanded. Here Wilton shook his head.

"Bad lot," he said. "Never tells the truth. You noticed that?"

"I've noticed that he resigned from that chess game when he was clearly winning," I replied. "That seemed a bit strange."

It was a shot in the dark really. Because I didn't know enough about Emperor Chess to be able to tell whether he was winning or just arranging the pieces. But the shot failed to rattle Wilton.

"Silly, wasn't it?" he said.

I paused.

"Didn't know you played chess," I said.

"Didn't know you played golf," Wilton answered.

"Why did you tell him he was losing?"

"Wanted to know what he'd say. Very tricky these chess players."

"And did he say it?"

Wilton nodded.

"In the end," he replied. "It's rather a sad case. Just nerves. That's why he had to give up tournament play. It was a perfectly straightforward game."

"Then perhaps you know everything about Bansted, too?" I asked.

Wilton shook his head.

"Not very much," he said. "They're all the same, those Bisley characters. Too fond of firearms. But he shouldn't carry that revolver of his about with him. Gives quite the wrong impression."

"It does rather," I agreed. "So do his dinner companions."

Wilton raised his eyebrows. "I know," he said. "He's for it."

"Arresting him, too?" I asked.

Wilton's eyebrows returned to normal. The expression was pure Neanderthal again by now.

"Not my affair," he said. "Pity she's a married woman. He'll hate being cited. Tried to pretend the encounter was accidental. That won't help him any."

"Checked up on her character?" I asked.

"Horrible" Wilton answered.

"Like Rogers's wife," I suggested.

It was the grin's turn again.

"He mentioned her to you, too?"

"And to the rest of us," I told him.

"Poor old Rogers," Wilton said, and touched his forehead with his forefinger.

"*Comment?*"

"Hasn't got a wife," Wilton explained. "Doesn't want one either. It's a Ph.D. that he wants. Felt a bit out of it among all you clever chaps. Invented the whole thing just to make himself at home."

He paused.

"But you go on," he said. "I'm just listening."

Here I paused at full Wilton length.

"The rest," I said slowly, "is largely guesswork."

"Don't apologise," Wilton answered. "that's what I'm arresting you on."

I pretended that I hadn't heard.

"For a start, I'm dubious about Mellon," I told him.

"Why?"

"Spends too much time in that car of his."

"So would you if you were looking for a forebear."

My face went vague. I could feel it happening.

"Forebear?" I repeated. "Don't get you."

"Searching for cousins," Wilton explained. "Old West Country family, the Mellons. Told him to be careful. People round here don't understand."

This was my chance.

"It's a blind. Won't wash," I said. "Told the last one she had hair like his mother's. I heard him. Should have said 'father.'"

"Not necessarily," Wilton answered. "Pa and Ma were cousins too. All Mellons marry their cousins.

235

There was a pause.

"Know anything about the girls?" Wilton asked at last.

Here I strayed off half a pace. I'd overcome most of my inhibitions already. But there are limits to the impression which even a really deep heel can afford to make.

"No success there," I said. "Not their type."

Wilton was looking at the clouds, and seemed to have forgotten all about me again.

"Una get rid of her gun all right?" he asked.

This needed steady handling.

"No trouble at all, thank you," I said.

"You're wrong there," Wilton answered. "Plenty of trouble. Everybody's been hunting for it."

"Whose was it?" I asked, still in the same carefully casual kind of voice.

"Search me," Wilton said. "Didn't even know she had one until Ma Clewes found it."

"Snooping?"

"Not her fault," Wilton replied. "I asked her to."

"Then why didn't you arrest Una?"

"Wanted to see what she'd do with it."

"And did you find out?"

Wilton looked down at the ground as though inspecting the worm-casts.

"Not properly," he said. "Recovered it from Bansted's room in the end. But with your fingerprints all over it. Gave it up finally."

"So did I," I told him.

We'd passed the sixth hole by now and were sauntering down the middle of the fairway. There was a road that crossed the links just beyond the seventh, and then there came the long climb back up towards the club-house. At this rate I should still be a free man by lunch-time. Or longer, if I had my way.

"You haven't said anything about Gillett," Wilton reminded me.

"If I did, you'd only knock it down."

"Not necessarily."

"Well, to start with, he killed Dr. Mann."

"Only figuratively."

"Why did he do that?"

"Didn't like him perhaps," Wilton suggested.

"Or he wanted to make it look as though Mann was guilty."

"Could be," Wilton replied.

What I really wanted was to keep the conversation going until I got to the road. It's no good trying to run on a grass surface.

"And there's another thing . . . " I began.

But Wilton laid his hand on my arm again.

"Don't mind telling you at one time I thought it *was* Gillett," he confided.

"Then what made you change your mind?"

"His answers all came out straight," Wilton said. I paused.

"And mine didn't?"

"Yours didn't."

Wilton waited long enough to scrape away a worm-cast with his toe.

"Any views on Hilda?" he asked.

"Nothing there," I told him. "She's just gone R.C."

But it wasn't quite the bombshell that I had expected.

"Apart from that I mean," he said.

"Well, you kept the Communist papers," I reminded him.

"Only overnight," he said. "In any case, they're cancelled now. Doesn't need them any more. She knows they're true."

It was only another twenty-five yards to the roadway. But I

needed every single one of them.

"How did her confession go?" I asked.

As I asked it I had a sudden chilly feeling. Perhaps he had been playing with her, too. For all I knew he was proposing to go back and arrest her as soon as he had finished with me. But he seemed open enough.

"Fine," he answered. "Very intelligent girl, Hilda. Said she'd given you the opportunity of coming clean. But didn't think you meant to take it."

I paused, remembering the coldness of our only kiss.

"So it was that, was it?"

"Did she actually ask you to arrest me?" I inquired. Wilton shook his head.

"Hilda's not the interfering kind," he replied.

"Only public-spirited."

"Only public-spirited," he repeated.

"Say why she suspected me?"

Wilton shrugged his shoulders.

"All rather vague," he admitted. "Something to do with your sincerity. Said you were a bit too glib to be genuine. Always inventing things."

I breathed more easily.

"But that's not evidence," I pointed out. "That's purely a moral judgment."

"Just what Hilda said."

There was another of those awkward silences. Then I spoke again.

"If it isn't rude," I asked, "what are you arresting me for?"

"Being a Communist," Wilton said.

"That's not a criminal offence," I pointed out.

"Not declaring it is," Wilton replied.

"You mean that form I had to fill in?"

Wilton nodded.

"You signed it."

We had now mounted the crest of the last bunker before the seventh hole. It was the secretary's prize exhibit, that bunker. There was a ten-foot cliff in the centre, and Wilton and I had reached the lip of it. This seemed as good a place as any. But I still wanted to wait for the cub-Captains to catch up with us.

Wilton helped by beckoning them to come forward. We were now a nice tightly bunched little group just as I wanted us.

Wilton turned his long neck towards me.

"Sorry about this," he said.

"That's all right," I answered. "Do as much for you any day."

Then I broke off.

"What's that policeman want?" I asked.

As a device it wasn't much better than first-form standard. There was no policeman that I could see. But it worked perfectly. Wilton and the two cub-Captains swivelled round and stared incredulously up the course. And as they did so I gave them a shove from behind. Wilton was the first to go down, and he upset the others. There was a lot of rather aimless clutching about in mid-air and then, under the full load of M.I.5, Bodmin branch, the secretary's nicely kept grass edge broke off like a piece of biscuit and the three of them disappeared into the bunker.

As I turned round and started to run for it, I realised that I must have second sight. Because there was a policeman. Only he was behind me. I even knew the policeman. It was the ice-eyed Inspector who didn't like me. And to show that he hadn't warmed up in his feelings he was holding a shotgun at the ready.

I put my hands up.

"Hold your gun, sir," I said. "I think the Colonel needs you."

Chapter XXXVI

Wilton seemed to have thought of everything. There was a police car as well waiting just out of sight around the bend. And, as soon as someone had dusted the sand off my party, they came along and joined us.

It occurred to me then that pleasantness on my part ought to be the keynote of that ride. After all, it might be quite a long trip to Bodmin Jail or Dartmoor or the Tower of London or wherever it was that we were going. And when I heard Wilton say, rather anxiously: "Have you got him there?" I was the first to answer.

"Don't worry about me," I said. "I'm all right. I've got the arm-rest."

Wilton wasn't taking any chances, however. He came over and pressed his face up against the car window. That was my second cue.

"I'm an old friend," I told him. "Look—we're inseparable."

So we were, too. The Inspector had put handcuffs on me the moment he got me inside that car. And handcuffs evidently satisfied some very deep pre-natal longing in his nature. I'd never seen his eyes so tender as when he produced them from his pocket. But for some reason he seemed to dislike any sort of exhibitionism.

"Put 'em down," he said sternly.

"Very well, constable," I answered, and let my hand rest lightly in his lap.

But by now I was listening to a conversation that was going on between Wilton and the two cub-Captains. Seating-room was apparently the trouble. The car was only a Wolseley twelve horse-power. And with the driver and the Inspector that made six of us. Wilton had just told the dark-haired Captain to make his own way back to the club-house and take Wilton's own car on from there. That was cue number three.

"I wouldn't hear of it," I said loudly. "Not at his age. He can have my place, I'll walk."

In my eagerness to make myself heard I may have leant forward a bit too far. At any rate, the Inspector yanked me back into the seat with a jerk that nearly dislocated my whole shoulder. I turned towards him.

"Careful," I said. "We don't want to snap them."

"Where are we off to?" I asked, as soon as the car began to move.

The Inspector did not seem to have heard. Either that, or he didn't want to tell me. But Wilton replied for him. "Bodmin," he said.

I sighed.

"Seems so aimless somehow," I pointed out. "Just backwards and forwards. Why didn't you arrest me up at the Institute?"

"Guessed you might try something violent," Wilton answered.

I could see his eyes in the driving-mirror, and I shook my head at him.

"Not with my nature," I said. "That's more the Pyknic type."

Wilton did not reply, so I turned towards the Inspector.

"Hope I'm not crushing you," I said. "It's not really me. It's the corners."

When it became obvious that he wasn't going to reply, I tried again.

"And could I have the sun visor down, please?" I asked.

"Otherwise I can't see you properly."

I saw the driver glance up at the sun visor. It was dead horizontal. Even so, he shoved it up a bit. I took this for a snub, and decided to sulk instead. I was still sulking when we got to Bodmin. That was what made the police station stuff so difficult.

"Morning, Sergeant," I said. "There's been a silly mistake. I'm not taking any further part in it."

"Can I have your full name, sir?" the sergeant asked.

"Sorry," I said. "My lips are sealed. I want my solicitor."

That ditched them, and there was a little conference between the sergeant and the Inspector, with Wilton right away in the background, staring out of the window.

Then the sergeant looked up.

"May I have his name and address?" he asked.

"Whose?"

"Your solicitor's."

"Oh, him. Certainly. Can you write?"

The sergeant drew his lips in and waited.

"But I'm afraid it's rather a long one," I began. "I'll spell it. I-V-A-N, that's one word. V-A-S-S-I-L-O-V-I-T-C-H, two s's. And better put 'and Sons.' I think he's got the boys in with him. Now comes the difficult part. One-one-eight-seven P-R-E-O-B-A-R-D-S-K-J-Y, that's one word— P-R-O-S-P-E-K-T. Prospekt with a 'k,' of course. Nidjni-Novgorod. I don't need to spell that.

242

The postman'll know it. And better make it air mail. I'll pay," I paused. "You might read it back to me," I asked. "I don't want to have to hang around here."

Wilton had sauntered over and was staring at me in that curious impersonal way he had. We might never have met before.

"Why are you doing all this?" he asked.

"Playing for time," I told him.

"You're wasting it."

"We're all doing that," I said, and Wilton moved away again. I turned back to the sergeant.

"Of course, you can phone if you'd rather," I said.

"But the line's terrible."

It is difficult to keep your spirits up in a cell. What I most resented was that it was cold. Really cold. And after two or three attempts I gave up all thought of sleep. I'd asked earlier if one of the lads would mind cycling up to the Institute for a pill. But the answer had come back that he would mind.

There were bars at the window. And, despite the poet, you can take my word for it that stone walls and iron bars quite unquestionably do. In fact, as I lay staring up at the ceiling I realised that I was in a mess. A real mess. And jollying things along wasn't going to help me any more. If there is one thing that sets an Old Bailey judge against a man it is the slightest impression of *joie de vivre*. It is only the pale and the obviously dying that ever get mercy shown to them. That was about my only comfort.

What I didn't like was the fact that Wilton had got on to that Communist background of mine. But even then he'd got it wrong. Because when I joined the Party it was back in the old days when we all belonged. In my line of business you were a bit of an outsider if you weren't a member.

And as I lay there, it all came back to me. It was the Spanish Civil War that had finally decided things. There had been a strange feeling of being at a cross-roads. In one direction there seemed to be a reasonable, orderly Europe— not very exciting perhaps because any civilisation planned in concrete necessarily shows up a bit dismal, but at least with scientists given the place that this country gives to the Lords Spiritual. That suited me.

As a matter of fact, it was largely accidental that Spain should have come into it all. But I knew Spain, and the alternative that it offered didn't look too good. It seemed to consist mostly of rather flash young men wearing bracelets and driving about in enormous Hispano cars, while whole families were so poor that they were living in cracks in the cliffs. There seemed to be a racket on somewhere. And it was pretty obvious that it wasn't the cliff-dwellers who were the racketeers. I'd have been on their side even if there hadn't been a war.

Then when the trouble started, and the Nazis decided to start pocket-battleship practice on Guernica I felt that I couldn't just sit quietly in W. D. P. Inc. without being somehow mixed up in it. And the Communists certainly did work. United Front, it was called. I remember that at the time I used to wonder how long the front would have held if there hadn't been some pretty energetic Party secretary somewhere at base headquarters sending out the leaflets. But the public responded. The Liberals, who for years had been used to talking to two rows of empty chairs, suddenly found themselves addressing full halls. It may have been pure vodka in the speaker's carafe. But at least people became indignant again. And for the first time I began to understand what my father had always been trying to tell me about Mr. Gladstone.

It wasn't difficult to join the Party in those days. There were the high-grade conversions, of course. Top-liners got the same sort of publicity that comes to Hollywood actresses when they marry rajahs and go Moslem. But mine was a very quiet little ceremony with no photographs. I was merely told to report to somebody called Arthur whose real name I knew perfectly well was Oliver; and most of my work consisted of canvassing in the Harrow Road area. If you know the Harrow Road you'll realise that it was good hunting all the way. And some of the sights I saw once I had got my foot inside those front doors persuaded me that it wasn't only in Spain that someone was working a bit of a racket.

But I wasn't really the kind of recruit they were looking for. I recognised that from the very start, and they got into it not so long afterwards. There is colossal initial impetus in my make-up that carries me up any hill, but on the level my staying power is only so-so. And, above all, I'm a failure at listening to political speeches. I found myself always getting to the end of the sentence before the speaker. Then I used to grow restless and begin doing cube-roots in my head just to stop myself from fainting clean off through sheer boredom. It was always the same speech, too. Up to the cube-root point, I could have prompted even without the notes.

At the end of about three months, I was getting about zero for Party attendance, and had to be careful to avoid seeing a lot of Arthur. That wasn't difficult, however. Because round about that time I was being equally careful to make sure that I saw a lot of someone else. Elspeth her name was. She was a nice girl, and there was some idea of our setting up house together. Elspeth was in the Party, too. That was really the difficulty. Because she was the sincere, intense, zealous sort. Even if we had shared a flat, I wouldn't have been sharing it with Elspeth. I should have been living in sin with an abominably noisy typewriter, a Gestetner duplicating machine and about twenty comrades, aged eighteen but looking younger, who came in for coffee and Communism every Thursday evening.

But the fact that I was no longer active, as the phrase went, did not mean that I'd stopped being a Communist. I was still definitely of the Left. And that was all that seemed to matter. Every religion has its adherents who don't adhere so closely as to get in anybody's way. But they shouldn't be scorned. They still can be relied on for half a guinea when the Appeals Committee writes to them.

I was one of those. I remained that way right up to 1939, quietly confident that civilisation would reach Western Europe, like epidemic influenza, from somewhere east of the Vistula. Then something happened. Again, it wasn't a very dramatic something. That's because my mind doesn't work in flashes and revelations. I was never converted: I'd merely joined. And when I decided that I'd had enough of it, I didn't immediately do a penitential strip-tease in the market-place, and then apply for the post of news commentator on Vatican Radio. I just said, "O Gawd," and packed up.

It was the Lysenko affair that settled it. And this bit has got to be personal. Unless you follow it, you'll never know the sort of man you've been out with. I've given you one or two hints already. You know, for example, that I drink. You know that I'm the answer—usually only a short-term answer—to a maiden's prayer. And you know that I don't usually give a straight "yes" or "no" to any question, because with my sort of nature I've found that it's much more comfortable to go quietly cruising

246

about on the surface of most things than to wade in waist-high with jaws clenched. But if you imagine that I haven't got a moral standard of my own, and that I'm not an amalgam of Jew, Catholic, Moslem and Thug when somebody transgresses it, then you're right out on the limb so far as James Wendell Hudson is concerned.

My religion has to do with facts. Things that other people have found out. Things that I can find out for myself if I go through the same processes. And remember that in my religion it is just as important to find out that something is wrong, as it is to prove to yourself that it is right. More important, in fact. (I've never actually said that before, but I'd like to get it printed, and mailed off non-copyright to every schoolmaster, priest, politician, parent and Commissar in the world.) The one thing that I can never stomach is to find someone believing something merely because he's been told to believe it. And the one thing that I can never forgive —because it's the sin against my kind of Holy Ghost—is to find someone playing about with facts just to make them fit into some damn-fool theory.

Perhaps worst of all is to show up coy when asked to produce the data. That's criminal concealment. Because data are to theories just about what dough is to bread. And theories aren't just the bread-and-butter kind of bread in my profession. They're the bread of Life itself. And you see now why I call my science a religion.

That's why I mentioned Lysenko. Because the Lenin Academy of Agricultural Sciences, which had been as respectable as the Royal Society, suddenly went mad. It started a purge, and threw over all the old Neo-Mendelist regulars who taught (after checking up the facts) that heredity depended on something called a gene—and a gene is just a little bit of matter that determines certain characteristics in the process of fertilisation. Instead, the Academy preached something called Michurinism. This was a brand-new doctrine founded by Father Michurin with Comrade Lysenko as his altar-boy. It said that heredity could be transformed by environment. And, in case you don't know, that is about as startling to a biologist as announcing that water freezes at 100° C. With one breath we all began yelling for the facts. And we went without sleep and drink just waiting for the postman to call.

But nothing came. A lot of merry Moscow journalists, however, began banging out their bits about it. Overnight, it became pet propaganda theme for the whole of the U.S.S.R. That was because it fitted in so marvellously with everything else that they had been saying. Aristocrats made, not born, was the new siren-song. And when master Lysenko still hadn't produced his notebook, and even turned nasty when he was asked a few elementary questions a chill began to develop somewhere around what I call my heart. Because, if this was all hooey, it was easily the biggest racket of them all.

And that was the way it began to look. All theory, no data. All propaganda, no proof. At the end of the first six months when every genuine biologist had been turned away and told not to handle the exhibits, there could be only one conclusion. The Socialist sixth of the world was faking the facts and sending out missionaries into the other five-sixths to make people believe them. It was W. D. P. Inc. on the grandest scale.

That was when I and little Arthur's Asiatic comrades parted company. And I wasn't the only one. There was now a great big hole inside quite a lot of the Left-wing scientists. The bats were flitting in hordes. And to imagine the size of the hole through which they were escaping, you have to imagine how the faithful

248

in Rome would feel at the end of Urbi et Orbi if the Pope suddenly announced that from now on doctrine was under the direction of the Sports Editor.

I've got that hole permanently left in me. And it was because of the draught blowing through it, that I didn't see why someone else up at the Bodmin Institute who was still all solid casing, should remain in one piece for ever.

That was what made me determined to go on being bloody-minded. I still needed time to think.

Chapter XXXVII

1

It was six-thirty next morning when they called me. And, as nothing else happened until nearly a quarter to eight, I could feel the whole day going sour on me.

When the cell door did at last open again, I saw the Inspector and one of the cub-Captains as well as the Station Sergeant all standing there.

"Morning, boys," I said.

Then I noticed that the cub-Captain had a long strip of sticking-plaster down one side of his face. He must have scratched himself while the three of them had been romping together at the bottom of that bunker. And I didn't see why he should be allowed to forget it.

"Cut yourself shaving?" I asked. "Surely you don't have to do it every day."

The cub-Captain said nothing, and the Inspector cleared his throat.

"I have here a warrant authorising your transfer," he said.

I turned and faced him.

"You can't do that," I told him. "This may seem a poor sort

of place to you. But it's still home."

The Inspector ignored that one altogether.

"Captain Lawther will be escorting you," was what he said.

"I'll take every care of him," I promised.

Captain Lawther was the fair-haired one. The one I disliked. He was in mufti. That meant that he was wearing something pretty deplorable in the way of a sports coat. It had knobbly leather-covered buttons of the sort that should only be allowed on very small children's overcoats. And I resented the fact that his tailor had given the jacket two slits up the back. The two-slit style is something that should be reserved for men of my age and substance.

But I didn't want him to feel awkward or self-conscious about things.

"Well, come on," I said. "Let's get cracking. I haven't got all day to waste."

But they apparently had. In the result, it was nearly teatime, with the lamps of Bodmin shining palely in through the cell window, before we got started. And even then we had to go through the ceremony of the handcuffs again.

And this gave me an idea. As soon as cub-Captain Lawther had turned the key on us both, I spoke to him.

"Sure it's comfortable?" I asked.

There was no answer.

"Doesn't hurt anywhere?"

Still no answer.

"Quite sure it's firm?"

Silence.

"Better make certain."

The jerk I gave it brought Captain Lawther right into my arms with a rush. But I pretended not to notice.

"That's fine," I said. "Now it doesn't matter if you fall. I've still got you."

I was about three inches taller than Captain Lawther, and at least two stone heavier. The more I thought about it the more I was looking forward to being tied on to him.

And I had a feeling that it wouldn't very long remain that way round.

It was only the first part of the journey that was by car. After that, it was British Railways again. And that suited me perfectly. Captain Lawther was every bit as embarrassed as I was by having to go about like a slave-dealer making a trade delivery. There weren't very many people on Bodmin platform. Just an old lady and her daughter, a farmer with his hat too far on the back of his head, the Vicar of some-where or other, and a couple of porters. But I didn't see why any of them should miss the predicament that Captain Lawther and I were in.

"Show them the pass," I said rather loudly when we got to the barrier. And then, before my escort could say anything, I added: "You can keep it, son. I shall know where it is if I want it."

With that, I gave a knowing wink in the direction of the ticket collector, and began leading Captain Lawther up the platform. It was here that he made the mistake of trying to stand still. But I knew that if it came to a tug-of-war he wouldn't stand a chance. Soon he was sliding after me like a puppy.

"None of that, please," I said sternly.

The old lady and her daughter heard every word of it. And, as with all really nice people, their sympathy immediately went out towards the little man.

"Oo, see that, Mum?" the girl asked.

The daughter stood there glaring at me. The old lady,

however, evidently wanted to avoid a scene at all costs. She began to move away. But I saved her the trouble.

"That's all right, ma'am," I said. "He'll come quietly."

That was when I began to lead him up the platform in among the milk-churns. There were rather a lot of milk-churns, and he must have hurt his knee quite badly against one of them. I heard the little beast suddenly cry out in pain. And it was what I had been waiting for.

"Why not take these things off?" I asked.

"Not bloody likely," he replied.

He was wearing the kind of expression that suggested that at any moment he might burst into tears from sheer torment and vexation. But I could see that he was being very brave about it. And I knew that he was using bad language just to persuade himself that he was really tough and grown up.

"Well, better keep moving," I said. "Doesn't make us so conspicuous."

I led him through the milk-churns again, only a bit faster this time. And we got into trouble with a porter's trolley. Between the two of us the thing nearly went over on to the line, and I fairly barked at him for all the trouble he was causing.

It was then Lawther asked if I'd mind lowering my voice a little. That pleased me. It showed that the treatment was working.

"Don't you think we had better have them off?" I asked again, quite quietly. "They're only making your wrist sore."

This time he paused before replying.

"Not till we get in the train," he said.

"Just as you please," I answered. "But I'm not standing about here to be stared at by anyone."

I was really quite nice to him this time, and I didn't lead him anywhere near a farm harrow that I'd noticed lying on the platform near the parcels office. There was no need for it. He'd said all that I wanted him to say.

2

It was all quite simple and straightforward when the train drew in. The guard and the station-master both knew all about a reserved compartment, and I let Captain Lawther show the pass without saying anything. I even allowed the train to draw right out of the platform before I raised the matter of the handcuffs. Then I thrust my wrist out.

"You win," I said. "I might have bolted if you'd done it sooner."

Captain Lawther flushed. This was clearly his moment of triumph. He looked like a choir-boy who had just swamped the anthem.

"I know damn well, you might," he said.

But the rumble-rumble of the wheels evidently reassured him. And pulling out his key-chain with his free hand, he unlocked the handcuff that was on his wrist.

"That's all right," I said. "Don't bother about mine. You'll want to do it up again when we arrive there. I don't want to start getting you into trouble."

This seemed to relieve Captain Lawther. He sat there rubbing his wrist and the bad place on his knee where he'd hurt it on the handle of the milk-churn, and finally he lit a cigarette. I could see that he felt all big and magnanimous because he remembered to offer me one. But I only shook my head.

"No, thanks," I said. "Don't feel like it. It's all right for you. You're in for promotion. I'm in for about seven years."

That left him glowing all over with thoughts about being

Major Lawther, and it left me free to look out of the window. This was rather important. We were getting back towards the moor by now, and the train was putting on more speed than I cared for. The telegraph poles were beginning to whizz past us in the darkness.

"Mind if we have the window down?" I asked. "You'd better do it. I don't want you to think that I'm going to jump out or something."

Captain Lawther had learnt by now to do exactly what I told him. And he moved over towards the door like an obedient younger brother. This suited me perfectly. His back was towards me, and his overcoat was on the rack just above my head. It was a large mock-Harris ulster that he had been wearing, bought specially to go with that bogus sports suit, I imagine. But I couldn't have asked for better. There were yards and yards of the material. And when I suddenly wound them round his head and tied the two arms tightly together somewhere just under his chin, he must have thought that we had reached the tunnel. He kicked about a bit. But because he couldn't see what he was kicking, he didn't hurt me. And I didn't even want him to hurt himself. Just so that he shouldn't roll about and fall out after me, I laid him carefully on the floor and pushed him under the seat like a holdall.

Then I opened the door—hung for a moment on the foot-board, and jumped into the cold and the blackness and the roaring night.

There are some people—film supers and others—who spend their whole lives jumping off moving trains and fire engine escape towers. They know how to fall.

I didn't. I can see now that it would have been more sense to face the way the train was going. It may have been that fact, however, that saved me. Because after the first crack that felt as though I'd run smack into a brick-lorry at about sixty miles an hour, I began to do a series of back somersaults. I dimly remember three of them—all that part is a bit confused—with my face catching the ballast once every revolution. And then, with a final cartwheel that nearly separated my spine, I suddenly found myself feet upwards in a ditch.

I have to thank the extreme coldness of the water for the fact that I didn't drown then and there. It brought me to again and I fairly thrashed my way out of it. Then I lay on the edge of the embankment, gasping. I wondered if I was still alive, and felt pretty sure that I must be. That was because I was still thinking the same thought that had been uppermost in my mind as I jumped. "Silly little basket," it ran. "Who's going to be made a major now?"

But there was no time for gloating. Away in the distance there was the quite unmistakable sound of an express train putting its brakes on. That could mean only one thing. Permanent Captain Lawther must have got his nose out of his ulster, and he was evidently hanging on to the communication cord. That meant that I had to set off straight away across the open moor like a cross-country runner.

The Institute was the one place that I wanted to get to. I had everything worked out in my mind. I was working on one of my hunches—and of Dr. Mann's. Though I couldn't prove anything, I was now perfectly certain that it was the great Professor Sonnenbaum, alias Dr. Smith, who was the guilty one. And it all seemed to fit together—his anti-Americanism, the way he had kept out of it when Mann himself had been arrested, his absence during the search for Una's assailant, his striking complacency in

256

the face of an inefficient police force. But I was perfectly realist about it. I didn't even kid myself that I could prove anything. Romantics like me have our place in the world: we're the yeast in the human mixture. It is the cold, shrewd efficient type that usually does the job when the romantics have shown them how.

There was only one of the right type in the whole Institute —Gillett. I wasn't under any illusions about him. If he hadn't possessed a blood-stream that would have set a Newfoundland cod shivering, he wouldn't have chased Dr. Mann off to his suicide. There was nothing in the least over-heated about Gillett. The great thing about him was that he possessed the scientific attitude. And if I could drop the hint I knew that he'd go on from there.

I covered the mile and a half in about thirty-five minutes. I couldn't make it faster because I'd hurt my ankle when I jumped. And it was from the annexe side that I finally approached the Institute. I saw at once, too, that I was lucky. There was a light on in Gillett's room. I made my way straight towards it. Literally straight, I mean. I wanted to avoid meeting people. And rather than go up the stairs, I decided to use the window.

This wasn't difficult because the ground sloped up from that side of the annexe, and the bedroom windows were on practically bungalow height. Gillett's window was open about three inches at the bottom. I put my finger through, and drew back the curtain. And I felt a queer pang as I did so. It was the absolute innocence of Gillett's occupation that overcame me. He had his ski-ing kit out on the table before him, and he was adjusting the guard on one of the sticks. Then I drew my lips in tighter. I'd just remembered what I'd be doing while he was getting on with his jumps and Christianas.

It was at this moment that I heard somebody coming. Unless

I was going to be nabbed again before I had even had time to say my piece, there was nothing for it but to heave up the window, and do the "Spectre de la Rose" leap in reverse. But I was a bad Nijinsky. I landed on the wrong ankle, and fell almost on top of the table at which Gillett was working.

Then, to avoid the stag-at-bay kind of melodrama, I deliberately eased up.

"Just dropped in for a quiet chat," I began, thrusting my hand in my pocket because I felt a bit self-conscious about the handcuffs.

But it was Gillett who had the stag-at-bay look, not me. Evidently my sudden entry must have upset him more than I had realised. You could practically hear the hounds baying all round him.

"What the ... " he began, and then broke off.

He got up, and began backing away from me. Rather a poor show, I thought. But, as there was an audience of only one and as he could deny afterwards that it had ever happened that way, I supposed it didn't really matter. And he was rapidly putting on his act again.

"I suppose this place is surrounded?" he asked quite calmly.

"Afraid so," I said.

"Are they covering us?"

"Just about," I answered.

For my part, I was determined to keep the conversation light and airy. Otherwise, in his present state, Gillett still looked as though he might start yelling out for help. And that was the last thing I wanted.

"Had the pleasure of a long talk with Wilton to-day," I went on. "We discussed quite a lot of things, and finally we got round to you. That's why I'm here. . . . "

258

But that was as far as I got. For Gillett suddenly took over.

"So I was right," he said.

"I don't doubt it."

But Gillett wasn't listening. Simply wasn't hearing me. He was staring in front of him—at the table, I think it must have been. And because even a ski-stick might be quite a useful instrument if you start swiping about with it, I picked it up first.

Gillett looked up.

"You think you're damn clever, don't you?" he said.

"Used to," I admitted.

"Well, I knew who you were the day you came."

"Pity you didn't tell me," I said. "I've often wondered."

Gillett ignored that.

"Why didn't you have your face lifted?" he asked.

"I can't help my scar," I told him.

"It nearly kept you out of the Party once," he said.

"Too conspicuous."

I raised my eyebrows. That was because I had suddenly become suspicious even of my best hunches.

"Was that why you left that first note for me on my pillow?" I asked.

Gillett seemed to be wondering whether to reply or not.

"I thought you might still be one of us," he said at last.

"I might have been," I told him.

"Then I guessed you were in with the police. You and Wilton spent too much time together. Not very subtle about it, were you?"

"It worked."

"You dirty traitor," Gillett said.

He was moving up in the direction of the bookcase while he was speaking. But he still seemed quite willing to go on talking.

"And then you sent all those other messages just to get me foxed up?" I asked.

Gillett nodded.

"That worked, too," I said.

There was a pause.

"All one typing?" I asked.

Again Gillett nodded.

"And all intended for me?"

Gillett was leaning up against the bookcase by now.

"No," he said. "They were intended for Mann originally. I knew he was a Party member, too. I thought that was why he'd come here."

"So you did a sort of switch over?"

This time Gillett just nodded again.

"And you planted all the stuff on Mann?"

"I wanted Wilton to find it."

"Was it Mann's revolver?"

"Mann never had a revolver. It was my spare one. I put the case in the basket, and the revolver in his drawer. I guessed he'd know what to do with it."

"You guessed right ... " I began.

But the note of bitterness was all wrong. I didn't want to risk offending Gillett. Not yet, at least. There was still too much to learn. So from there on I kept everything deliberately light and casual.

"Oh, by the way, about that pass of mine," I went on. "It *was* you who pinched it, wasn't it?"

Gillet nodded.

"Nearly came in very useful," he said. "Got someone else in the Party to use it. With average luck all this trouble could have been avoided."

"Just what I was thinking," I told him. I was rocking up and down on my heels by now to show how much at ease I was. And I tried one line purely at random.

"Why did you break with Hilda?" I asked.

I was quite prepared for Gillett to go all silent and clamlike. But apparently he had put his inhibitions behind him.

"Because I didn't trust her," he replied. "She belonged to the opposite side."

"And is that why you tried to kill Una?"

Gillett frowned. It could have been either because he had tried, or because he had failed. With his sort of profile you couldn't tell.

"Found she'd been rifling my personal belongings," was all he said. "Too inquisitive."

"Not surprised," I told him. "You had us all guessing when you said you'd been fired at."

For a moment there was just a flicker of a smile on his face. It was an amused, superior sort of smile.

"Exactly what I intended," he replied.

We were getting along famously by now. So I led up quietly to the closing line.

"Well," I said, "better hand over the culture, and we'll call it quits."

Gillett suddenly reached his hand out to the bookcase beside him. But I had to take the risk on that.

"Not there," I said. "Una gave it to me. Then Bansted borrowed it. I think it's in the Black Museum by now."

Gillett smiled. It was one of the nicest, and most genuine smiles I'd ever seen on him.

"You bloody fool," he said.

As he said it, he pushed aside a copy of Simpson's *Morphology* and made a grab at something on the bookshelf. It was a revolver. A nice new one, too, from the look of it. I had the feeling that it had been bought specially for me.

"Did you think I was going to tell you everything, and let you get out of here alive?" he asked.

"Seemed like it," I replied.

And, as I said the words, I slung the ski-stick hard at him. It wasn't a bad shot. Another six inches to the right, and it would have got him full between the eyes. As it was, he side-stepped it. But it was the best I could do. A ski-stick was never made for in-fighting.

What's more, this particular one apparently hadn't even been made for ski-ing. It wouldn't have stood up to the strain of it. Because even the quite mild battering that I'd given it had knocked the end clean off. The guard came away completely, and a little metal capsule rolled out. It was the ink cylinder of a ball-point. Just like the one in which little Dr. Mann had stowed away his penicillin.

"So that's how you were going to get the culture out of the country, is it?"

Gillett looked down for a moment.

"Don't bother now," I said, "I'll pick it up for you later."

But this time Gillett shook his head.

"This is where I'm going to kill you," he said quietly.

It certainly looked as though we'd reached that point. And I couldn't think how to string things out much longer. But I had a queer feeling all the time that even postponing matters by a few seconds might make the answer come out different.

"Do you mind counting up to three before you pull the trigger?" I asked. "It's the bang I can't stand."

"You won't hear it," Gillett answered.

I shrugged my shoulders.

"I've given up being sure about anything." Gillett squared himself.

"One!"

"One what?"

But it was no use. I didn't seem able to distract him now.

"Two!"

I closed my eyes and waited. I was feeling rather swimmy by now.

"Thr . . ."

The report when it came sounded simply terrific. My whole head jerked back, and seemed to burst open from the concussion. It wasn't immediately that I even realised that the report had come from the wrong place. It had come from the window instead of from the direction of the bookcase where Gillett had been standing. And already a pale, tobacco-stained hand was drawing the curtains back. It was Wilton's hand. His left one. That was because he still had the revolver in his right.

"I told you it was either you or Gillett," he said.

"Then why the hell didn't you arrest both of us?"

My patience with Wilton had worn a bit thin by now, and I felt another attack of bloody-mindedness coming.

Wilton finally managed to get his long legs over the window-sill. Then he crossed over and looked down at Gillett. But there was nothing to be done there. At that range even I couldn't have missed.

"I wanted to see if he'd get careless once you were removed," he said.

There was a pause. A full-length Wilton pause.

"He did," he added.

I picked up the capsule, and handed it to Wilton.

"Well, that's about the end of it," I said.

"Not entirely," Wilton answered, without even remembering to say thank you.

"Meaning what?"

"Somebody's got to tell Una," Wilton remarked quietly.

I smoothed my hair down, and straightened up my collar.

"Not me," I said. "Not after this. The Old Man had better break it to her. Or you can. Anyone but me."

"Come better from you," Wilton answered.

I caught his eye as he said it. In a half-light it was quite an understanding sort of eye.

"Perhaps you're right," I told him.

And as I went towards the door Wilton stood back to let me pass.

A NOTE ON THE AUTHOR

Norman Richard Collins was born in Beaconsfield, Buckinghamshire, on October 3, 1907. By the time he was nine years old, at the William Ellis School in Hampstead, he displayed a talent for both writing and publishing. In January 1933, when he was twenty-five, he became assistant managing director in the publishing house run by Victor Gollancz. In 1941 Collins was forced to move to the BBC due to increasingly poor relationship with Gollancz, who resented Collins' talent and saw him as a rival. During this time he became known for his innovative programming which included *Woman's Hour*, which still airs today on BBC Radio Four. He rose to Controller of the BBC Television Service, later leaving to co-found what is now ITV after deciding a competitor to the BBC's monopoly was needed.

Alongside his busy career, Collins wrote fourteen novels and one work of non-fiction in his lifetime, most of which were popular successes, published begrudgingly by Gollancz. Collins also became well known for his innovative programming at the British Broadcasting Corporation during the late 1940s, and later for advocating and leading the movement toward commercial television broadcasting in Great Britain.

An unmistakable mark of Collins' power of application and creative energy was that he continued to write fiction throughout such an active working life. Although never a full-time writer he was a fluent and prolific author with sixteen titles and two plays to his credit between 1934 and 1981. An autographed edition of twelve of his novels was published during the 1960s.